CRIES OF BLOOD

CHRISTIAN MARTIN

Cries of Blood

Text copyright © 2020 by Christian Martin
Cover illustration © 2020 by Marina Kyriacou

All rights reserved.
ISBN: 9798635448984

Original title: Llantos de sangre © 2016 by Christian Martin

All rights reserved. No part of this work may be reproduced, stored in a retrieval system, or transmitted in any form or by any means, electronic, mechanical, photocopying, recording or otherwise, without the prior permission of the author.

This book is a work of fiction. All characters, events and some places are fictitious and any resemblance to real persons, living or dead, real stories or real places is purely coincidental.

Dedicated to:
Pablo, for encouraging me to write this story;
Sarah, for wanting to be in it,
and Angelines for believing in my evil side.

Content

Prologue .... - 7 -
1. The offer .... - 10 -
2. "Started badly" .... - 24 -
3. "In the middle of nowhere" .... - 36 -
4. "Just for a few days" .... - 46 -
5. "Scary film" .... - 66 -
6. "She's just a child" .... - 82 -
7. "Yäel, her name is Yäel" .... - 93 -
8. "Just a damned accident" .... - 111 -
9. "Is this *lead* to your house?" .... - 132 -
10. The diary and the call .... - 148 -
11. "Neither the good are so good, nor the bad so bad" ... - 170 -
12. "What do you want from us?" .... - 182 -
13. "Don't you want to be pretty?" .... - 195 -
14. "I'll be back in a minute" .... - 209 -
15. "Cries of blood" .... - 226 -
16. Final questions .... - 243 -
Epilogue .... - 256 -
Acknowledgements .... - 262 -

Prologue

The rain was beating against the sitting-room window.
The room was dark, but for the glow of a lone streetlight filtering through the curtains. Even so, it was easy to make out the silhouette of a figure pacing the room. From one side to the other, and back again . . .

It was very late. Late enough that cars outside in the street were rare, passing by only at long intervals. And still she was awake. Not so much a silhouette, but as a spectre in the middle of the night. With long, dark hair tumbling down her back. Barefoot. Hands hanging numbly at her sides. Eyes wide open, bloodshot.

She paced the room again, looking everywhere with eyes sunk in shadows. It looked as if she were expecting something to happen or waiting impatiently for someone to arrive . . . Across the room again, but towards the curtains this time. Raising her hand, she opened the silky curtain a little, just enough to look out through the misted panes.

She put her hand into her trouser pocket, took out a black mobile phone and a little notebook. She looked at them for a long time before seeming to reach a decision, unlocking the screen and opening the notebook. It was almost impossible to make out a single word or number; almost every one had a line through it and had been rewritten, as if someone had thought of an idea, rejected it and then come back to give it another chance, over and over again. Indecipherable numbers scribbled down mechanically and in a haste. And every one of them struck through and scribbled over, practically annihilated, overwritten dozens of times – except for one solitary number. Even so, it was hard to make out through the jumble of lines.

She stood looking at it for a few seconds, pressed the call button and keyed in the number. Then she put the phone to her ear and waited for someone to pick up. It was not long before the call was answered.

'Yes?' The voice was hoarse. A woman speaking.

The girl said nothing. Maybe she hadn't thought of what to say if she finally dialled that number. Perhaps she'd been obsessing so much over whether to call or not that she'd omitted the detail of thinking about what to say.

'Hello? Who is this?' There were rustling sounds at the other end of the line. 'For God's sake, it's five in the morning! Some people are sleeping here!'

'Julia, it's me,' the girl said simply, forcing each word out with and effort.

'Me, who? I hope you've got a good reason for calling me at this hour.'

Silence. Where could she even begin to find an answer? But there was no reply. A few seconds went by in silence before she said:

'It's Eva. You called me last week . . .'

'Eva . . . Yes, of course, Eva. How are you?' the woman said at once. Her voice had lost its dry tone in an instant and she spoke casually, with feigned detachment. She waited a few more seconds for her caller to speak, but when the girl said nothing, she asked. 'Is everything alright? It's five o'clock in the morning.'

'I couldn't sleep. I'm sorry if I woke you up.' There was a snort from the other end of the line, as if such statement wasn't obvious enough. 'I've been thinking about what you proposed and I've decided to take the offer . . . but under certain conditions.'

With each word Eva spoke faster. Julia, at the other end of the line, asked her to wait a second. There was a noise again, this time as if the woman had put the phone down on a marble table. But it was only a few instants later she picked it up and spoke again, this time more clearly.

'Of course, Eva. What I want you to be sure of is that you're doing this of your own free will. I don't want you to feel that you're under any obligation . . .' Her tone, relaxed and velvety now, failed to conceal her eagerness. This was the tone of someone trying to achieve a much-sought after objective – while clearly afraid that her chance of doing so could vanish into thin air at any second. 'Although I would like to be the one to take the project forward, of course . . .'

This time it was Julia who fell silent, waiting for an answer.

'Yes, I'm doing it of my own accord. I don't feel the least bit forced by you. I've decided – but like I said, only under a couple of conditions,' Eva repeated, stressing the last word.

'Great. If you don't mind, Eva, we could meet in my office tomorrow morning and talk it over calmly, when nobody's tired. I want you to be clear-headed when we discuss the arrangements,' the woman explained, allowing a professional tone to fill her voice. 'Would half-past nine suit you?'

'Yes of course, that would be fine,' Eva replied.

'Would you like me to send you the address?' the woman asked.

'No worries, I already have it.'

'Then I'll see you in my office at half-past nine. Get some rest. Goodnight.'

1. The offer

The morning dawned cheerfully after a long night of continuous rain.

Even the pigeons and the occasional bird woke early to welcome the brand new day. They flew through the sky, playing under the shy sunshine which gleamed through the last clouds that still refused to disperse away. And down on the streets the pavements were full of puddles, but clean; there was nothing better than a good rainy night to clean the streets of dirt.

It was amazing to see how the city woke up, beginning with the first cars and trucks rolling down the streets. The first to open their businesses were the small grocery stores. Their managers – somehow all from the Middle East – shouted to the delivery men who tried to take the stock out of the lorries and in through tight back doors. Nobody who walked by seemed sure whether the yells were complaints or friendly greetings.

After the grocery stores it was the turn of the coffee shops. Out of their doors came the gasping of coffee machines and jingle of plates at the counter, followed by the appealing scent of the first round of doughnuts, sausage rolls and toasts with butter and jam that would welcome the early bird customers. These would come out a few minutes later, their coffees releasing playful clouds of steam in the bitter cold.

Then, step-by-step, more people would come out of their houses under big, warm coats zipped all the way to the top. It didn't matter their age; they were all in a rush, their faces tired and unfriendly as they carried their backpacks or briefcases. Each and every one of them went straight to their cars, tube stations or took one of the buses that passed by. But if there was anything amusing at such an early hour, it was to see the immaculately dressed women in their business outfits, all of them pretending to feel comfortable in their designer heels. None of them would be wearing them by the end of the day – instead they would walk back home in old sneakers that tore apart their smart images.

Only tourists strolled down the streets calmly, in no apparent hurry. They all enjoyed the first puff of their morning cigarettes while deciding where to go and what sites to visit later.

The streets were delightful then. Listening to the doors unlocking to let in the good-looking sales assistants, some of them struggling to hold their heavy bags as they pushed inside; and, of course, giving a chance for the cheekiest, flirtiest bloke nearby to show off his fake kindness to help them. All they ever wanted was the girl's phone number, but none of them seemed to realise they had no chance.

Easy, fun moments. But not if you were trying to hail a taxi ... And even worse if you were in a rush: the few taxis visible on the street would be already taken. And then there'd be the smart-ass who'd ignore your complaints after taking the taxi that clearly stopped just for you.

But that was not an issue for Eva. A girl like her could afford a room at a prestigious hotel, able to take advantage of their drivers' services. Even so, she had chosen instead to have a black taxi waiting at the hotel doors for a good half an hour. The driver had smoked more than one cigarette while the meter ticked ever higher without a single drop of petrol used.

When the spotless black and gold uniformed doorman of The Ritz Hotel greeted the girl wearing black sunglasses, the taxi driver quickly threw the last cigarette on the pavement and moved hurriedly to open the back door for her. Once both were settled in the vehicle, she asked him to take her to Trafalgar Square. The cabbie, a native Englishman in his forties, started the engine and pulled onto the main street.

He allowed himself for a few glances at the girl in the rear-view mirror as he drove. When she'd come down the stairs from the hotel entrance, he'd thought there was something familiar about her. One look at her face had told him she wasn't good in the mornings. The sunglasses clearly failing to hide the bags under her eyes. She was in her mid-twenties, or perhaps a year or two older. She had soft, shiny brunette hair, and tanned skin a shade darker than could surely have been obtained in a country where the sun was as scarce as this one. She wore tight clothing under a couture coat, which limited the opportunity for the indiscreet driver to see more.

'Your face looks familiar,' said the man cheerfully, trying to make conversation. He looked at her again in the mirror. 'I don't know exact–' he continued to watch her in the mirror, his curiosity apparently rising. After a few seconds he seemed to remember. 'That's it, you're Eva Ro-dri-gues . . . It's been ages since I saw you in the press.'

'Domínguez, Eva Domínguez,' she corrected him, mirthlessly. 'And if you don't mind, I'd prefer not to talk right now.'

The girl had not answered bad-temperedly; she had been refined and tactful. And the man nodded and turned on the radio in return. He would always have it on when he encountered a not very talkative customer. He found it a useful remedy for those uncomfortable silences.

He focused on Piccadilly Street, which at that moment was quieter than usual, although still full of tourists heading towards the most popular shops and blocking or delaying the passage of the people walking behind them. Only when the girl asked him to stop the car, absurdly just a five minutes walk from her hotel, did he dare open his mouth to ask her for the one hundred and thirty pounds shown on the meter.

When she opened the door, the man seemed to hesitate whether to say anything else. He managed to mumble a few unintelligible sounds. The girl looked back at him; but he'd turned his face to the road, looking sorry and ashamed.

Eva got out of the cab and looked around dejectedly. Once, not so long ago, people wouldn't have hesitated to ask her for an autograph for a friend or relative. In most cases, those "friends" curiously shared the same gender as the person who made the request. But at least they'd asked.

She shook those thoughts from her head, shut the taxi door and started walking.

With the National Gallery on her left, she crossed the square crowded with tourists. They were spread throughout the plaza, taking pictures at the two central fountains or around the lions surrounding Nelson's Column, which rose majestically above all of them, watching the city with his cold, granite stare. She crossed the road and walked down Whitehall Street, following the statue's gaze towards Westminster. She had always loved that part of London, with its pompous buildings twice as big as normal, making anyone who passed them feel important.

A few minutes later, she crossed a few other roads to end up in Whitehall Court, where she found the building she was headed to. She pressed a button on the intercom, and once the door released open she entered a luxurious lobby, a few seconds later heading to the top floor in the lift.

There she took a quick look at herself in the mirror. The bags under her eyes seemed about to explode, and her bloodshot eyes didn't look much better. But she didn't even bother to brush her hair or straighten her coat.

Once the elevator signalled that she had reached the third floor, she stepped out and heard a door opening in the hall. This floor looked even more luxurious than the lobby downstairs, with polished, marble walls and floors that could easily pass for a Picasso painting. On her right were two doors. The one that was opening at that same instant, jet black and made of what looked like half a ton of iron, made way for a woman of stunning beauty.

From the pristine, beige high heels to the long blonde hair, perfectly coiffed and tied up in a simple ponytail, every aspect of her appearance seemed to have been meticulously studied.

She was the prototype of the perfect professional woman: thirty to forty years old, stylishly dressed, attractive and slender, with pert breasts, full, seductive lips, and deep green eyes enhanced by well applied makeup.

'Good morning, dear. Have you been able to sleep at all?'

'I've tried to sleep a bit,' Eva answered, with a soft voice that didn't match her countenance. 'You're Julia, right?'

It wasn't a question, though. She knew perfectly well who the woman before her was. She had watched many of her TV shows, even heard about her books. And even without any visual reference, the woman's voice was difficult to forget. It had something special that over the phone she'd been able to perceive from the first sentence. It was a cosy, velvety tone that invited confidence, which on-screen helped to build the image of a direct but self-assured woman. Maybe that was the reason she was the only name Eva had never crossed out in her notebook, not one single time.

'Please, come in,' Julia said, opening the door wider to let her into a bright reception hall.

Eva took a few steps inside. She was surprised by the woman's taste in decor. She hadn't really known what she was expecting, but it certainly wasn't what she now saw.

When the woman closed the door and motioned to follow her, she realised that Julia didn't have the typical office with dark carpet and outdated furniture. Eva had always thought of those places as unfriendly, with any distinctive detail merging with the rest of the room, making it hard to spot without a thorough look around.

Instead, everything in that room was welcoming, light in colour if not completely white. And at that time in the morning, with the timid September sun sneaking through the blinds, it looked more like the doors to heaven than a serious and cold office.

However, Eva did not waste time observing the room in detail. She didn't give Julia a chance to offer her a seat, but began to speak right there in the middle of the room, hands clenched around the handle of her handbag. 'I have only one condition. Meet it, and I will give you what you, as too many others, have been trying to get from me for so long.'

Now, she paused to let the woman sit down while she herself took a breath and glanced briefly around. Everything was clean and neat, but it wasn't as if someone had just tidied up. It seemed to be its natural state: the books were ordered on the shelves; white roses stood in a glass jar on the coffee table; business cards, all properly aligned, were at one of the corners of the desk; and the few photo frames in the room were polished brightly.

'So you want to get to the point, huh? I like that. Would you maybe like a tea while we talk?' Julia asked, smiling. Eva nodded and she invited her to go on. 'Spit it all out.'

Eva looked at her, as if for the first time. It seemed as if the girl was hoping to read Julia's intentions in her eyes. After what appeared to be a whole minute, Eva said, 'I don't care how you tell the story. All I want is for you not to omit even one single word I'm going to say to you. Not a single comma or a detail, even if you think they're insignificant,' she finished saying with a somewhat abrupt tone.

Julia stood quietly for a few seconds. When she spoke, she used the same soothing voice that she used on all her TV shows.

'Allow me my curiosity. Why are you doing this? Why not hold a press conference instead? And, of course, why have you come to me on the first place?'

Eva didn't hesitate. She was clearly determined.

'I'm doing it because I've already suffered a lot during my long silence, as has my career, my family and those of my . . . friends. I think it's time for people to shut up for once and stop spreading lies around. My friends' families need a rational explanation and not a front-page headline with quotes from a random policeman. We're sick and tired of other people trying to explain something they neither lived through nor understand at all, even with all the existing evidence that they have received to date. So, I finally decided to accept your offer: I don't think there's anyone more appropriate or experienced than you . . .'

'But don't you think it would be better to meet your friends and their families and tell them yourself?' Julia persisted, then hurried to add, 'but this doesn't mean I don't wish to break the news myself, of course. It all just seems strange to me. I'm sure you've received hundreds of calls from reporters, all wanting to get the real story for a tasty price. And here you are, choosing me to tell the story instead of facing your friends and their families yourself.'

'I'm not doing this for them to know everything, Julia. They already know the story I want to tell you, and they've all given me their consent. They believe that it will be the best thing for me. I've already suffered a lot,' the girl repeated, ducking her head and staring down at her bitten fingernails. 'I don't expect you to understand it now. But when you know everything, you'll understand then.'

She paused and looked away, trying to clear her mind. The more she thought about it, the more anxious she became, and more tears came into her eyes. She sighed and reached into her handbag. From it she took out some papers folded in half and placed them on top of the desk.

'You'll find there the signed consent of the families and my own,' Eva informed her, seeing the clear bewilderment in Julia's eyes. 'And I believe you'll be pleased to know that neither the families nor myself are seeking to get a penny out of this. We would all rather donate any amount to organisations that would do some good with it.'

Julia was speechless. She didn't know what she was meant to say about the papers in front of her. Her face was a poem: the joy and shock had produced a betraying, nervous tic on her lip. It had never been so easy for her before; not that she hadn't fought hard for that moment. A long time had passed since she'd got interested in the girl who sat across the table from her now. She'd called her incessantly and almost searched under rocks for her. She'd sent her letters and gifts, and had talked to anyone who was close to her. She'd tried everything and more.

It was almost two years since she'd submitted her resignation letter to her boss, at the same TV channel that first gave her all the power she still possessed. After years of experience gained with prime-time TV shows, her own morning show, the most watched television news across the UK, the highly praised articles in newspapers of international circulation, exclusive interviews with top film stars and politicians, four books reaching number one in more than twenty countries . . . she was still looking for what she called her "Fucking Boom!" She kept searching for the job that would make her stop wanting more and more. The job that would finally let her go to bed and wake up in the morning refreshed and happy.

She needed that story. She knew the first moment she had heard the headlines. Because this girl had managed to attract the attention of national and international press with her story. And from then on, something inside Julia had screamed out, telling her she needed that whole story just for her.

So far only fragments of the story and many, many lies had made it to the headlines, one after another. She trembled with emotion when thinking how much she would get from undressing, shaping and revealing that story exclusively for the first and last time to the world. The one and only true version of the events. For that reason, she'd told herself she wouldn't rest until she got it . . .

And now that same girl was in front of her, saying those exact words and showing no hesitation. It was making her heart race uncontrollably.

'So, I'll be ready whenever you want to start,' Eva finished her speech.

Julia was perusing the papers Eva had just given her. Meanwhile, the water started boiling in the kettle behind her desk. On the same shelf she had teacups, saucers, a box filled with biscuits of different colours and some pots with different types of tea bags. When the kettle switched itself off, she left the papers on the desk and turned around to prepare two cups of tea.

'Very well, I have only one more question for you. I believe that when you told the truth in the police interrogation, and later on in court, you mentioned that you weren't present throughout all of the events. But if I'm not mistaken, you said that your house – where everything happened – was fitted with security cameras in the main rooms. Have you . . . watched them for yourself?' She hesitated for a moment. She didn't want to come across as edgy or too inquisitive. 'I'm asking you this, Eva, because if you . . . '

'If your question is whether I have watched the tapes and I unmistakably know what happened, my answer is yes, I have. I wouldn't have the nerve to talk about something without being sure of it,' the girl said, sharply, leaving clear any doubt about it. 'Once the police officers made copies, they returned the originals to me. It took me some time to watch them. But I couldn't get it out of my head. At first, I refused to even touch them . . . But in the end, I told myself that if I didn't watch them from beginning to end, even though the coroner's report was detailed and clear, I would never be free of it all.

'I assure you they are utterly horrible. It took me a while to accept what I saw, but the truth is always the truth. And even if it hurts, it is what it is, no matter how impossible it may seem. But even knowing the truth, no matter how many times I watched them, I couldn't believe it . . . I still struggle to force myself to think about it.'

The office went silent, except for the roar of the cars passing down the street outside.

All the information she had about the case wasn't helping Julia understand what the girl was really talking about. There were many gaps in her story, gaps she couldn't wait to fill. And if she was sure about something, it was that the girl wasn't lying. The coroner's verdict had been given a few months after Julia's resignation two years ago, soon after the events were covered by the media – against Eva's will. However, the world's press couldn't resist exposing what they knew about that bombshell.

Of course, they always told the story that interested them the most or whatever would sell more papers, no matter if changing one or two words here and there distorted the facts. She knew it well. She had once been one of those pieces in that chess game without checkmate, a game in which nobody cared about rules or feelings. The important thing was to be fast, to be heard and to get a good cut. It was just business.

She couldn't stop thinking that the truth, when revealed in its entirety, would be an unforgettable story. And Julia knew that if the girl was going to let her reveal it, it wasn't because she wanted to clean up her image: like Julia herself, it was a long time since Eva had appeared on TV. If the girl was doing this now, it was because she really wanted to get that dead weight off her shoulders – that weight she'd been carrying longer than necessary.

She had seen Eva on the news so many times. The cameras showed the reporters harassing the girl with hundreds of sordid questions. Cold-hearted journalists filled TV programmes with statements against her. At the same time, there'd been so many others on her side; but none of them would stop putting their fingers in the wound, a wound that for Eva couldn't heal.

Julia didn't hesitate any longer. This was a huge opportunity. The girl had only asked her not to omit a word or detail and, for some reason, she wouldn't even take a penny from it. If the girl had any other conditions, so what? She was giving Julia the chance of a lifetime, valued in millions of pounds and what would become the final pedestal in her career.

'Very well, then,' Julia said, leaving a cup of tea in front of the girl and sipping a little from her own. 'As I explained when we spoke before, my offer is pretty simple. After a few calls to my old boss at the BBC, I've got a deal for an interview to be aired in two parts: the first part one day, and the second the day after. In both parts we'll mix the interview that I'll have with you, in this same room, and the images from the security cameras from your house. I know some parts of those videos won't be able to be shown on TV, so there'll be some reconstructions with actors too . . . The only people in the room as you're interviewed will be you, my husband, who'll be in charge of the shoot and material editing, and me.

'Moreover, I would love to write a book about the events, separate from the programme. On this you'll be absolutely free to approve or veto whatever you want or don't want to be included. Obviously, I'd like to make it crystal clear that in comparison, neither you nor I would be in charge of what is broadcast in the final edit of the programmes. I know you're well acquainted with how television works, and I'm not going to lie about that. You know I can't make any promises, except with the book, in which you'll be the one to give the green flag.'

She paused, took the chance to have another sip of her tea and tried to read the girl's thoughts through her eyes. She opened the top desk drawer. From inside she pulled out a blue folder, opened it and left it in front of the girl. And she placed a pen next to the papers inside.

'These are the contracts you need to sign before we start. And if you want and are able to, I could have everything ready for the interview tomorrow morning. We'll need the tapes of the security cameras and, if it's possible and you give your consent, the same diary that the police confiscated and used to understand everything. Without any of those elements, I might miss the smallest details of the events and couldn't ask you the right questions. About you . . .'

She paused again, this time watching her words. The situation had shifted since she'd started speaking. It had been the young girl who had set out every point at the beginning of their meeting; now it was she who was doing so, but abruptly and without softening her words the way she would normally to avoid scaring anyone away. Was she asking a lot? Was she being too ambitious? She didn't want the girl to have second thoughts.

'As I mentioned last night,' Julia proceeded, smiling and smoothing the conversation, 'I need you to rest to gain strength and show up with the best possible presence. It's obvious that you need to calm down and sleep well to look rested and revitalised. We need the best from you, and I know that a girl with your talent can deliver that.'

Eva smiled for the first time in the whole day.

Ordinary people always thought that celebrities were like gods. And Julia, being a celebrity herself, knew that wasn't true. They were as human as everybody else. They didn't have perfect skin that had never borne the marks of acne or tiredness. They didn't wear designer dresses every day. And the girl loved how Julia had just reminded her, after softening her up with her fine verbiage, that her appearance that day was inadequate for their business.

'Of course, I appreciate your sincerity,' Eva said, still smiling. She began to read quickly and carefully through the contracts and signed in the boxes that had been highlighted with green marker for her. When she was done, she put them back in the blue folder and asked, 'Do you need anything else?'

'No, I think that's all. Make sure you sleep well tonight and bring me the best of your smiles. You're gorgeous when you smile, and it seems it's been a long time since you've been able to do that.'

'You're right, it's been a long time . . . By the way, could I have some sugar in my tea?'

The next day, after having slept quite well with the help of some new pills recommended by her doctor, Eva felt more cheerful. She was ready for her interview with Julia. And she thought about what she was going to wear for it. Eva knew how it would be: people would criticise or applaud the smallest detail. Nothing would pass them by.

So when Julia opened the door of her office, the beautiful girl waiting on the other side surprised her. Eva was wearing white high heels that showed off her long, slender, sun-tanned legs. But what Julia's eyes most adored was the cream dress that fell to Eva's hips, skimming over her breasts on which a fine white pendant was resting. Her hair tumbled over her shoulders in simple curls, and the little makeup she wore, showed her natural beauty, just as Julia had requested.

But that was not the only change that had occurred since the previous day. Julia's office had been transformed overnight. Where before, by the window, there had been a chair with a small coffee table, now there were two red "U" shaped seats contrasting against the white walls. Between them there was a huge plasma screen. To the right, left and centre there were three cameras facing in different directions and surrounded by enormous lights.

But there wasn't time to dwell on their surprise. The voice of a man, who appeared in the room by a door Eva hadn't noticed the day before, interrupted them.

Short introductions were made.

Sam, wearing jeans, a shirt and a quite attractive two-day stubble, was Julia's husband. And once they had gone step-by-step through how the interview was going to work, he asked them both to sit on their respective seats to adjust the focus on each camera. He increased and decreased the lights one by one, gave them each a microphone to hide under their clothes, and he prepared the DVDs Eva had brought with her. He inserted them into a DVD player connected to the huge screen . . .

And without further ado, the interview began. Julia turned to one of the cameras and presented the reasons why the girl was there that day, ready to tell the story that had never before been heard: the one and only true version, told by one of the protagonists of the events, backed up by all the evidence that would once and for all dismember the lies told to date.

Julia took a deep, quick breath, grabbed her notes and the diary Eva had brought with her as requested, looked across at her and inquired, 'Tell us, Eva, where does your story begin . . .'

2. "Started badly"

Everything was dark. The car's headlights hardly showed a few feet of the road in front of us due to the heavy snow. And the merciless cold wasn't exactly helping the situation. It didn't matter how much we played with the controls, we couldn't make it even a single degree hotter inside the car.

'Would you mind wiping the mist from the windscreen? I can't see shit,' Daniel told me, frustrated by having to lean over the steering wheel and still not seeing much.

'Hey, don't talk to me like that just because we haven't arrived yet!' I reproached him, taking some tissue paper out of one of the pockets of my puffer jacket, which I'd zipped all the way up to my nose.

'Oh, yeah, so now it's my fault! What an asshole I am; I have no fucking idea about these roads, right?' he mocked me, while concentrating on the satnav. 'If this pile of shit had indicated the roads properly, we would have been there by now.'

'You mean that if you'd set it up before you took the wrong turn and got lost, we'd have been there by now!' I corrected him, whilst bad temperedly wiping the windscreen. It was *so* not my fault that we'd got lost.

Stacey's cry of disgust came from the back of the car. She poked her head between the front two seats, frowning, and removed the scarf from her mouth. 'Look guys,' she said forcefully, 'if you don't shut up, I'm getting out of the damned car. For god's sake, you haven't stop arguing since we left London! My head is screaming and I don't have a single painkiller on me. It's damned cold in here. And look at me, my face is dead white!'

'Well, you can use that ton of makeup that you *bring*,' we heard Dave's low voice at her side, without much enthusiasm. The poor guy's English faltered at times.

Stacey stared straight ahead, almost possessed. The tendons on her neck tightened just before she suddenly turned to face the figure of the boy. Even in the darkness I knew she'd be able to see his face, slightly lit by the screen of the iPhone with which he was playing, not a bit deterred by anything around him.

'Excuse me, what did you just say, *David?*' she asked, stressing a funny accent when pronouncing his name.

The boy removed the headphones from one ear and stopped whatever he was doing on the phone. He looked at her with an expression between regret and indifference that demonstrated his hatred of being called David. He detested how it sounded in English, and Stacey always made sure she used that pronunciation to annoy him. When he spoke, his tone was calm and measured. 'I *say* that now you can give use to all the makeup that you *bring*. If you wanted to be warm in the middle of December, you *should go* to the Caribbean.'

'Look, arggghh . . . This is just–!'

I spun around in the passenger seat and looked at the both of them.

'Don't you two start arguing now! That's the last thing we need. We're so sorry,' I said, emphasizing the "we're", not wanting to sound too sarcastic. 'We haven't exactly given you an ideal journey. So now we're all going to relax and enjoy whatever we have left of the trip.' I turned back in my seat, looked to the satnav and smiled. 'Anyway, it's not going to take us much longer . . . Or so I think.'

'But didn't you say you used to come here every summer?' Daniel asked me. He was pulling weird faces, narrowing and focusing his eyes on the road ahead, still trying to see beyond the car lights like an old man trying to see the numbers on the remote control.

'Well, yeah, but it's been a long time since I've been able to. Between work and how busy we are around the TV series, it's been a few years now since I came up here.'

I stared at the road, irritated. For as much as I could see around us, I had no idea of where we were. The satnav indicated that we were ten minutes away, but I was unable to recognise a single stretch of asphalt.

Cries of Blood

Driving in the summer was a different story: the night fell later and anyone would be able to recognise at least parts of the road. But it wasn't summer, and rather than being lost in the north of Scotland, it seemed as if we were lost in the middle of the North Pole.

As I'd just told them, it had been a few years since I'd travelled there with my family, before I joined the TV series where the four of us were now working. And although I'd gone there many times through the years, we were now driving in a dreadful snowstorm. We knew the storm had been affecting the north of the country for days, but we hadn't expected it to turn that ugly in just a few hours.

All of a sudden, the satnav's screen began flickering and producing funny noises. I knocked it, uselessly. Every second that passed it worsened, with increased flickering and higher, acute noises.

'Chssst, turn that shit down, it's going to wake up my little Daisy,' Stacey whispered, covering her Bobtail puppy's ears, even though the dog had passed the whole journey dead to the world.

'Oh, come on, she is not going to *woke* up after the pill you *give* her,' said Dave, his eyes fixed once again on his phone screen.

I was struggling to turn off the device without any luck. Then unexpectedly, it went quiet and the screen turned as black as that night. I sighed and placed the device back on its stand to charge.

'Turn right in two hundred yards,' we heard it saying, out of the blue. 'Turn left in two hundred yards. Turn right in three hundred yards. Turn around . . .'

'Oh, for fuck's sake, stupid satnav! Turn that shit off!!' Daniel shouted at me, exasperated.

'Take the third exit at the roundabout. Stop the car in one hundred yards. Stop the car . . .' the device went on and on, as if playing all the options in its memory, still with its screen completely black.

'Shut up, we're not stopping the car, you nutter!' I blurted out as I grabbed the satnav as if I were a crazy woman.

'Turn around in one hundred yards . . . Turn right in fifty yards . . . Stop the car in twenty yards . . .'

What happened next was all really fast. I felt a hand pulling the device from mine. I heard a window opening. The icy wind produced a prolonged, sick shiver all the way down my spine. A second later, the window was closed and Daniel sat comfortably next to me, a broad smile on his face.

'And *voilà*, enough with the satnav. I knew that for ten pounds it couldn't be a good one.'

I started laughing uncontrollably. My giggling was contagious, and moments later the three of them were laughing with me. And at last, after a long day on the road, a good feeling took possession of the interior of the car. I felt so cheerful that I even willingly cleaned the mist on the windscreen again.

'Oh, yeah, it's funny now,' Daniel half murmured by my side, in an abrupt tone of regret.

'What do you mean?' Dave asked, still laughing.

'Well . . . I mean that without a satnav, I don't know how we're going to get there. Not even those of us who've been here hundreds of times before know where we are.'

I gave him a little punch on the arm and focussed my eyes on the road, as if I'd just seen something. 'No, wait. I think this looks familiar.' I cleaned my passenger seat's window and looked around. Then I tried to discern something through Daniel's. 'Ok, if I'm not mistaken, once we go around this side of the mountain, the road will be surrounded by lots of trees. I think we're close to the neighbouring village near my house.'

We all sat tight, coats zipped all the way up, waiting to go around the side of the mountain. And indeed, at the end of the bend we found the road I remembered, all surrounded by tall pines and covered in snow. It went down a slope, towards a kind of hollow. The long "S" shaped bends didn't stop, but at least, through all the trees, we were able to sight a small, distant group of lights.

The snow was scarce once we reached that sheltered part of the road. We could still spot it on top of the branches, though, piled up in thick layers that threatened to drop on us when we passed beneath them. But I didn't care.

Finally, we were arriving.

After over more than thirteen hours with heavy traffic, visiting each and every of the service stations on our way because, when one of us didn't need the toilet, Daniel needed to fill up the tank, or someone else needed to stop for a cigarette (since Daniel wouldn't allow anyone smoking inside his car), or was craving a milkshake from Starbucks . . . The tug of war between Daniel and me, Stacey complaining every twenty minutes and Dave asking me to charge his phone every hour . . .

That moment felt glorious.

Soon after, we reached the tiny village of Guildon Forest, so small it barely appeared on any map. It was quiet and remote or, as Stacey would call it, a "dead horse town". At that time of the night, not a soul could be found on its streets.

The majority of people living there were elderly; the younger residents in their forties at least. Many of them had long since gone to the capital or other parts of the country, sometimes returning to work in the nearby ski resorts during the ski season.

Some houses were in very poor condition, abandoned. If on some of them you could count two standing walls, it'd be a miracle. But on the other hand, the inhabited houses were well kept, adorned with pots of flowers in the small front gardens, Christmas decorations on the doors and windows, and elaborate gates at the front of each home.

The village consisted of seven or eight streets. The furthest one had a tiny church and what decades ago had been a small coal factory, once the lifeblood of the village and the reason for its existence.

On the main street, where the better looked after buildings were and where the few inhabitants of the place lived, was the only store for the whole village. It sold anything you needed: from food to books, tools, and medicines. The owners, Mr and Mrs McGregor, were old friends of my mum. That was the reason they were still open; I'd called them letting them know I was on my way and would need some food for a few days. Obviously, it was money they couldn't turn down – especially in a "dead horse town" like that one – no matter how late it was.

When we entered the store, we were thankful for the warm air embracing and welcoming us. It was followed by an intense and sweet smell.

'Oh, God, now it really *seem* it is Christmas,' Dave half shouted, at the sight of a tray of freshly baked muffins at the counter.

The guys split up to gather the things we needed while I talked to Mr McGregor, an old man whose standing up was already a phenomenon. When I used to go there as a child, he was already quite old.

'You are so beautiful, dear,' said the man, giving me a loving pat on the cheek. He had always been kind to me, almost like my own granddad.

'Thanks a lot, Mr McGregor. How are you and your wife?'

'Very good, thank you. Although she is becoming even more irritating every day: all day long complaining. When it's not back pain it's her fingers, or if not it's her knees. So, here I am.'

I smiled at him. He and his wife were always complaining about each other. And though it was funny, I had to listen to the same moans every single summer. I was sorry to see he was always somewhat depressed, going on about troubles that only seemed serious to him. His wife, on the other hand, was a happy woman, the kind of person you couldn't talk to without smiling.

However, it brought back so many good memories from when I used to summer around that village. Moreover, I was thrilled we had arrived and that I was able to speak with someone I hadn't been stuck with, hour after hour, in the same car.

'I bet she's not that bad . . . By the way, my mum sends her love and she hopes that you two are well. And now, if you don't mind, I'd better get on with my shopping since I made you stay open so late in the eve–'

'Oh, before I forget. Congratulations, dear! My wife told me this last spring that you were chosen for . . . What was that called?'

'Do you mean the TV series?'

'Beg your pardon, what was that?' asked the man, turning his head to one side to hear better.

'TV . . . SE-RIES . . .' I repeated, raising my voice.

'Oh, yes, of course, for one of those . . . My wife is up to date with all those gossip magazines, but we haven't been able to see you since in here we don't get a TV signal–'

Then, as if in a comedy film, Stacey's head popped up from behind a shelf of bottles. 'What?! There's no TV in this place?!'

'Don't worry, we have one at my house. They just don't get much signal down in the village, and much less in this weather. But calm down, we shouldn't have any problems at my place.' I turned back to Mr McGregor. 'Don't you worry about anything. Now, if you don't mind, I'm going to hurry and get some stuff. With this horrible storm, we've had a tiring journey and we can't wait to get to the house and get settled.'

I picked up a basket and rolled my eyes when I turned around. Half the planet knew who I was, but the old man wasn't aware of the world-famous TV series I starred in. So he'd happened to hear about it "last spring". He was definitely not up-to-date, the poor man. I went to the back of the store, where I discovered Daniel browsing through some gossip magazines.

'Hmm . . . Aren't you supposed to be doing something right now?'

'Oh, yeah, sorry. I've just seen this magazine,' he said, while still leafing through an article under a picture of himself, posing. 'Look, it says, "Daniel Fergusson, the handsome redhead of nineteen years old, originally from Kent, has just finished shooting his third film, 'Trivial'.

Since July, he's starred once again in the series that made him famous last year, 'Prodigies'. Where will the schoolgirls' favourite boy spend Christmas this year? Last year he was seen in a Cuban beach resort. Will he show off his hot body once again in an exotic location? Most probably he'll opt to spend some family time with his new girlfriend and co-star, Eva Dom–" '

'Right, that's enough,' I interrupted, giving him an unfriendly look. 'If we've come all the way here, it's precisely to get away from all that,' I reminded him. I'd never liked those kinds of magazines.

But he ignored my prompting to put away the magazine; he turned his back to me and kept reading. 'Yeah, but look, they also talk about you. "We've seen the nineteen-year old American-Spanish actress, Eva Domínguez, happy with her new boyfriend (Daniel Fergusson). Recently, we caught them outside a shopping centre in Paris, where they were promoting the show in which they met. They didn't mind showing off their love in public until they spotted our cameras. Right after they sped away in a taxi. Eva is now shooting her next film under the direction of Charles Still, in which she co-stars with her mum, the Spanish and Oscar-winning actress, Olivia Domínguez. This will be Olivia's first film role since the death of her husband . . ." '

That was it. I took the magazine from his hands, placed it back on the shelf with the rest and turned around.

'You *have* fucked it up,' I heard Dave telling Daniel behind me.

'Excuse me?'

Dave followed me to the next isle, carrying a basket full of food. He knew what Daniel didn't seem to understand. I didn't take it well when reminded about my father. It was three years since his death by then, and I still hadn't really moved on. When Dave reached me by the drinks shelf, I was yanking some soda cans into my shopping basket. He just stood there by my side. It was clear by his long silence that he didn't know what to say. So he ended up using the not so clever question, 'You ok?'

'I'm great! Now, leave me alone!'

Cries of Blood

Dave turned away immediately, flushed. He didn't like how everyone took out their problems on him. Enough people preyed on him on set, where he had to put up with all the rudeness and bad manners of others.

He'd met me at one of the final stages of casting, just before we all found out our respective roles. I was so sad for him when I found out that he and Daniel were fighting for the same role; Daniel was far better known than Dave. However, the producers were impressed with him and decided to keep him as a special extra on the show. He had come all the way from Spain in search of an opportunity as an actor. I think he'd been studying in a school of acting in Guildford before we started shooting.

At first, he thought I was like Daniel and Stacey: brats and snobs who had come out of nowhere with huge egos. But soon he realised I wasn't like that. He knew my mum and I, since he was also Spanish. And when he saw I was an ordinary girl, he was surprised. On many occasions I didn't eat with the rest of the cast, preferring to join him and the rest of the extras – which most of the actors thought was plain weird.

Our friendship grew quickly and we hung out together in our spare time. We told each other everything and he'd come over to my house. Now and again he tried to make his excuses, because he didn't want me to believe he was so close to me just for my fame. He had many hang-ups about his stagnated career as an actor. And he didn't want to seem like he was using me to progress his career.

I always told him he was an idiot, that I would never think that of him. And as many times he refused to go somewhere with me, the more I planned to spend time with him.

Like this holiday.

Unfortunately, when I'd insisted on going to my house near Guildon Forest and asked him to come along, he'd refused at first. In the end, he'd ended up accepting, even though he didn't like Stacey or especially Daniel. Every time Daniel saw Dave and me together at the filming set, he'd approach as if I were all alone and would start kissing me, pretending there was no one else around. He made up a hundred excuses to snatch me from Dave's side. I didn't really know if it was out of jealousy, or simply that his ego made him preen in front of everyone.

But I never turned my back on Dave, as many times as I could scape on the set, I'd always go around and talk with him.

So when he'd left me alone in the aisle of the store, hurt by my furious reply, I ran after him and apologised.

'I'm so sorry. I can't take it anymore.' I blew my nose and wiped the tears from my eyes. 'I'm sorry if I've been edgy with you, but between Daniel being a cold idiot and Stacey being a dick–'

'Yes, I know, they are a present from *a* expired Tetra-Brik of milk.'

I pushed him as I laughed – although, as I've said, the poor guy wasn't quite successful with some comments or jokes – and asked him to come with me to get the rest of the shopping.

And I don't know why, but as we were piling groceries into the basket, he told me something I would never forget.

'Anyway, I *knew* this trip started badly, but you will see how everything is not so bad.'

The car was dead silent as we drove up the mountain. Since the moment we got in the vehicle, Daniel and I hadn't spoken a word to each other except for me to guide him where he had to go, as my house lay just outside the village.

After moving to the UK, my parents had bought land nearby and built a house out of anyone's sight. It was there where we used to summer every year, far, far away from the fame and from the rest of humanity.

On the back seat, Dave was once again focussed on his iPhone, connecting to Facebook. Next to him, Stacey was busy reading an interview she had done a few weeks back for a gossip magazine.

Occasionally, she let out a "What! Such scumbags", "I didn't say that!" or "he's just a friend". Dave, who was listening to her exclamations, seemed to be laughing his ass off and, most probably, the least he would be thinking about the girl was a "Fuck you".

Outside, there was more of the same: continuous, huge amounts of snowflakes falling from the sky, getting bigger and thicker by the second.

Daniel was driving faster than before. I guess without realising he was doing so. He was pissed off. He didn't like that Dave had come along with us. I knew he detested everything about him: all the time on his phone; his wishes of becoming an actor, even – as one day Daniel told me – believing that one day he was going to be given a role in the series and finally stop being just an special extra; his being such a good friend of mine, knowing me better than Daniel himself. The thought of Dave possibly being in love with me didn't get out of Daniel's mind. We had spoken about it, and it had caused one of our many arguments.

More than that, the weather wasn't helping his mood. The windscreen wipers were squeaking in front of our eyes, hardly giving us better visibility . . .

All of a sudden, I was startled from my thoughts. 'WATCH OUT!!' I screamed as we rounded a sharp bend.

I saw Daniel's hands gripping the steering wheel and his foot pressing hard on the brake when he realised that, in the middle of the road, there was something moving.

The wheels turned on full lock.

My friends were shouting . . .

Stacey's puppy was barking . . .

The car bumped onto something on one side . . .

And then it stopped . . .

'What *happen*?!'

'God, are you all ok?!'

'What the fuck was that?!'

The little dog kept barking, turning her head back to the side of the road where we had just skidded through.

I wrapped my hands around my head; I had banged it against the passenger window. When I could see clearly, I made sure that everyone was unhurt. I asked Stacey to make her dog shut up and opened my door. And I looked back.

I couldn't see anything. The rear lights of the car were creating an irritating red circle around the snowflakes, which fell like icy knives from all angles. In the lights they changed from pure white to a dark, blood colour.

The ground under my feet was icy. I took a few steps away from the car and tried to discern something beyond the darkness.

For a moment, I thought there was nothing whatsoever on the road and that Daniel was going to be furious with me, especially after bumping his car. Perhaps it had been a trick of the light, the weather confusing my senses. Or maybe it had been a stupid owl flying in front of us just before we launched the car into the ditch.

But there was something on the road after all.

And it was not a stupid owl.

I will never forget those freezing moments. They'll remain engraved on my memory until the end of my days.

3. "In the middle of nowhere"

'It can't be . . .' I remember that I whispered.

The blood froze in my veins, as did my breath in the air. For a moment, I stood still in the middle of the road. Nothing could have roused me from the stupefaction that invaded each and every one of my senses.

I heard my three friends on the road behind me. They were all trying to see through the falling snow.

All three suffered the same shock as me.

As if time had stopped, the four of us stood quiet and motionless, holding our breath. Snowflakes were falling on us as if we were just another tree or rock on the mountain. Until, as if I had just woken up, I said. 'It's . . . a little girl.'

In the middle of the road, as if it were normal at that place and under those weather conditions, was the standing figure of a little girl. She was wearing only a simple, white nightgown. Jet black eyes shone through the snow. Piercing but sweet and innocent eyes, surrounded by a mass of dark, damp hair blowing heavily in the wind. In her arms she seemed to be hugging some kind of bundle. I couldn't tell what it was from where we were standing.

The most important thing was that the child was the shape I had seen on the road, just a few feet away.

No one said anything else for a long while. We should have asked if she was all right, but only silence invaded the scene. A silence only broken by the whistling wind, fiercely buffeting the treetops over our heads.

A single bark from Stacey's dog brought Dave back to reality. He approached the girl.

'What . . . are you doing here? What *you do* in the middle of the road?'

The girl just stood there, staring at him impassively, as if the question wasn't for her.

'Are you ok?' I asked this time, getting closer step by step.

She only tightened her arms around her chest, squeezing the lump she was hugging. When I arrived where she was standing, I realised that the poor creature was barefoot, in the middle of nowhere and in that snowstorm. But it didn't seem to bother her at all.

'Oh, come here, sweetie,' I urged her to get covered with my own coat. 'God, you're shivering . . . What on earth are you doing barefoot in the middle of this road?'

Once again, the girl didn't say a word.

I looked around. From what little I could see, I couldn't find any trace of car tracks besides our own. If someone had passed through there before us, it must had been a long time ago. Other wise the snow would still be showing a trace to be seen.

Not a single house. Not a light from any home around, as I already knew there wouldn't be. The village was about two minutes' drive . . .

We all hurried to get inside the car, except Daniel. The boy stood outside, having a look at the driver's side of the car that had bumped against a guardrail. While he was ranting about the accident that "my car!" had suffered, the three of us were busy looking at the little girl. I made sure she was all right; not a scratch to be found.

'But what were you doing in the middle of the road?' I asked her again; but she didn't say a thing. She held my gaze while still hugging whatever she was holding against her chest, as if her life depended on it. 'Where's your mum? Where's your dad?'

I got the same reaction from her.

Silence.

A silence now disturbed by Daisy's barks, who was trying to jump to the front, curious. The Bobtail puppy was so cute, with the grey-back fur on the back of her body and her front all white. Cute, but annoying.

'What's your name?' asked Stacey, at the same time holding her dog in her arms.

'Well, it's clear the girl isn't going to speak. Maybe *he* is in shock or something, *no*?' Dave surmised after a couple of seconds of silence when it was obvious we weren't going to get an answer from the child.

She returned our gaze as if she couldn't understand us, as if she was foreign and didn't know in which language we were talking. Now that I think about it, there was something strange on her eyes. She didn't look at us as if we were unknown people. She didn't seem to be shy, nor frightened of us, even though she'd almost been hit by our car. She stared back at us from the inside of my coat.

'Jesus, she looks so young. How old must she be? Six? Seven?'

The girl nodded.

It had been a simple move of her head, almost imperceptible. It made me wonder if it had been an actual nod. Perhaps she'd just felt a chill . . . Or, maybe, she really had nodded.

'Are you seven years old?' I repeated.

This time she didn't move in the slightest. She just held my gaze. Such a motionless and innocent stare from a cold little face, white as paper.

The driver's door opened, flooding the interior of the vehicle with freezing cold air, accompanied by a shower of snow and an even more pissed off Daniel. When he closed the door, he wiped the snow from his hair and looked at the child.

'Is she ok?'

'Don't waste *you* time, she is not saying a word,' Dave said to him, succinctly informing of the situation.

The four of us sat quietly, looking at the girl.

A curious situation. Surrounded by huge amounts of snow. On the ditch of a road in that God-forshaken place. After being very close to running over an innocent girl, the same girl who was now looking back at us as if nothing of what had happened had anything to do with her. As if she wasn't there, or as if she thought she was invisible.

'What are we doing, then?' Daniel asked, worried. 'Should we take her to the village? Should we go around and see if we can spot a house somewhere? I don't know, she must have come out from somewhere, right?'

'Let's go home,' I said drily.

'What do you mean?'

'Is it so difficult to understand what I just said?' I snapped, without looking at him; I only had eyes for the little girl in my arms. I held her close to me and massaged her back to bring her back to warmth.

Daniel looked to the front, put the keys back in the ignition and turned on the engine. He sat there quietly for a few seconds, listening to the wind fluttering around the car, while a thick curtain of snow continued to fall from all directions. He took a deep breath, reversed the car back on the road and continued in the same direction up we'd been travelling in before we'd swerved to avoid the little girl.

The next few minutes passed in complete silence. Even Daisy remained quiet except for the occasional soft groan. She kept her eyes fixed on the child. No one dared to say a word until Dave's phone made a weak noise.

'*Perfecto*, no signal,' he said with a snort.

'Turn right, just on that side road,' I pointed to Daniel when we approached a thick wooded area on our right.

He reduced the car's speed and turned where I told him to, like an automaton. He drove the car through the mountain as I'd directed, taking a rocky but quiet, wild path. Tall trees surrounded us on both sides. Their branches quivering in the strong wind.

A few feet ahead, the path turned darker, as if the cold was absorbing the headlights of the vehicle. With the ground covered in snow, it was difficult to guess which way we had to go. It could have had diverted somewhere else and we wouldn't have noticed. But since I didn't say anything, Daniel kept going cautiously forward: he didn't want to damage his new car again.

Around half a mile later, the route grew even fainter. I pointed out which way to go through the trees, and Daniel took my instructions without protesting or asking how long it would take to get to my house. At least we knew where we were. That was the only thing that mattered.

Delving deep into the trees had its positive side, even though we still couldn't see much around. Gradually, the wind reduced in ferocity and the snow was ceasing. Finally, the car's heater managed to maintain a pleasant temperature inside. The windscreen began to get misty, though, and Daniel had to wipe it off all by himself to be able to see the path, which turned away its cold, white face to show us yet more wet and muddy ground. It was the right route to my parents' house.

The house was a bit quirky. All of my parents' friends who'd visited it – and even I myself when I was little – had been impressed by its American style. A two-storey wooden house with its façade covered with light grey cladding, a slate roof and spacious interior, would shock at first sight. Especially with that house being situated in the north of Scotland.

On this occasion, however, the situation was different.

We'd endured all those uncomfortable hours of the journey, being in that horrendous snowstorm for the last couple of hours, practically lost and far, far away from home. Daniel and I were pissed off with each other; Stacey had complained every single second; and then there was Dave, who wouldn't have come in the first place unless I'd insisted . . . To top it all, we'd almost run over a little girl in the middle of the road . . . Yes, the expressions on our faces when we finally saw the house emerging from the trees was completely different.

We were more relieved than anything else.

Even when I gave Dave the keys to the gates, surrounded by bushes and more trees, he got out of the car without complaint. He didn't seem to care about the cold outside, walking through whatever conditions in order to end the car journey; he just wanted to reach the house, get warm and rest.

That had been a bumpy trip.

A trip in which there were still more things to come.

'Well, the heating is on,' I told them, closing the door that connected the garage with the house. I'd gone down there fifteen minutes earlier, after getting settled with all the suitcases inside.

When we'd entered the house, I'd taken my suitcase in one hand, the child hugging herself to me as we climbed the stairs followed by my three friends. Those stairs were made of wood and creaked so creepily that no one would be brave enough to use them at night, especially in the dark. On the first floor and on my right, I quickly reached my room – the one my parents would normally stay in – and left the girl sitting on the bed for a second.

Right after that, I showed each of the others to their bedrooms on the opposite side of the corridor. And when I say "each of the others", I mean it. Daniel stood quite silent when I indicated which of them was his; he'd obviously assumed he'd be sharing a room with me. But after he hadn't listened to me when I'd asked him in the store to stop reading that article, and after he'd gone on to mention my deceased father – well, that wasn't happening now.

Later on, we all went downstairs, except for the little girl whom I left shivering in my bedroom. Dave removed the dusty sheets that covered the furniture, which made Stacey's dog sneeze a few times. Stacey and Daniel put all the food and drinks in the fridge and kitchen cupboards. I prepared a cup of instant soup for the child to warm up a little. Only after I'd made sure she'd drunk it all, I went down to the garage to turn the heating on.

My mum had left some instructions on a sheet of paper that took me a long while to understand. The boiler had a huge petrol tank and far too many buttons to push and dials to spin. At first, I couldn't have said if it was colder outside or inside the house. However, after much struggling with the boiler, it finally produced the growl I remembered being scared by when I was younger.

'I think it's going to take at least half an hour to warm up the house,' I told the guys, when I went back upstairs.

Daniel approached me from behind and took me gently by the arm.

'Yes?' I asked him with a menacing tone, looking at his hand.

'Can we talk?'

'Right, tell me. What do you want to talk about? About your car, your fame, your money, your films, stupid gossip magazines in which–?'

'That's enough, please. I'm sorry, babe. What's done is done, and you know I didn't do it on purpose.'

I took a deep breath. I hadn't deigned to face him while he was talking to me. I admit that sometimes I can be a bit dramatic, but I didn't want to look at him. Not after he'd done what he wanted, without caring about my feelings . . . But, above all, not after he'd mentioned my dad, whom I'd only ever discussed with him once. Therefore, I turned around and began speaking slowly and firmly, still not looking at his eyes.

'No, Daniel, it's not enough. You want to talk, thinking about yourself as usual. Meanwhile, in my bedroom, covered with my coat and in a soaking nightgown, there's a little girl of six or seven years old, maybe even younger. The poor thing is just waiting to go to bed after being in the road for who knows how long, alone and separated from her home and family.

'So, if you don't mind, I'm going to see her, unless you have a better plan than talking rubbish, smoking weed or taking the alcohol in from the car. If I'm not mistaken, that's all you're interested in right now.'

Nobody said anything more, so I went upstairs and left the three of them in the living room. When I got to my bedroom, I closed the door behind me. The child was standing in front of the window. She'd left the coat on the bed, where she'd been sitting before I went downstairs and asked her to wait for me. I hurried to open my suitcase and gathered up a few things.

'Come on, sweetie, put this on.'

The girl turned slowly and looked at the long pink t-shirt I was holding out to her. Yet again, she didn't mutter a word; instead, she moved her hands in circles. When I understood what she wanted, I smiled and turned around, pulling one of the silly faces people make when children are around, trying to make everything funnier and win her trust.

'Take off the nightgown and leave it on the chair next to you: it's soaking wet.'

I started biting my nails as I waited for her. It was a bad habit of mine when nervous or after an argument. Somehow, it relaxed me and helped me think calmly. Unfortunately, it was something that was becoming a routine since I'd started going out with Daniel. It was obvious we weren't having the best time. We hadn't even been together for long and working on the same project wasn't helping – quite the opposite.

On one hand, I was a girl who (thank God) had famous parents, with money and properties dotted about the globe. But I was also an ordinary girl who only wanted to be treated like anyone else, and for now and again to get as far as possible from people wanting to know every detail about my life.

Daniel, on the other hand, was the opposite. He seemed born to be an actor. Fame, money, fans, flashing cameras, red carpets and interviews . . . He loved them all. Although that didn't stop him from complaining about the persistent fans and paparazzi on the street, whom he ignored, facing straight ahead with his aviator sunglasses on.

Sometimes, I would ask myself how it had happened that I was going out with a guy like him. We didn't share the same values, hardly had any interests in common. I just knew that, we'd started going out after he'd badgered me for a date.

But that wasn't something to waste time thinking about now. We were far away from the rest of the world, in the middle of nowhere. That had been the plan after all. What we hadn't planned was to nearly have an accident when a child appeared barefoot in the snow on the road in front of us.

What was I supposed to do?

Who was I meant to call?

We were in the north of Scotland, near a village too small to have a police station. The nearest town was at least fifteen minutes' drive away, and that was without the snowstorm. And even if the village *had* had a police station, that wasn't a place for a little girl. What would they do with her until someone came and claimed her?

No. It was decided. The best thing for her was to stay with us until we found out where she came from. Someone must have been looking for her, so we'd wait till the next day, let the storm calm down, and in the morning I'd ask Daniel to take me to Guildon Forest so I could ask Mrs McGregor about it. She knew all the gossip. She always knew what was going on in the nearest town, despite never getting out of the village herself. And in a case like ours, it would be great to have her around. I knew that if the child had come from the village, it would only be because she'd been visiting grandparents or other relations for Christmas. Mrs McGregor would definitely know who was missing her.

Thousands of questions came to mind.

How was it possible that the girl had appeared in the middle of that road, so far from the village or any other house?

What kind of parents would let a helpless child leave the house wearing only her nightgown?

What was she doing outside at that time of the night?

Had something bad happened to her family?

But most strange of all, where on earth were they?

Suddenly, I realised that the girl had fallen asleep on the edge of the bed. She was still hugging that lump she had been pressing against her chest when we found her. At last I could take a look: it was a light brown teddy bear – or, at least, what at some point had been one. It was gnawed and shabby. And even though it was wet, she had fallen asleep squeezing it tightly to her chest, as if to make sure no one would take it away from her.

I didn't want to disturb her, but her hair was soaking wet and I had to raise her up to get it dry.

She remained with her eyes closed, even with the noise of the hairdryer, exhausted from her adventure outside. I just got a little smile, almost imperceptible on her tiny lips, when I laid her back on the bed, covered her with the duvet and used the hairdryer to warm the sheets beneath it, as my dad used to do when I was little.

When the bed was warm enough, I put on my pyjamas and took my diary from one of the compartments of my suitcase. I sat quietly on a small armchair in the room.

There I began describing all the events of that day, under the small beam of light from a side lamp. From the start of the journey in London until the arrival at my mum's house. And, when I felt satisfied I'd covered everything, I curled up next to the girl and went to sleep myself.

We would need to wake up early to go to the village. And since I didn't want to make any more noise, I decided to take a shower in the morning.

4. "Just for a few days"

It was Christmas Eve. I was glad to wake up early, look out through the window and see the landscape covered in snow; but the storm hadn't calmed down at all. In fact, I'd say it was worse than the night before.

The truth was it worried me. It wasn't just because we'd have to go down to the village in a few hours to try to solve the predicament we were in; but we'd agreed to stay there for three days at most. We'd disconnect from work, friends and family, and afterwards we'd spend the remaining few weeks of the holidays with our loved ones. But now I didn't know how or when the snowstorm would end.

What if we couldn't get back to our families on time? Had it been such a good idea to insist on all of us going up there to Scotland in the middle of such horrible weather?

Looking back on it now, the only thing I'm sure of is that we deserved a break from everything and everyone; but we didn't deserve what happened to us.

You don't realise how beautiful privacy is until you find yourself in a situation like ours. No one would have bet a penny on the success of our TV series at the start, but it had become one of the few British shows to be aired across half the planet at the same time. Wherever we went there were people who knew us, stopped us and harassed us with questions about things that weren't any of their business.

I remember what happened the previous Christmas, a few months before the show was aired for the first time. My mum and I had gone to New York to spend a few days with my dad's family. After his death, we'd barely had time to be with each other. But whilst I'd had a great time there with my grandparents and uncles, I was constantly pestered by the press. Plus people would interrupt us at any restaurant to take a picture with us or just to say hello, since they "knew" us.

So, I had my reasons for being happy to see all that snow. I'd never cared about its consequences in London, where salt was thrown on even the darkest corner of the city whenever the weather turned icy. I was used to having others deal with it for me, so it hadn't occurred to me what a curse it could be for us.

Now I tried not to think how difficult it would be to move outside the house to enjoy the magical views the weather was gifting us.

I found Stacey downstairs and in high spirits. She was happily moving around the large open space that served as kitchen, living and dining room in one, looking through the window every now and then and humming Christmas songs while Daisy scampered after her. She was wearing pink pyjamas with a pattern of white dolls and her slippers, also pink, were decorated with fluffy balls on each instep that the puppy was trying to bite. So they began to play around the room, only to end the game two minutes later when Stacey got tired of running.

Over by the fireplace, Daniel was trying to set a match to some logs, making me smile.

'Heating's off and it was a bit cold. I thought of using the fireplace,' he said to me, somewhat intimidated, not knowing if I was going to get angry with him for not asking me first. 'I saw you had some dry logs outside and I'm just trying to–'

'Thanks,' I said simply. I approached him, gave him a kiss on the cheek and turned on a tiny switch next to the fireplace. 'You need to switch the fan on, so it helps keep the flames burning.'

The poor boy was speechless. He never knew how I would react to things, and I often surprised him the day after an argument with a different attitude. It was as if a good sleep made me forget all the bickering. It was an approach that, on one hand was good, but on the other hand had allowed people to take advantage of me on more than one occasion. However, it had helped me many times to solve tiny or huge problems that I had with someone. And for good or ill, that's just the way I was . . .

Cries of Blood

'How's the little girl? Has she said anything to you yet?' Stacey asked me as I was opening the door to the garage.

'I think she has a fever. She was fidgeting and shivering all night long. But no, she hasn't said a word yet; seems the cat's got her tongue ... I think my mum must have kept some old clothes from when I was a child that would fit her. I'm just going to take a look.'

I turned the garage light on and followed the steps down.

It was a disaster. My mum loved to keep everything for its memories. From toys to drawings, dolls from my childhood or even furniture, paintings, clothes, a couple of spare beds in case we ever needed them, papers, bills, magazines ... Anything we'd stopped using at our London house had ended up there. You can imagine the crazy amount of stuff piled around.

At least the garage was quite spacious and everything was more or less organised. In the centre of the room there was enough space to walk carefully among all the junk.

I started looking for any box with my name written on it, and it didn't take me long to strike it lucky. At the top of a stack of boxes, all with my name and dates on them, there was one that had "Eva's clothes. Little" written on the front, followed by the smiley face that my mum used to draw on everything. But as it was too high up for me to reach – and I don't remember any time when I tried to climb anything that didn't end up with me bleeding on the ground – I called to Daniel to come and help me out.

A few seconds later he appeared at the bottom of the stairs, rubbing his dirty hands with a cloth.

'Oh my God. Now I see why you didn't let me put the car in the garage,' he remarked, laughing, while looking to all the boxes and trash that surrounded us.

'Come on, help me getting that box. Luckily, I'll find something that will fit the girl.'

'I didn't know you were so motherly, babe,' he said in a tone between shy and comic.

'Well, there're lots of things you don't know about me,' I replied, putting on an air of mystery.

'Anything I should be worried about?'

'Mmmm . . . Wait a second,' I said after spotting an album of pictures from when I was at school. I rummaged between its dusty pages, the paper infused with a fetid, musty smell, looking for a picture that I was certain had to be in there.

'Let's say that I haven't always been skinny or *attractive* . . . By the way, this isn't coming out of here,' I warned him, pointing to him while holding the picture against my chest; although it's *funny* that it turns out to be me who is revealing what I confessed to him. 'When I was seven years old, after I'd moved to London from Spain and changed my friends, school and home, I ended up a bit depressed and found a passion for cakes. I must say that I had braces on, that I'd put on quite a few pounds and that . . . I'm so embarrassed. You can be proud of going out with "Miss Cake Eater" from my school.' And I showed him the horrible picture of me, smiling next to an empty plate.

'OH-MY-GOSH! Where did you hide that ass?' he burst out laughing, almost crying. 'Actually, I must say that you've got worse since then.'

'At least I'm not the one who hid his willy between his legs and pretended to be "Daniela" . . .' I replied in the same cheerful tone he had used with me. That's the way we were with each other sometimes, coming up with little games, laughing and picking on each other in a friendly way.

But on that occasion I knew I'd won, because he blushed and muttered something like, 'Such a big mouth! I'm never letting you alone with my mother again.'

He took the box down while I was still laughing. Those pleasant moments would occur when least expected; but they didn't happen very often. I wanted to make that one last as long as I could. I hated to be angry; I'd never liked it. And I think that it was those kinds of moments that had kept us together.

'Here you go. And please, do me a favour: keep my friends in shape,' he whispered in my ear, grabbing my hips. He hugged me from behind and kissed me on the neck.

He knew how to make me smile and feel good sometimes. That was one of those times.

We spent quite a while digging through the box full of clothes from my childhood. I tried to pick the items that were in better condition and, of course, the ones Daniel couldn't find a way to make fun of. My mum used to dress me in bright colours. She'd always said the country was miserable with so much rain, and what better way to brighten it up than with her very own little "doll".

Anyway, for the short time we spent in the garage, we both tried to laugh and not get angry with each other. Only once did something happen that made us remember why I'd got angry with Daniel the previous night. But this time, I knew what to do.

It happened as we were about to go back upstairs to the house. Daniel found a bicycle and made an unfortunate comment about it. He didn't do it on purpose, and much less knew that the bicycle didn't belong to me.

'It was my dad's,' I confessed to him.

'I see . . . Mmm, Eva, I know that yesterday I shouldn't have kept reading out that article, but we all have things that hurt, things we're embarrassed about . . . or whatever. But if we're together, we'll have to . . .' He sounded as if he had spent all night preparing that speech and had just found the moment to use it.

'I know. And I'm sorry. I don't know . . . what to say. I would just like you to understand me better sometimes, to open your eyes to someone other than yourself. I don't think I'm ready to talk about . . .' I hesitated for a second, 'About my dad. Obviously, I haven't had a good time since then and I've tried to find some support through my friends and family, without talking about it. I'm so sorry about my mood swings, but I want you to understand that it's a part of me that I don't know when I'll feel ready to open up about.'

I was happy about clearing things up and I think we both felt relieved that we'd been able to speak to each other like adults for once, without arguing.

I knew that Daniel wasn't really to blame. It was just that sometimes his attitude and the way he did things got on my nerves. And even I would have to admit that I'd get cross with him over the slightest thing. (For no reason some people knew me as "The Española Girl.") Every now and then, I'd realise that defect of mine and, like that time in the garage, I would try to force myself to stop being so dramatic.

'Would you mind if we talked about your father?' Julia interrupted Eva from her seat in the armchair opposite.

Eva shook her head, knowing that she didn't have a choice.

'As many people know,' Julia started narrating, looking into the camera, 'Liam Lawrence was an American film director. He met Olivia Domínguez while shooting a film, the same one that won the actress her first Oscar. Some time after, they got married and had Eva. They chose Spain as their permanent residence, but their constant jobs in Hollywood and in the United Kingdom brought them here. So, they decided to move and start a new life.

'I remember it as if it were yesterday,' the presenter muttered, looking to one side. 'I was still young, but I remember seeing them in all the magazines. "The perfect family", with a marriage envied by everyone, and a beautiful daughter.'

She stared at the young girl, who didn't look unfazed by the compliments.

'But little has been said about the unfortunate loss of your father, Eva. Would you mind telling us how it all happened? Perhaps some people may better understand your words when you talk about all those hidden feelings at that time, why you couldn't talk about him.'

The girl cleared her throat and looked at the woman with a bitter smile.

'It was tough,' she affirmed. 'Everything was perfect, as you said. Or, at least, that's how I remember it. Both my parents were the best and our home life was wonderful. We managed to live far away from fame and be an ordinary family, with our highs and lows. But we were happy. I don't remember a single argument between my parents. They were laughing all the time . . . Until my dad, who had been very busy with several projects in Hollywood, went to the doctor. He had complained on more than one occasion about stomach-ache and, apparently, he had trouble going to the toilet.'

She shut her eyes for a moment and took a deep breath, trying to stay calm and not be overwhelmed by the memories that had hurt her so much. With every word she spoke, images from that time flashed across her mind.

'He was diagnosed with colon cancer. But it was too late to treat it. They found metastases in his small intestine. And everything happened very quickly. He had to retire immediately from the film industry; even my mum had to cancel a film she was expected to be in. But neither of them told me anything.

'We dedicated some time to travelling, enjoying our last moments all together. But it was brutal to see the change that cancer made to my father. It almost happened overnight,' the girl remembered. 'He became extremely thin, every day losing more weight. And I wasn't stupid. I realised that something was wrong. On many occasions, my dad ended up bedridden, unable to pretend any longer that everything was fine . . . The only thing that the disease failed to take from him were those beautiful eyes he had –'

'Eyes that you two had in common,' Julia added.

She looked at the girl's lovely eyes. For the first time, she didn't know exactly what colour they were. The light was playing tricks, creating shadows on the iris. One moment they were pure grey, the next they'd changed to a blue or an ambiguous greenish colour.

'Yes, I know,' the girl admitted. 'Don't think that it isn't painful. Nobody expects to lose their father so soon. But I had to pull myself together as much as I could and try to get on with my life. Even if every time I looked in the mirror I saw my dad, I had to go on.'

We tried to fix the boiler, but it seemed to have decided not to work ever again. So, we went upstairs and closed the door, just after I had a last look at my father's bike.

I prepared a bowl with warm milk and some cereal for the little girl and went up to my room.

The girl was awake and looking out the window, gripping her teddy bear tightly. She turned when she heard me coming in, and I saw the flush in her cheeks. I didn't need to place my hand on her forehead to know that she definitely had a fever.

I left the clothes and the bowl of milk to one side, rummaged in my bag until I found my medicine box, took a pill out and split it in half. Obviously, I read the instruction leaflet first: I didn't want to give her a bigger dose than necessary. I offered her the half of the pill and a bottle of water, which I always had beside the bed.

'Oh, don't worry, it's going to make you feel better,' I told her when she turned her head back to the window.

I stood there staring at her for a few seconds and then went to her side. She turned her face to me, looked at the half pill and bottle of water and turned her back once again, returning to the bed with her teddy bear. At that point I couldn't stop myself laughing.

I said, carefully pronouncing each and every word, 'Ok, no worries. You don't want to take the medicine? That's fine. But I'm afraid that after your trip last night on the snow, all barefoot, the fever will get worse. You're going to sweat a lot and your head is going to hurt quite a bit . . . And I'll have no choice but to call a doctor to come and see you . . .'

I didn't need to say another word. A second later, she almost tore the pill from my hand, put it in her mouth and drank a big gulp of water. Then she opened her mouth to let me see that she had swallowed it down and got back in bed, covering herself with the duvet up to her neck.

'And what do you say about breakfast, sweetie?'

She sat up again and, without a word of protest, carefully took the bowl of warm milk and cereal and blew at every spoonful she took to her mouth.

If I can say anything today about that girl, it would be that she was no fool. Behind those innocent eyes and butter-wouldn't-melt expression, she was hiding a clever side. And with that scene – which made me smile and talk about it later on with the guys – she made her cleverness very clear. But the problem was trying to prise open the shell in which she was hiding. I hadn't had time to speak to her properly since we'd found her. I'd assumed that children were children and, no matter how shy or embarrassed they might be, in five minutes they'd overcome it and start babbling like parrots.

But this was another kind of girl. Something had to have happened to her to end up in the middle of a road. Especially at a time when she should have been fast asleep and dreaming. And I was wondering why she hadn't made a single sound when we asked her where she came from, or where her parents were, or why she was standing there in the snow.

I had an immense curiosity to find answers to the puzzle that we had inadvertently come across, the one I was turning over and over in my head. As any adult would in such a situation, I thought it was all very weird . . .

'By the way, I brought you a present.' As I'd guessed, it got her attention. She turned to me and looked at what I was holding. She wasn't pleased to discover that I meant my old clothes – although in her current mood I wouldn't have got a better reaction from her if I'd been holding a bag full of sweets. 'Tomorrow is Christmas Day and, as we're going down to the village to find your mummy and daddy, Santa Claus has given me these clothes for you. That way, you'll be warmer and able to get better in a jiffy. I'm going for a shower. When I come out, I'll give you a bath. Let's see if your fever goes down, ok?'

I wasn't expecting any response from her, although I stared at her for a few more seconds than necessary before I picked up my own clothes and headed to the shower. When I came back, I wasn't expecting either for her to protest about the bath.

The girl, compliant after having eaten all her breakfast, didn't argue about coming with me for her bath. I didn't need another trick, like when I'd threatened her with calling a doctor.

But once again she refused to take her clothes off in front of me, so I closed the shower curtain after she got in. A second later, she gave me back the t-shirt I'd given her the previous night. She left the teddy bear on the edge of the bathtub and followed my instructions to wash herself. From behind her ears to between her toes. I could hear her rubbing with the sponge while I was telling her a silly story, trying to earn her trust. I had always loved children.

'When you say "I had always loved children", do you mean that you don't want to be near one ever again?' Julia's voice interrupted her again.

Eva fixed her eyes on the presenter's. The woman was looking at her with a neutral expression, almost determined with her whole being to study all her facial expressions. Eva found herself back in the office as if awakening from a dream.

For a moment, she had been engrossed in the story. She was trying to answer the questions that Julia threw at her every now and then, questions designed to stop her from getting side-tracked with irrelevant details and drawing out more about the individuals who were involved.

It had been two years since those events and, step by step, she became more deeply immersed in the story. She remembered and was surprised by the new nuances that came to her down memory lane. Some of them were memories from which she, for all that time, had tried to run away, just as she'd tried to run from the death of her beloved father. Recollections that, with the delicate nudges from the presenter, came back to her mind in sharp images.

Those images had trapped her in their sticky web, blocking the rest of her senses. They didn't allow her to see the pale glimmer of the sun – which at that moment was being blocked by a cloud in the sky –, nor see the white blinds, and deprived her from feeling the drop of sweat that ran down her neck.

'No . . .' she muttered to herself. When she saw the woman's expression, she rushed to explain what she meant. 'I don't think that because you fall off a bike, you shouldn't try cycling anymore. At least that's how I see it after these last two years in silence. What happened then shouldn't mean that I don't like children anymore; although, obviously, I think I'll need to heal my wounds before feeling confident enough to approach to another child . . . or have one myself,' she finished with a forced smile, trying to soften her words.

Julia appeared pensive. Then she wrote something on the notebook that rested on her crossed legs. That position gave her an air of sensuality, unique to her. After that, she looked to the girl and tried to link their conversation back to the story, tactfully.

'All right, Eva. So, you are in the bathroom with this . . . lost girl, who you found in the middle of a snowstorm. And, as you were saying, at this time she was getting more confident, but still wasn't saying a word to anyone. And since she didn't refuse to have a bath, we could say . . .' she paused theatrically, sipping from the glass of water that rested on the arm of her chair before continuing, 'that you were gaining ground with her. Did you get anything out of her?'

The young girl took a deep breath and took her eyes from the woman's, staring into the distance. 'To be fair, at that moment I didn't feel like I was gaining "anything". That wasn't my aim. But I must admit that the way I behaved, trying to get her to come out of her shell, it could look like that. It was just that I had so many questions about her,' the girl said, returning her gaze to the woman, 'they stormed over any other thoughts. And I didn't know how to treat or talk to her.

'Put yourself in my situation: under the care of a minor, being who we were and in such an out-of-the-way place,' she challenged the woman after a small pause. 'Like any other decent citizen, I knew I should treat her with care and respect, just as I'd want someone else to do if it had been my own daughter. But kids are delicate and they're all different. I just wanted to reunite her with her mum . . . But when I tried to hold her hand and take her to the car to drive down to Guildon Forest, she refused.'

The girl was dry after her bath and was wearing jeans, a sweater and a pair of wellies. The wellies were a bit big for her, but she'd be seeing her parents soon and she'd have her own clothes again. But when I asked her to hold my hand so we could go and look for them, she just shook her head and gripped the teddy bear tightly to her body.

'No, come on, sweetie, we have to go. Your parents must be so worried about you.'

She turned, with the slow grace of an elderly and ill person, went back in the bedroom, took the boots off and got back into bed. It seemed as if that was her hiding place.

'Look, I know you're ill, but the sooner you get back with your mum, the sooner you'll get better. I'm sure she'll put you in your own bed, sing you a lullaby and you'll feel well soon.'

Silence overtook the room. Until that moment, when she stared at me with those eyes of hers – small, dark and feverish – and started moving her hands trying to tell me something, it hadn't crossed my mind that she might have been mute. She moved her hands in such a subtle and yet explicit way that I understood at once what she was trying to say.

'Do you want me to go and you stay here sleeping?' I interpreted.
She nodded.

'No, you can't stay here: this isn't your house. You have to come with us to look for your parents, otherwise we won't know who they are. *I* don't know who they are.'

There was only one thing I knew for sure about children: the moment you repeatedly said "no", you'd lost them.

She shook her head again and gestured with her weak hands that it was too cold outside.

Long story short, after too many attempts on my part had been met with hand signs, and when it was getting late, I decided to leave her with Dave and Stacey. I couldn't just force her to come with Daniel and me. We could always go back for her or, actually, her own parents could go and pick her up. After all, it was them who had lost her, not us. Surely, we were already doing enough.

So, after getting something to eat in the kitchen, I got in the car with Daniel and we set out for the village.

The route from my house to the road, and even the road itself, were pretty bad after all night snowing, so we had to be very careful. We didn't want to get stuck in some godforsaken ditch.

At least we had a better visibility at that time of the day. The dim sunlight, filtered through dozens of dark grey clouds, allowed us to see the road quite well. That was why, a few minutes later, as we passed the place where the night before Daniel had had to brake and we'd found the little girl, I asked him to stop the car. Perhaps in the daylight I'd be able to see some clue we'd missed.

I approached the guardrail and looked down the mountain. I could only see the village, looking very little from where we were. And I could see, as I'd known the night before, that there was no house between the village and that part of the road. In the other direction, looking up, I could only see more and more treetops buffeted by the wind and the snow.

Not a sign of life, except for a squirrel running between the branches, looking for shelter.

I got back in the car and we went down to Guildon Forest. I didn't need to show the boy where the shop was. When we entered together, shaking the snow from our shoes, we found only Mr McGregor there. He told me that his wife was at home making dinner, and that we were more than welcome to join them there. So, we went out onto the street again and walked to the end of the road, where there was a small, dark brick house with Christmas decorations on the door.

Mrs McGregor was passionate about Christmas, and I knew she always found time to put up lights, figurines and tinsel all around the house.

'What a surprise, sweethearts,' she welcomed us, smiling and almost throwing herself at us.

'Merry Christmas. Would you mind if we took some of your time?'

'Are you kidding me? You can take a whole day off me, if you please . . . Let me have a good look at you. You are so cute and grown up . . . And who's this dashing and handsome friend of yours?' That was just the beginning of what ended up as half an hour of continuous compliments and small talk about each other's families.

I told her about my mum, who sent all her love and asked to be remembered to them both and asked her about her health. Meanwhile, she brought us both a bowl of soup to warm up. And we very much appreciated it.

Mrs McGregor was a splendid cook and could prepare anything you wanted if you just gave her the right ingredients. Even after months, you could recall the wonderful flavours of her home cooked meals. I can still remember the mushroom and carrot soup we devoured in a flash that day.

Aside from being a good cook and a cheerful woman, she was a hypochondriac like no one I'd ever met before in my life, too chatty and a little eccentric at times; but woe betide you if you insinuated she was a busybody. That was the worst thing you could ever do.

So slowly, not paying too much attention to her chatter, I skilfully introduced to the conversation the reason we were there . . . among other things, I hurried to say.

'Did I just hear right?' the woman said, grabbing my arm, surprised by my story.

'Yes, you did. We found a girl of about six or seven years old, not sure exactly. Up there, in the middle of the road.'

'Barefoot and just wearing a nightgown?' She opened her eyes wide, unable to believe what we were telling her. This was going to be her gossip of the year.

'Well, Eva told me,' Daniel jumped into the conversation, 'that you know your neighbours well, so we wondered if you knew of any of them who had . . . I don't know, a visitor or something.'

The woman got up and took a cigarette from a packet on the coffee table between us. She didn't say anything for a good half a minute and Daniel, huddled next to me on the small sofa, looked at me puzzled. But we didn't say a word. She was a rather old lady and sometimes she struggled focusing, so when chatting with her you'd have to remind her what you were talking about. This time, however, we let her think.

'No, I'm afraid I don't,' she said eventually, while giving a puff on her cigarette. 'I know that the lady at number five has some family over, but her children must be as old as your parents, and their grandchildren would be one or two years older than you. The rest of the neighbours don't get visitors. So it makes me so happy that you two came to see me . . .'

Her voice broke into a choking cough, as if her lungs were going to burst through her mouth at any second. As I said, she was old, plus she would complain about anything. I think I heard her mumble something like, "Oh, I'm dying".

'This is a small village, as you well know, Eva. It doesn't matter whether it's spring, summer or winter: it's always empty. Only occasionally do we get some visitor, like the lady at number five, who became a widow last year, the poor thing. What a dreadful time she's had–'

'Yes, I understand,' I interrupted her seeing that she was about to begin another long story. 'But this girl must have come from somewhere. Besides Guildon Forest, the nearest town is a good fifteen-minute drive from here. A little girl like her can't have walked that far without getting a single scratch. Especially not practically naked in this cold weather.'

'Have you talked to the police?' the woman asked, becoming serious.

'No, we haven't. We were hoping you'd know where she was from. Perhaps her family have been asking door by door or–'

'No, sweetheart, no one's come around at all.'

'Then, what should we do? The girl's got a fever and surely her mother should be looking for her,' I said, worried.

How could it be possible that no one had been asking for her? How many times had I seen stories on the news about children and adults going missing, and all the uproar that their families had created just a few hours after their disappearance?

If that girl had come from somewhere, it had to be from Guildon Forest. As I told the old lady, it was impossible that she had managed to come all the way from the nearest town. I'd made sure I'd taken a good look to see if she had any scratches or cuts to her body; her arms and legs were uninjured. In addition, her nightgown was pure white and in one piece. If she'd walked a long way it would have caught on a bush, or she might even have been attacked by some wild animal of the mountains. And in that freezing weather she would surely have died of hypothermia, being so small, thin and half naked. If she weighed three stones, it'd be a miracle.

It was clear to me that something didn't fit.

'Go back to the house, get her fever down and see that she is in good hands. I'll try making a few calls to the neighbours and see if they know anything. If needed, I'll call the police myself, but with the condition of the roads in this damned weather I don't think they'll be able to come right over. And I doubt that they'll do anything about it on Christmas Eve.'

'All right, but I feel horrible for not being able to do anything else for her. She's very shy and I'm sure she's looking forward to being back with her family.'

'Of course, she must indeed,' the woman agreed with me, folding her arms under her breasts and nodding, as I remembered she always used to do. 'But before you go, please tell me what she looks like and anything else that might come in handy, so I can do some investigating.'

Even in the seriousness of our situation, Daniel and I struggled to stop ourselves laughing. On the way there I had warned him how much Mrs McGregor loved all kinds of gossip. That village was practically dead, with hardly any fresh news since they all knew each other so well, and it was difficult to keep any secrets. It was pretty funny to see the woman so excited about having some "work" to do. I knew she would do a good job, so I gave her as many details as possible: time of discovery, clothing, teddy bear, hair length, facial features . . .

'I hope there aren't too many missing girls in the woods, don't you?' Daniel joked when we were back in the car.

'Well, she was just making sure she knew everything there was to know,' I answered. 'What really surprises me is that there hasn't been anyone looking for her . . . No mum . . . No dad . . . I don't get it. I just don't get it.'

'What if nobody is looking for her?'

I remained quiet, trying to understand his question. His voice had been neutral, emotionless; maybe he was just analysing the situation. And I didn't really know what to answer, so I asked him, 'What do you mean?'

'I don't know. Just imagine that nobody is in fact looking for her. What are we going to do with her?'

I couldn't answer that out loud, but thousands of ideas flashed through my head. We'd never planned to stay at the house for too long, so it was a scenario worth thinking about. Because who would we leave the girl with when we left? With the police? What on earth would they do with a little girl? Would she end up in an orphanage? Could we maybe leave her with Mrs McGregor? But how would she cope with a little girl when she already struggled with her own health? I didn't have much of a clue about those things, but I was sure that social services wouldn't let an unknown person take care of a minor just like that. So, in theory, what we were doing wasn't even right.

Would we get in trouble?

What would the press say if they heard about it . . . ? I was already seeing the headlines in front of my eyes.

'Oh, Daniel, don't think like that,' I almost spat out, trying to get all the bad thoughts out of my head. 'Of course her parents, wherever they are, must be worried and looking for–'

'All right. But how long are we going to have the child in the house?' he interrupted me, trying to get to the crux of it all.

That question might have been the most important thing he'd asked me in all the time I'd known him. Today, I think I know the answer I should have given. But unfortunately, it's quite different to the one I gave then.

'Until we hear something from her parents. Just for a few days. I guess . . . that if it's time for us to leave and we still haven't heard anything from them, we'll have to take her to the police.'

He stayed silent, reluctant.

I tried not to say anything for a while; but, whenever you have doubts, the best thing is to try and clear things up on the spot. How many times has someone been unsure of someone else's meaning, but hasn't done anything about it? That only creates paranoia; but, over time, we always realise those ideas are far from reality. And we both had experience of that. So to be sure I asked him, 'Don't you want to have her in the house?'

'Look, babe, don't get me wrong. It's not about me wanting or not to have her there,' he said very serious, even taking away his eyes off the road for a second to look at me. We hadn't fitted snow chains to the wheels, so he was having to drive at a crawl. When he returned the eyes to the road, he continued talking slowly, trying not to upset me. 'I don't know whether she should stay or not. We know nothing about her, her family, where they are, where she came from, not even how she ended up in the road. I don't think either Mrs McGregor or us are the appropriate people to do any kind of "investigating". And our house might not be the best place for her to be found by whoever is looking for her. We have the police for this kind of things.'

'So . . . You don't want her.'

'Oh, Jesus. It's not that. Let's put it this way. We are just a bunch of guys on holiday. We came here to relax and disconnect from everything. And we start off from the first minute with something like this? Besides, what's the point in keeping her with us if she's going to end up with the police anyway? That's like giving candy to a child and then taking it away.'

'So, what you're trying to say is that we should take the girl out of the house by force and drive her to the nearest town? Possibly get stranded on the way, trapped in the middle of nowhere, just for the chance to leave her with some strange policemen in an office?' I placed more emphasis on that last word, raising my voice. 'In a cold office, without a place to lie down and feel comfortable, without people who will look after her properly?'

Daniel pulled a stupid expression, the way he did when he was in a good mood. And in return I punched him gently on the shoulder.

'Gee, you're on fire with this girl thing, babe . . . If you want her to stay with us, fair enough, but don't get too attached.' Somehow, I knew that he'd said that so I wouldn't raise my voice again. 'Because, when her family show up, they'll take her away in a flash. Snowing badly or not. At the end of the day, four of us came here and only four of us will go back. Just a few days and then goodbye, so nice to meet you, sweetie.'

I nodded and smiled, happy that I'd won the argument . . .

God, thinking about it now, if I were able to go back in time, I'd go to that car and give myself a good slap across the face.

The – could we call it a "funny thing"? – the funny thing is that, at that same moment, while smiling and looking out of my window, I knew what I was doing was completely wrong. Ok, we were helping a lost girl and welcoming her to our house. But after all, she was a child and we had no right to grant ourselves a responsibility that didn't belong to us.

But who in my place would have foreseen the consequences of doing so?

Who would have thought that that act of good will would result in such horrible events?

5. "Scary film"

The journey back to the house wasn't as easy as the one into the village had been. Once we were on the road that led all the way through the mountain to my house, we entered a muddy area. The snow was piled up everywhere, freezing the ground below it. Time after time, we found ourselves driving through icy patches buried under the snow. And once I thought I'd have to get out of the car and give it a push. But Daniel, bad tempered, instructed me to stay in the car.

If that boy was passionate about anything, it was overcoming any kind of barrier to living his life the way he wanted to. This icy road was just a small obstacle on which he would impose his will.

A good three or four minutes went by, during which I had no idea what to do. If I dared say anything, he would get pissed off; if I didn't say a word, I was sure he would scold me for sitting with my arms crossed; if I suggested anything at all, he'd just say how stupid it was, or that I had no idea about cars. But finally, after he'd pumped the accelerator then the brake, inching forwards and backwards all over again, we suddenly heard a new type of squealing and the car jolted forwards and took us home.

When we got back, we surprised the guys.

After we'd said goodbye to Mrs McGregor, we'd stopped by the store to say goodbye to her husband. A second before we left, I spotted a pile of Ferrero Rocher on one of the shelves. I knew that none of the guys could resist them, so I said to myself, 'Why not?'

Of course, that wasn't the only surprise. Mrs McGregor had offered us some of her "left overs" from her Christmas decorations. I'm sure that her husband would have appreciated it if he had been present. So I accepted them, since no one in my family had spent Christmas in that house . . .

We'd only gone in summer, when the weather was more clement and we could go out and visit the beautiful castles still standing in Scotland. Or like on one occasion, when I was desperate to try and take a picture of the Loch Ness monster – although a few minutes later I'd been more interested in tumbling on the grass.

Anyway . . . Daniel and I weren't the only ones welcoming the decorations with a smile.

'I'm afraid we have some bad news, though,' I pointed out, cutting off the instant joy that had invaded the living room as they took a string of lights from the box of decorations and, in the corner, Dave struggled to swallow three chocolates at once.

Both Stacey and Dave – who'd complained about not having signal on his phone the instant I'd got back – looked at me scared.

'Is it about the girl's family?' Stacey asked. She'd already had in her head a somewhat macabre story about the child's parents' whereabouts.

'Oh, it's not about them,' I calmed her down. I told them all about our meeting with my mum's old friend down in the village, and the decision that had come out of our long conversation with her.

When I saw that they'd relaxed, I told them the bad news. 'I'm afraid we don't have a Christmas tree in the house and, to be quite frank, the whole place is rather dusty. So, if we want to enjoy our time in the house for a few days, two of us will have to go and get a tree from the forest and the other two will have to stay and clean the house . . .

What happened next was a big surprise. I'd have lost loads of money if I'd dared bet on it. Both Daniel and Dave, jointly and willingly, took on the task of finding a Christmas tree. They looked at each other and smiled. Dave rushed out to get changed into warmer clothing; Daniel practically ran to get an axe from the garage for the task. They met again at the door and out they went like the wind, followed by Daisy.

'It's incredible what guys will do just so they don't touch a broom,' Stacey blurted out, incredulous.

The two of us knew about the issues between the boys perfectly well. In fact, everyone on the set knew. If there was one thing that was true in our profession, it was that there was envy and gossip all around. You only needed to show a bit of reticence towards someone, and everyone around would have found out by the next day. So, seeing them running to do something together, without anything in it for them, as if they were good friends . . . it was something from a parallel world.

'So it seems we don't get to choose, right?' I asked Stacey, my voice heavy with irony.

To be truthful, stupidly though it was, I'd been hoping to stay with Dave whilst Stacey went out to get the tree with my boyfriend. That would have been something I would have loved to see. If you wanted help from that girl, it'd better be about choosing clothes or nail polish colour; you'd never get her to do anything that required physical effort . . . And so it was, even though someone hearing her honest comment about the boys might have thought she was ready to help me start cleaning, she left after less than two minutes to get her daily injection of insulin.

Thank God, there wasn't much to clean. I was expecting maybe a bit of dusting of the shelves and the rest of the furniture (which had been covered with sheets during our absence), a quick hoover around, then loading the washing machine with the dusty sheets and taking a mop to the floor. But I didn't need to, because the floors weren't dirty. So, I just brought some order to all the fashion magazines Stacey had left on the sofa, placed Daisy's bed in a corner, and filled up her water bowl.

It took five minutes at most.

When I went upstairs, I made sure I stopped by Stacey's room and let her know that everything was done. I caught her sorting out her vials and syringes of insulin and . . . bottles of makeup, nail polish, mascara and eyeliners, concealer, lipsticks and lip-gloss, blush, nail files, tweezers . . . making sure everything was perfectly lined up.

I just couldn't resist saying: 'Take your time.'

'Did you get along with Stacey Martin?' the presenter interrupted her story.

Eva seemed to think about it, trying to pick the right words.

'In what you're telling us,' she heard Julia saying, 'I keep sensing a certain, special tone when you say anything about her . . . I wouldn't know how to describe it properly. Supposedly, you two were good friends.'

'Oh, we were. Often, I hated her for the things she said or did; but, at the same time, I'd need thousands of beautiful words to describe her,' she hurried to clarify. If she took more time to think, let silence fill the space, she would only give the woman a chance to imagine more problems in her relationship with the girl than there really were. 'Stacey had it all: both good and bad. Quite often she'd surprise you with a sweet, caring attitude, as if she were an angel, only later to step over you as if you were bubble-gum on the floor, not caring about you in the least.'

Eva paused to drink from the glass of water that lay by her armrest. She had already finished three of them. The continuous storytelling and the dozens of answers she was expected to give were seriously drying her throat. Moreover, it wasn't an easy story – at least, not a story she would choose to recall for pleasure.

'Let's say that she and I had a love-hate relationship. Love, because very often she showed that beautiful and respectful side of hers; hate, because her life had led her to hold fiercely to some values that went against my own. And like any true friend,' she assured the woman with a serious voice, leaving no room for doubt, 'I adored her for better and worse. No one is perfect. We all make mistakes, even though we sometimes don't like admitting them.'

Cries of Blood

'Speaking of mistakes, what happened next with the little girl?' Julia asked coldly, an iron smile fixed to her face. She knew Eva had gently closed the door on an intriguing part of her story.

And who was this impertinent girl to stop her doing her job? This was show business. And she was the best at it. If she had to dig deeply into the girl's mind to get some dirty stories and increase the value of that interview, she'd do it without hesitating. This wasn't Julia, the lady next-door; this was the one and only Julia Stevenson, investigative journalist *par excellence*.

To be fair, we had an amazing time the rest of that day. The girl seemed to be feeling better. Her fever had gone down and she smiled when I told her that we were going to decorate the house for Christmas.

As a punishment for escaping without cleaning, I entrusted Stacey with the huge task of untangling the lights that were tangled together in not one, but three big balls of wires. The little girl and I had to contain more than one shared giggle as we watched her struggling with them from our station in the kitchen.

Meanwhile, the child and I were getting the food ready. She wasn't able to help me much, since I wasn't comfortable leaving her with a knife in case she cut herself. But I saw her deeply involved in making some gingerbread cookies. I had prepared the dough before we travelled to Scotland, since it had to settle in the fridge for a few days. So, we only had to cut them out, giving them all sorts of shapes. We helped ourselves with some cutters that I'd bought and, when they were ready, we let our imagination go wild decorating them.

The girl surprised me when I saw her so committed to the task. Perhaps it was that she didn't have a fever anymore. She showed me, smiling all the time, that she was better than me at decorating. I felt as if I were the child, the different colours of icing running over the edges of my cookies.

I had such a good time that I almost forgot about the boys. I didn't know where they'd been or what they'd been up to. I just know that they came in covered in snow, something I told them off about after all my work cleaning the house. I told them to go outside and shake it off.

'Daisy, bad girl!' I reprimanded the dog, who was running around the living room, energetic, getting everything covered in snow and mud. She stood very still, looking at me.

Daniel, who was the strongest of the two, was dragging a huge and quite beautiful pine tree behind him. He told us how difficult it had been for them to find a nice tree that wasn't too tall. Many of them had the right height but were missing lots of branches, and the ones that were perfect for a magazine cover were nine feet or more in height. What's more, they'd had to carry it around by themselves. (I should say that none of us knew then that it was illegal to cut down a tree without permission.)

'Thanks, love. It's perfect. Although, actually, I don't know how we're going to keep it standing up,' I said to him while laughing uproariously. Stacey had come up with that same question a few minutes before, and it was a good point.

'Look, babe, if you tell me we've gone traipsing around the stupid mountain and now we're not able to –'

'Take it easy, we could try using a big pot and some rocks from the back of the house,' I calmed him down with a kiss, and hugged him to get him to warm up. When I looked to the kitchen, I saw Dave with the child and the cookies, so I raised my voice with a thick Spanish accent. 'David Campos, don't you even think of touching a single cookie!'

After that, we all got down to work. We finished untangling the lights, took a big, stone pot from the back, and looked for some rocks and soil. It didn't turn out easy to put the tree up. When we held it and Dave told us that from his position in the kitchen with the child (and the cookies), it looked right, we would let it go, only for its weight to make it instantly lean to one side or the other. But it was nothing that a few extra rocks in the right place couldn't solve.

We all helped. We passed around tinsel, balls, glittery icicles, and the blue, red and gold ornaments. The child helped Dave and I to hold the lights over the windows, while Daniel and Stacey put theirs between the aromatic pine needles.

I won't ever be able to forget that moment with my four friends, all together, and the little girl. The laughter, smiles and complicity. That was the Christmas magic, spreading over all of us with its warmth and happiness.

That way, the four of us set the table for dinner. The girl stayed watching cartoons on the TV, on the only channel that seemed to work. And we could talk about adult stuff, swearing and making bad jokes. And when everything was arranged on the table, we all sat down, holding hands.

'What is this supposed to be? Thanksgiving?' Stacey asked.

'No, it isn't. It's called sitting down at the table and, whether you're religious or not, giving thanks for the food and the company,' I said. I had that same tradition in my house. My mum had raised me in a home free of religion, but one where we had respect for everyone. It had been years since she'd gone to church, although she took me on special occasions. And my dad, who hadn't been raised in a religious family, only believed in something beyond us when it interested him. So, on special days, we always held hands at the table and made our own "thanksgiving".

Everyone, except for the child, said all the things for which we were grateful. The little girl just waited politely to start eating, devouring not just one, but two portions of food.

In her office, Julia was getting impatient. She was going over the notes and questions written in her notebook. For a moment, she didn't know how to make the story more interesting.

Every now and then she interrupted the girl to ask a question and clear up some point of doubt. But if she let Eva talk and talk, she knew they would take forever. Furthermore, although it was just the girl, her husband and herself in that room, it didn't mean that the moment was just for them. Millions of people would be tuning in on prime-time to watch that interview.

'So, none of you realised there was anything unusual about the girl?'

'No, we didn't. At least not then,' the girl answered, sounding dejected. 'She was quite bright and we were just too busy enjoying our time off.'

When she turned her head and found the muted images the plasma screen was playing, they seemed to take her breath away. She had been too busy relating the details of her story to realise that, at the same time, Julia's husband was playing the corresponding images of the events.

The screen was divided into four windows, three of which were black and headed with a corresponding camera number. The fourth window showed images, with the date and time running at the top. And Eva saw herself, happily eating the stew she had prepared that day while Daniel and Dave were cutting down the tree.

Julia observed Eva watching the film in silence. She could almost feel her sadness.

'On the screen, as you can see, it's the five of you. Which brings me to the next question,' said Julia, leaving a dramatic pause, knowing that (once the footage was edited) it would look amazing. 'It's assumed that your house is next to Guildon Forest, a small village which I'm sure many of our viewers have never heard of before. And, as you've well described, it's in the "middle of nowhere". So why is it that you had cameras around it? Surely you only set security cameras in a business, not a house in the middle of the countryside?'

Eva looked away from the screen and fixed her eyes on the woman's. It looked obvious that she had already been forced more than once to explain why those cameras were there. When she spoke, Julia detected a note of ennui and exhaustion.

'A few years earlier, when we'd gone on one of our summer holidays to the house, we found the place turned upside down. Someone had broken in and stolen some of my mum's jewels. They weren't of much value,' Eva explained, vaguely, 'and some paintings she had painted herself a long time ago.'

'Was the robbery investigated?'

'No, it wasn't. We got the police to open a case, but it ended up being filed in a dusty folder. We never heard anything from them. Not that we blame them, of course,' she added quickly. This conversation was being filmed, and she didn't want to get in more trouble than necessary. 'We couldn't provide any evidence, since we didn't have any security system in the house. Why would we have thought someone was going to rob our house? Like you said, it's literally in the middle of the countryside.'

'And it was then that the cameras were installed,' concluded the presenter.

'Yes, my dad contacted an American company that sold some not too expensive cameras, ones that didn't require any private company to monitor them. They were programmed to save energy, only recording when they detected movement.' She pointed to the three black windows on the screen. 'The footage was stored on a hard drive.'

Julia wrote something in her notebook and tried, once again, to go back to the crucial points in the events.

It was Christmas Eve, so we each called our respective families. We took turns with the landline, which wasn't working very well due to the snowstorm. Occasionally, we heard strange noises on the line, but at least we were able to speak with everyone for a few minutes each.

Our families had been worried. They had tried to contact us on our mobile phones, but, as we didn't get any signal, they hadn't been able to get through. So we calmed them down and told them we had arrived at the house safely, in the company of a child whom we'd found in the road.

'Excuse me?' my mum asked, not sure if she had heard properly or if it was a crossed line.

'Yes, mum, but don't worry. We have Sergeant Mrs McGregor investigating the case,' I blurted out laughing.

'Well, be careful and make sure she's ok.'

And after promising to call her in the morning with any news from Mrs McGregor, we said goodbye.

It was quite late, but we were young. We hadn't had a single moment of peace with the promotion and filming of the "Prodigies" series. And that was before the additional roles we'd occasionally landed. So, we were beaming with happiness at the chance to do whatever we wanted, without the constant monitoring of any assistant director trying to tell us what to do. We didn't have to go through makeup, hair or the costume departments . . .

We were all lying on the sofas, talking about things of no importance. It had been an hour more or less since the TV had stopped working at all. While the child was watching her cartoons, the screen had simply turned to black and white dots.

'Why don't you get your laptop so we can watch a film?' I suggested to Daniel.

And that's when the child, for the first time, left us open mouthed.

We had agreed on Daniel bringing his laptop and Dave a hard drive loaded with hundreds of films. But apparently, for some reason, he'd forgotten to put it in his suitcase. So, we were in the middle of nowhere, practically stuck due to the snowstorm, without TV and no Wi-Fi whatsoever. No neighbours to whom we could turn to ask for a film or DVD. No store we could pop into in a second.

The only option we had left was to watch one of the films saved on Daniel's laptop. But Daniel was a horror film fan, and the only ones he had on his laptop were the scariest films ever.

'But how are we going to put on a scary film?' I almost shouted at him, bringing his attention to the child, who sat on my lap playing with my hair. 'I can't let her watch any of your films! She's just too young.'

'Aren't you sleepy yet?' Stacey asked from the other side of the "L" shaped sofa, while stroking Daisy.

The girl shook her head, without taking her eyes off the plait she was making with my hair.

'Don't you have anything but horror?' I asked Daniel.

He didn't need to look on his laptop.

'Scary film or go to bed. You choose, babe.'

I hated to ruin things for the others. I had already made enough decisions that had affected them, and I was feeling guilty about it. I was the only one to blame for the child still being with us.

Should we have taken her to the police?

Was it worth the risk to drive, without snow chains on the wheels of the car? It would take at least fifteen minutes – not considering the extra time it would take us in that weather – to get to the nearest town.

But I didn't even have time to think about a logical answer to that. Suddenly, we heard the child's voice.

'Scary film.'

Yes. Those two simple words. Well pronounced and without hesitation.

The four of us sat quietly, just looking at her. None of us had been expecting her to say anything, and the surprise showed on our faces. Above all, it was the peculiarity of the occasion on which she'd decided to talk for the first time.

Had all the previous questions we'd asked not interested her in the slightest? Why hadn't she spoken before? Why now?

'Fuck. She *speak* and all,' Dave stammered.

'You heard it: scary film it is,' Daniel concluded.

I didn't do anything to stop them. We were four responsible people. If the others were willing to let the child watch a scary film, I wasn't going to be the one contradicting them. I wasn't their mother.

Stacey opened a bottle of wine and made some popcorn. Although she was diabetic, she used to drink sensibly every now and then. She always took care to control her glucose levels to avoid them rising or falling. She shouldn't have had any problems, as we had eaten well during the day. The popcorn only lasted five minutes, and she had to make a second batch.

Clinging to each other, we started watching "The Strangers". We had tried to connect the laptop to the television screen, but we didn't have the right cables, so we huddled together side by side.

For the first few minutes I concentrated on drinking from my glass of wine. I believe I was the only one to think how strange the scenario was: a group of young adults with a child, in the early hours of Christmas Day, in a house struck by snow, surrounded by Christmas decorations and lights and . . . all of us watching a scary film. What was wrong with us?

I had never seen that film before, so I didn't know what to expect from it. I just knew that my boyfriend had good taste in films. And that was precisely what I feared the most. For those first few minutes, I made sure that the little girl was ok.

'If you get scared, tell me, alright?'

'Deal,' she answered.

This time her reply didn't surprise me. But it did strike me that her tone was a little too sweet.

The little one was in my arms, between Daniel and me. I would have loved to have been able to sit right next to him. For him to hold me in his arms. Feeling him close to me at any moment when I could get scared myself. Those kinds of films made me quiver.

Daniel kissed me and looked into my eyes for a couple of seconds. He put his arm over my shoulders and caressed my hair as I used to like him to do.

The other two were whispering things to each other.

And the little girl . . . Well, maybe after everything that's happened, I remember it all through different eyes. But I know that at that moment

Cries of Blood

her eyes caught my attention. Dark as the inside of a wolf's mouth. Attentive to every second of the film.

At the beginning, there was a couple going through some problems, all somewhat unclear, to which the girl paid little attention, bored. But then the plot began getting interesting . . .

I didn't imagine it; I saw it perfectly.

A glow crossed her eyes in the dark.

There was something odd about them, although at the time I didn't think it could be real. However, there was definitely something that kept drawing my attention back to those eyes. I couldn't stop looking at those black spots in the darkness of the room, highlighted by the brightness of the laptop screen. Their power drew my own eyes to them . . .

I was just about to cover her eyes when the first shock happened in the film. Stacey shivered noticeably on the other side of the sofa, next to Daniel. At our feet, the little dog jumped up and started barking.

'Chist! Go back to sleep,' Stacey hissed at her.

And the child . . . didn't flinch in the slightest. She just fidgeted, shifting Daniel away from her side. We had been close to each other and she must have felt uncomfortable.

I had no time to absorb any further detail. Just a few minutes later, a creepy, hooded person appeared on the screen.

'You should probably take the girl upstairs now,' Stacey suggested while biting her nails.

I pressed the pause button, grabbed the girl and took her from the living room. I was glad that at last someone had seen reason. But when we got to the stairs, she refused to go up. She abruptly shook my hand from hers, looked at me firmly and said, 'No.'

'You have to go to bed,' I whispered.

'No.'

'Beg your pardon?!' Stacey cried. 'It doesn't matter whether you want to watch the film or not: it's too late and it's been hours since you should have been in bed.'

'No,' she replied again, arms crossed.

The boys were watching the scene.

'Do you want to have nightmares?'

'Thank you, Stacey.' I appreciated the back-up. I didn't want to look like the bad cop.

The child, holding her teddy bear tightly, looked intensely at Stacey.

'I am not going to bed,' she insisted.

'Excuse me, but who do you think you are?' Stacey snapped, getting up from the sofa and raising her arms. 'Eva is in charge here. It's her house, not yours. And if she says you're going to bed, you go to bed and that's the end of it. Besides, this is not a film for kids like you.'

'But I want to watch it!' the little one cried out, surprising everyone. How had she gone from saying nothing to that intensity?

I don't know why, but she calmed down then, tears shining in her eyes as she looked at me, almost begging me to let her watch the film.

'I'm sorry, but it's not a kids' film. You've heard Stacey,' I warned her and took her upstairs.

She didn't complain again. I took her to the bathroom, so she could use the toilet before taking her to bed, and after that I left her in my bedroom. There was not a single word about that scene when I went downstairs. We started the film again and watched it peacefully. This time, I was hugging Daniel, and Dave and Stacey were quietly bickering about the last remaining popcorn.

I didn't pay any attention to the film. I didn't enjoy it in the least. For the first time, I was regretting my decision. I just wanted the best for all of us, for my friends to enjoy the stay in my house and for the child to be well looked after and happy. Were those hopes incompatible?

It was then that I understood Daniel's earlier question, the one he'd asked in the car that morning as we were returning from Guildon Forest. How long would we have the child with us? Would another scene like that one happen again?

Cries of Blood

If it wasn't enough being engrossed with my doubts and those problems, I had a difficult conversation with Daniel later on.

Both Dave and Stacey had gone to their bedrooms. They hadn't even stayed to watch the end of the film. They'd had a busier day than anticipated. And Stacey apologised, whispering to us that she was tired and needed to check her glucose levels after drinking wine. So, the two of us stayed alone on the sofa.

I rested my head on his lap and he stroked my hair. And when the film finished and the end credits came up, we stayed quiet. In a way, I was afraid of what he was going to say, but I feared more that my pride could get in the way.

'Do you think we're doing the right thing here?'

'I don't know if it's right or not, but it's what we must do.'

'Are you sure?'

'Don't start, Daniel,' I cut him off, feeling a bit dizzy from the wine. 'If you think this is all my fault, I have to say that there are actually four adults here . . . Four adults with our own opinions. And I don't care that we are in my house: if any of you don't want to keep her, just say it and be done with it. I'm not any of your mothers.'

He placed a finger over my lips, breathing slowly. 'I'm not trying to say that this is your fault. It's just that I doubt we'll be able to enjoy the rest of our time here if we're going to have that tadpole around us.'

'What do we do, then?'

'Tomorrow morning, as soon as we wake up, we call your mother's old friend. I guess she must know something by now, but she might not have called us as it's late. I don't think it'll be too difficult to find out where the kid's parents are.'

I nodded, serious. It was the logical thing to do.

And he looked back at me and pulled one of his silly faces. He pursed his lips and said, 'Where are my kisses?'

'The snowstorm took them away,' I scoffed back at him, smiling and closing my eyes while I let him fondle me with his soft hands.

After several minutes filled with games and ridiculous sentences, we went to his bedroom and spent the night together.

Those moments were the essence of the type of holiday we'd expected to experience. We'd never imagined ourselves stuck in a house with a child that, despite our help and kind treatment, would answer us back so rudely . . .

6. "She's just a child"

A timid light filtered through the curtains that covered the windows. Outside, the wind continuously crashed against them, throwing snowflakes at the glass. It was colder than the previous morning, which made me shiver and wrap myself in the duvet. I rolled under it and discovered that I was all alone in bed.

'Daniel?' I called in a shy whisper.

He wasn't there. And I hadn't heard him get up.

I had slept very well, feeling his comfortable warmth as I lay in his arms. Not finding him there made me feel unprotected. I got up and looked out of the window.

The snowstorm hadn't stopped for a second. The snow was piled higher than the previous day. I'd been hoping that it would at least have weakened, so the sight depressed me somewhat. Nothing was going according to plan.

I had thought about going outside with the guys and showing them the mountain. It had been a long time since I'd been in Guildon Forest and enjoyed the beautiful views it offered. In earlier years, instead of going out with my parents to enjoy nature, I'd stayed in the house watching TV. And now that for once I was excited at the idea of going out there, the storm was ruining everything.

I went down to the living room and saw the little dog sleeping in her corner. From time to time she shivered, as the fire had gone out overnight. At least I discovered, with a smile on my face, many presents under the Christmas tree for everyone. No one had woken up yet. No one except Daniel.

Where was he?

I looked in the bathroom and the garage, at the back of the house and even checked whether he was with his beloved car. But the vehicle was alone, snow building up over it.

The night before we had agreed on calling on Mrs McGregor. Perhaps he had called and talked to her. Maybe he'd told her where he was going. So, I picked up the phone and searched for her number. I found it written in a little phone book next to the telephone. I dialled the numbers and waited for an answer.

'Hello?' A woman's voice came down the line.

'Hi, it's Eva.'

The woman made a small rumbling growl. 'Are you all right, dear? Do you know what time it is?'

I was surprised by the question. I hadn't even checked the time, something I regretted when I looked up at the clock on the wall by the mantelpiece. It was seven o'clock in the morning.

'Oh, sorry, I didn't realise how early –'

'It's ok, sweetheart, when you get to a certain age you no longer sleep much,' the woman reassured me, with a loving grandmother's voice. 'By the way, merry Christmas.'

'Oh, yeah, right, merry Christmas to you both,' I chanted, caught between being ashamed and happy to remember the date. 'Has Daniel called you, by any chance?'

'No, dear, he hasn't. Why would he do that?'

And then I felt stupid for expecting him to have looked for her phone number and called her. I should have waited for him to return from wherever he was. He couldn't be very far. And if he had actually called Mrs McGregor, he would have left a note for me.

'Oh, well, we were wondering if you had found out anything by now about the child's parents.'

'No, dear,' the woman informed me with an unhappy tone. 'Yesterday, right after you left, I went by the neighbours' houses. They don't know anyone who could have a child of her age. Much less anyone asking after her door-by-door. Just me.'

I remained quiet for a few seconds, thinking about what she had told me. It didn't make any sense.

'But that can't be right. Where has the child come from, then?'

'Oh, dear, I wish I knew,' she said.

'Have you called the police?'

'Not yet; my husband has an old friend who works at the police station there, so I'm waiting for him to call his friend and talk to him. Maybe he can tell us if someone is looking for her. But don't you go taking the car anywhere,' she warned me, with a very severe tone. 'All the roads are closed due to the ice. Half the country is in the same state; it's the only thing I keep hearing on the radio . . .'

I could not believe it.

Why had we had to go there?

Why had I had to insist on going up there?

Although, if we had never driven along that road, God knows what would have happened to the little girl. She could have died of hypothermia in the forest. But we had driven that way. To our misfortune, I had insisted on the trip long and hard enough to convince them all.

'Well, call me as soon as you know something,' I asked her, not able to say anything else.

The only thing I could think about was how the rest of the guys would take the news. None of them had complained about the matter. Or, at least, they hadn't dared to . . .

I stopped thinking about all that and thought of my mum.

This was the first Christmas we had spent apart. Ever since my dad's absence, I had been protective of her. I'd never seen her cry, not even a single tear shed in front of me. But I had heard her sobbing in private; even though she never knew. And she had urged me to go away with my friends. She didn't want me around her all the time. 'I'm going to be just fine, sweetie,' she told me, so I wouldn't feel bad about making plans with my friends.

I wanted to call her, but it was too early and she wouldn't be in a good mood if I woke her up. So, I went up to my parents' bedroom and saw that the little girl was still sleeping peacefully, with that angel's face that aroused anyone's protective instincts. I made as little noise as possible as I picked up my diary and returned to the living room.

I tidied the room a little. The wine glasses from the night before had been left on the coffee table. Neither Stacey nor Dave had been bothered to take the popcorn bowls to the kitchen sink.

When I'd finished clearing up, I sat on the sofa, covered myself with a blanket and opened my diary.

I loved its yellowish pages. Every now and then, I would sprinkle them with perfume: it made the experience of writing on them more pleasant. It soothed me to ramble through my ideas, quietly and alone. I would even say that the scent of the diary made me think more clearly and objectively.

Step by step, I wrote down what I remembered from the previous day and the conversation I'd just had with Mrs McGregor. Perhaps, if I described all the doubts that pestered me, a little light would light up in my head. I re-read all of it and . . .

Nothing. No line made any sense whatsoever.

It seemed rather as if I was reading the thoughts of another girl. I couldn't understand why all this was happening to me and what I could do to solve my problems.

I closed the diary, hid it between the sofa cushions and went to the kitchen to get a nice bowl of porridge with sugar and cinnamon.

'Could *have* I have one as well, please?' a sleepy Dave asked me, down from the top of the stairs.

So, the two of us sat together, enjoying the warm porridge. It was one of the few quiet moments we would have for the rest of the day.

Once Dave had finished his bowl, he went to the Christmas tree and picked up a small package. It was wrapped in golden wrapping paper and, on the top, it had my name written in delicate calligraphy.

'Open it,' he urged me. 'I hope you like it.'

I smiled. I felt bad for opening the first present, and even more that it was only the two of us there. But I didn't wait for Daniel to come back or Stacey to come down to the living room. And I discovered that my present was a lovely silver bracelet with letters engraved on the top.

' "A", "P", "S".'

'*Amigos Para Siempre*. Or Best Friends Forever,' translated Dave from Spanish.

I blushed and didn't know what to do or say, except just to give him a hug. I had never had a friend like him before, and much less a male friend.

'Open yours,' I said reaching for a box wrapped up with silver paper, and I put on the bracelet he had given me.

I had spent days thinking about what he would like for a present. I knew him very well and I had a few ideas in mind, but he didn't like to possess lots of stuff. He'd had to move house quite a few times since he'd been in the United Kingdom and he had struggled to carry around all his belongings. His family lived in Madrid, Spain, so it wasn't like he could just drop his stuff at his parents' house while moving.

'OH-MY-GOD, I love them!' Dave exclaimed, pulling out the exact headphones that long ago he told me he wanted to get.

He stared at them in his hands, disbelieving. They were expensive and I knew he couldn't afford them, so I was glad to see his surprised reaction. He was so excited, smiling broadly, that he threw himself at me and kissed me on the cheek . . .

Just then the front door opened, dragging in a noisy, icy wind that made us shiver. Among the shrieks of the snowstorm outside, we heard Daniel's laugh. He came in followed by Stacey.

The dog woke up with the gust of cold air and ran, delighted, to greet her owner.

For a second, I stood there shocked. I had no idea that Stacey had woken that early and that she had left with Daniel. I'd thought it was just Daniel who was missing from the house. And it surprised me even more to see her helping with a basket loaded with logs that both of them were bringing in.

Daniel saw Dave and me standing close to each other . . .

'What the –?'

I looked at Dave. He looked back at me. And we both separated from each other instantly.

'Don't you dare put your hands on my girl!' Daniel shouted.

Dave and I jumped, startled by his scream.

'Da . . . Daniel, I was just . . . I only . . .' the poor boy managed to stammer.

Daniel came towards us and pushed Dave. Dave tripped over the headphone cables and fell backwards, making a loud noise against the floor.

'Daniel, no!' I shouted. I rushed to help Dave, who seemed to be in one piece, although his elbow looked a bit painful after he'd landed on it. When he got up, we both saw the headphones lying on the floor, broken. I turned to Daniel and shouted at him. 'What the fuck do you think you're doing?'

'What the fuck do I think I'm doing? No, babe, what on earth is he doing putting his hands on –?'

I slapped him across the face with all my strength. I couldn't contain myself.

I knew what that scene looked like. I couldn't blame him for it, really. But a misinterpretation and violence were two completely different things. I wasn't going to allow him to hurt my friend, and much less over a misunderstanding.

'He was thanking me for the present I gave him!' I cried out, no longer in control of myself.

'And why would he be kissing you? I don't kiss my friends when I thank them for anything,' he snapped back at me, pressing his jaw with one hand.

'Well, I don't say *night-night* to a car, but apparently you *do*. Next time you dare raising your hand over –'

'What? What are you going to do?'

Daisy began barking at the two of us, so Stacey had to grab her by the collar.

'That's enough, guys. I can't believe you're adults,' she said, shushing the dog. She ordered Daisy into her corner and closed the front door.

I helped Dave to sit down, even though he claimed to feel alright. It had been a stupid fall. Fast, but stupid. So, we stayed sitting quietly for what seemed like an eternity. Dave, holding his broken headphones; me, shaking my head, not able to believe what had just happened.

We heard Daniel and Stacey tidying up the logs of wood behind us. They piled them in a stack by the wall, next to the cold fireplace. When they'd finished, Stacey went to wash her hands and Daniel sat on the edge of the hearth.

I didn't know what he was doing and I didn't want to know. I was busy holding back tears from my eyes. He had never behaved that way while we were together. I had never seen him being violent with anyone. Not that he was a saint, but I would have sworn he would never have raised his hand to anybody . . .

But that trip had already begun changing all of us.

'I . . . Eva . . .' I heard him saying behind me.

Dave just looked at his headphones, frowning. He was moody and trembling, the way he always was when he was angry. I turned around slowly, telling myself to keep calm, count to ten. I looked Daniel in the eyes and waited for him to speak.

'I'm sorry, I'm really sorry,' he mumbled.

What was I meant to say back? That was a conversation just for the two of us, and this wasn't the place to discuss it. We had already poisoned the environment enough. Besides, we never properly argued in front of anyone. I always kept the big arguments for our moments alone, so as not to bother anyone else with our problems.

But this was a situation that had gone over the line. I knew that nothing good was going to come out of that talk, so I would wait for later on to speak to him, privately, and clear things up once and for all.

But when I tried to tell him that . . .

We all jumped up.

We had heard through the ceiling the unmistakable noise of glass crashing against the wooden boards of the floor upstairs. And I don't think I'd be wrong to say that suddenly we all remembered that we weren't alone in that house. We had that little girl under our care, and it had been a long time since any of us laid eyes on her. God knew what she had just done.

We hadn't had time to react when the dog bolted up the stairs. And, as the storm raged on outside, we all ran noisily behind her. I was just hoping for the girl to be alive and unhurt. We followed Daisy, who didn't go to my bedroom, where I had left the girl sleeping. Instead the dog went straight to Stacey's bedroom.

And the four of us rolled into a ball in the doorway . . .

What happened next is stuck in my memory.

'Noooooo! What the fuck have you done, you little bitch?!' Stacey bellowed, holding a hand to her heart.

We could see the look of surprise from the little girl. She looked back at the four of us, shocked by our hasty appearance. She pressed her hands tightly around her teddy bear, while we focussed our eyes on the puddle on the floor that was reflecting the light from outside. The broken pieces of glass were spread out around the child. And we didn't need Stacey to tell us what they were . . .

They were the insulin vials that the day before Stacey had placed next to her makeup.

The glass from two small bottles was now scattered across the floor.

'Why?!' Stacey demanded an explanation.

But the child just held her teddy bear tighter to her and tried to meet my gaze, without saying a word.

'Ok, calm down . . .' I started saying to my friend.

'What do you mean, calm down?! Calm down?!' she yelled back at me, almost swooning with each and every word. She looked at the child and lunged for her. But Daniel's swift arm stopped her just in time.

'Let's not do something stupid, ok?' the boy growled, standing between her and the child.

'Do something stupid? Really?! After you've almost beaten the crap out of Dave just for thanking your girlfriend for a present?! This stupid brat has broken my insulin vials!' She shot a glance back to the little girl and shouted at her, 'Do you even know what that was for?! Do I touch your stuff?!'

And quick as lightning, without Daniel being able to stop her this time, she snatched the teddy bear from the child's hands. She raised it in the air and threw it against the nearest wall. The child started shouting and crying, as if possessed, running towards it. And when the teddy bear hit the wall and then the floor, we didn't notice the unusually heavy thuds it made.

It had taken a split second. In that moment, the sounds were imperceptible to our senses, overwhelmed by the hysteria of the child.

She became even wilder after realising her teddy was missing an eye. She looked for it angrily and, when she found it, she ran out onto the landing. None of us went after her; we stayed with Stacey. Even Daisy stayed with us, whimpering with her tail between her legs. I shuddered when I saw Stacey's pale face.

'Are you alright?' I asked, taking her by the arms and helping her to lie down on the bed.

But she felt even dizzier that way. So, she sat on the edge of the bed and rested her head between her legs. She hardly lifted an arm, pointing towards her desk. With a glance I realised what she was trying to point at.

I took her glucose monitor and, as I'd done on more than one occasion before, I helped her to check her sugar levels.

'It's all good,' I let her know. 'Relax and breathe.'

After a minute, she calmed down and her ragged breathing soothed.

'She's done it on purpose,' she whispered.

The three of us looked at each other, our hearts still beating like crazy in our chests.

'I don't think she's done it on purpose, Stacey,' I dared to say.

'I agree with Eva,' Daniel supported me. 'She's just a child.'

Stacey raised her head. She stared at Daniel for a second, as if seeing double. Then she shook her head as if he had somehow disappointed her. It was a look I didn't understand at the time. After a few seconds just staring at him, frowning, she said, 'Yes, she did it on purpose. It's not easy to break those vials. I've dropped them many times and never broke a single one.'

'I think you're just being paranoid . . .' the boy answered her.

'Didn't you hear the same thing I did?' she asked Dave and me, her eyes pleading. 'It wasn't the sound of bottles falling down by accident . . . She smashed them hard against the floor.'

She stared at us, puzzled that nobody believed her. But why would a child want to break her insulin vials on purpose? The three of us assumed that the little girl must have been playing around with Stacey's makeup, and the vials must have fallen and broken by accident. After all, which child has never broken anything? They are masters of mass destruction wherever they go. Their curiosity is always attracting the cry of some mother.

This situation couldn't be any different.

Stacey grabbed Daisy by the collar and left the room looking deeply hurt. We followed them to the front door, asking her to calm down and rethink. But she showed us a certain finger and stormed out, pulling the dog after her by the leash.

We stood there, stunned, in what seemed like the essence of our trip: a miserable silence that surrounded us and was only broken by the ticking of the clock on the wall.

I went back upstairs, leaving the boys alone. I opened the door to my bedroom where, as I'd expected, the child sat on the bed hugging her teddy bear. She didn't look up, just sat there silently with her eyes closed.

'It's Eva, your friend . . . Everything is fine, sweetie.'

I slowly got closer and sat next to her. I watched how she held the bear with one hand, while in the other she held the eye that had fallen off it.

'Do you mind if I try fixing it?'

I couldn't see any sign that she was listening to me.

'I can probably fix it with a bit of superglue . . .'

Again, she didn't let out a single syllable.

I thought the only way to comfort the child would be by putting the eye back on the bear's face. But then, just when I was an inch away from it, the girl shouted at me. 'Leave me alone!'

'All right,' I whispered, surprised by her ferocity.

'Don't touch Johnny.'

'Ok, ok . . .'

And I remained still, arms by my side, thinking about her having given her teddy a name.

Johnny the bear.

7. "Yäel, her name is Yäel"

I didn't go down to the living room until half an hour later. The wait for the child to fall asleep felt eternal. And when she finally did, I left the room softly, trying not to make the slightest noise that could have woken her up. God knows that was the last thing I wanted.

Downstairs I saw Dave, who looked as if he hadn't moved from the sofa the whole time. In his hands were the headphones I had given him as a present, now wrecked. He looked heartbroken, turning them over and over again, trying to fix them. But they were unfixable. I knew how much he had wanted those headphones and now they were ruined, just seconds after he'd torn off their wrapping.

He wasn't a materialistic guy, but he appreciated the little things. He was simple and open. And I could read in his eyes that he was devastated because the headphones had been a present from me. I had remembered that day we passed by a shop window and he'd told me, so excited and rambling for ages, that he was going to try to save the money to get them. Maybe he expected me to forget about them; but I would never have done that. Because he was my best friend. Because I cared for him. Because he meant something to me. And, just like the bracelet he had given me, those headphones were worth their weight in gold for their sentimental value.

And so, the anger inside me began to emerge. Making it a struggle to breathe.

Why did Dave always have to be the one to suffer? He didn't harm anyone: he lived and let live. He was polite and kind to everyone, even the people who taunted and teased him. Some people could mistake him for a wimp; I knew him for what he was: a boy with a good soul, but one who'd have to deal with this kind of things over and over, unless one day he found it in himself to fight back.

Therefore, knowing that he was not going to do anything about it, I asked him if he knew where Daniel was. I put my coat on and went out to the front of the house, where I found him smoking a cigarette.

'We need to talk,' I told him, in a tone I had never used with him before.

Daniel offered me a cigarette and I lit it up. I knew from his silence that he realised what was going to happen. He was leaning on the railings of the porch, looking into the distance. To a place nobody had ever been. He was preparing himself for the inevitable.

I sat down on a white bench in the porch. Then I took a few puffs of my cigarette, filling my lungs, and let out the smoke slowly, watching the wind blowing it away.

For the first time in a long while, I cleared my thoughts from the thick fog that had settled around them.

'I think it's time for us to take a break, Daniel.'

He took a last puff of his cigarette and threw it in the snow. He didn't say anything. He just put his hands in his coat pockets and sat on the other side of the bench. Actions had consequences, and he couldn't fight the ones he had created with his own behaviour.

I looked at him for what seemed an icy eternity, the two of us sitting there on the bench at the mercy of the snowflakes. They melted with the heat of our bodies, making our clothes damp. After all that time together, all that time when I'd thought I knew him, I couldn't believe he wasn't going to say anything.

Wasn't he at least going to fight for me?

Wasn't I important to him?

Was he going to let me go without saying a word about what had happened?

'Are you going to say something?' I exploded.

He looked at me, his ginger hair fluttering between his blue eyes. He didn't blink. In those seconds the anger and pain he was feeling were palpable. Finally, he started to speak.

'I've screwed up and I'm sorry, Eva. I love you, but I don't like Dave. You know I can't stand him, and I don't want him near you . . .'

'We've already talked about this a dozen times, Daniel. How many more times are we going to argue about it?' I shouted, exasperated. I couldn't take any more of this jealousy.

'As many times as it takes for you to stop hanging around with him.' He didn't take his eyes from mine.

I looked down at the snow. I had to count to ten, twenty, thirty . . .

'If you really loved me as much as you say you do, you'd respect my friendship with him. He hasn't done anything to make you doubt him; it's you. You're the one who turns your back on him, the one who makes a fool of him at work . . . And now you're going to beat him up? I can't deal with this anymore, Daniel,' I burst out, afraid my darkest and deepest feelings were going to come out once and for all. I hated arguing like this, but I had to carry on. 'I haven't been sure whether to be with you or not, if there was something worthwhile in this relationship, if I loved you . . .'

He was surprised by my words. I didn't need to look at him to feel his pain. But it wasn't my fault. He was the one who tried to tell me who I could be around. Who was he to tell me what to do?

'Do you love me?' he asked me, solemnly.

I didn't need a second to think about it.

'No, I don't. I don't love you.' The words came out of my throat, almost scraping my skin with their burning claws. 'I can't love someone who doesn't respect me, who is jealous, who is violent with my friends. I don't know who you think you are to behave this way.'

'Excuse me?'

'That's right, Daniel. I'm not a piece of meat!' I shouted, desperate. I was getting more pissed with him by the second. 'You make me feel like that with your words, as if I need you to protect me, as if you're in control of my life . . . I want a break, because I don't know anymore if it makes sense to stay together.'

'I've only asked you for one thing: to keep your distance from him!' he exclaimed, getting up from the bench.

'No, you didn't ask me; you ordered me.' I made my point clear. 'And if I'm honest, I don't want to see that violent side of yours ever again. I can try to tolerate you being jealous, but I can't ignore you being aggressive.'

We gave each other a few seconds to breathe.

'Do you like Dave?'

'What?' I babbled. I hadn't understood the question, although it seemed to be quite clear; I had no idea what he was talking about.

'Do you like him as more than just a friend?' Daniel asked pointedly.

I didn't reply. I had answered that question over and over in our arguments. I couldn't stand having the same conversation one more time. It was a vicious circle we couldn't seem to end.

'I see ... A break ...' he whispered, turned around and headed back towards the door.

Before he reached it, we heard Daisy's barks and saw her running back to the house. Stacey was walking slowly behind her, arms tight around her body and with her scarf all the way up to her nose. It seemed the walk had done her good, although she looked freezing cold. Even when she walked up the front steps and one of them shifted under her weight, causing her to fall awkwardly, she didn't act dramatically about it.

Daniel rushed to help her. He gave her his hand and raised her from the pile of snow in which she had landed.

'I think that step needs fixing, doesn't it?' Her tone was unusually cheerful.

'Yes, it does. We'll do it tomorrow – if the storm stops, that is,' I said. Daniel and I shared a quick glance. He knew I wasn't referring to the snowstorm.

Stacey didn't notice. She was getting rid of the snow that had worked its way under her scarf.

'What are you doing out here?' she asked, looking puzzled.

'So, you didn't like Dave?' Julia asked, writing quickly in her notebook.

Eva closed her eyes for a moment. After that she looked at the plasma screen next to her. She watched Daniel, Stacey and herself go back to the house, the little dog following them and running around the living room. The puppy stopped to drink deeply from her bowl of water and spun around a few times before she lay down on her bed. Eva was standing staring at Dave, who had now left the sofa to try lighting the fire.

'No,' the girl answered, without thinking about it twice, her determined tone putting an end to further questions.

The presenter reread her notes and looked at the screen.

'It does look, indeed, like Stacey came back to the house in quite a different mood to the one she left in. Wasn't she worried about having no insulin left?'

'Actually, she had more. She had kept another vial in the fridge. We were only meant to stay there for three days, but she had brought a vast amount of insulin. She would never have needed that many vials, but she was cautious, which on this occasion saved her life,' said Eva, happy to change the subject. 'And she didn't mention her theories about the girl's intentions again. In fact, she acted as if the child wasn't there at all. We started cooking the two of . . . Well, I started cooking while she fetched me the stuff I needed. It almost felt like nothing had happened.'

But the other three of us couldn't act that way. We didn't have that skill. We couldn't act as if "nothing" had happened.

Many things certainly *had* happened, and in just one morning. As a result, Dave wasn't talking to Daniel, or at least he was talking to him even less than usual, if such thing were possible. I had just asked Daniel for a break, because our relationship didn't make any sense. Daniel was avoiding looking or talking to Dave and me. The child, again devouring two portions of food, spent her time shooting dirty looks at Stacey between spoonfuls, while Stacey pointedly ignored her. And strangest of all, I occasionally perceived a somewhat cold tone towards Daniel from Stacey, who was the only one to whom he was speaking.

After we'd all finished lunch, everyone else went to their rooms, while I stayed with the child in the living room. The television seemed to work properly again, more or less, so we sat on the sofa watching cartoons. She sat on my lap, playing with her teddy bear and paying attention to the screen. I decided to tidy up her hair with plaits, as it was quite long and getting tangled. Besides, I needed something to stop me from thinking. I felt my head was cluttered with problems: poor Dave with his headphones, Stacey with just enough insulin for the rest of the holiday, and my own issues with Daniel.

Even though I had finally opened up, I still had more things I needed to discuss with him. More I had to reproach him with. They would need to wait. This wasn't the time or place to do it.

I was glad to clear my mind, sitting down and watching television, while plaiting the child's hair. Now and again, she said a few words. She even gave me a kiss on the cheek and apologised for having shouted at me before in the bedroom.

'Why did you break Stacey's vials?' I asked her.

She looked at her teddy bear, now one-eyed.

'I didn't want to break them,' she answered me, with an innocent voice.

I told her that she couldn't touch other people's belongings without their permission. I told her why Stacey had reacted that way and why she had gone that mad with her. And I explained to her that Stacey needed the insulin because she had a problem that none of us had.

'Is that why she didn't eat any gingerbread cookies?' she asked me.

When preparing the dough for the cookies, I'd forgotten to make some without sugar for her. 'Exactly, sweetie. That's the reason she needs those vials and her other stuff. Stuff that you should never touch,' I clarified, finishing a plait and starting a new one.

However, when I said she should apologise to Stacey, she refused to do it. Stacey had broken one of Johnny's eyes, her poor teddy bear, and she wasn't going to say sorry until the girl apologised first.

'Hey, I don't like that behaviour,' I reprimanded her, surprised by her answer. She had given it with the same innocent and calm voice she had been using until that moment with me. Even so, I didn't like it at all.

I said, 'Hasn't your mum ever told you not to be spiteful? At the end of the day, you shouldn't even be with us. You should be with your family.'

She turned around, frightened. 'Are you going to kick me out of your house?'

I felt so sorry for her. Of course I wasn't going to kick her out of "my house". I wasn't a monster who would leave a child in the street. But I did want her back with her own family and for us to be able to get on with our lives, try and settle our differences and enjoy the rest of our stay in that house.

'No, I'm not. But we're leaving the day after tomorrow, and we need to know where your family is.'

Suddenly, I realised that in all that time it hadn't occurred to me to ask her name.

But she didn't answer; she turned around to play with her bear.

'And what about your mum?'

But she didn't answer me, just shrugged her shoulders.

'And your dad?' I asked her a little wearily, seeing she had begun answering my questions only when she pleased.

And once again, no answer.

On one hand, I supposed it might be normal that she didn't know her parent's names. Children know their parents as "mummy" and "daddy" – that's all they need. But for sure the child should know her own name at least. And it had begun to bother me that, whenever we asked her something personal, she wouldn't answer. She had already gone over the line of shyness, far over it in some cases. She didn't seem to be afraid of asking and talking to us about our personal lives. But still, she wouldn't let us do the same about hers.

I remembered that Mrs McGregor had told me her husband would call an old police friend of his. The police would need more than a few short descriptions of the little girl. And a name would be the most important thing. It had been more than twenty-four hours since we had found her, so her family should have reported her disappearance by now. But what could we do to find out her name if she wouldn't tell us?

'Have you tried her nightgown?' Dave asked me.

I had left the child in the living room, alone and watching the cartoons, to go up and memorise my lines for the next episode of our TV show. Dave was in his bedroom, playing on his phone, and smiled when I asked him to help me. He always loved to help me memorise my lines: it helped him hone his memory for when he had lines himself. So, humming on the way, he came to my bedroom without me asking him twice.

But I couldn't focus properly. Dave asked me what was wrong, and I explained the issue about the child's name. It was then that, out of the blue and without hesitating, he asked me that question.

Only when I returned him a puzzled look did he explained what he meant by that.

'I don't know, but when I *were* a kid my brother and I had the same identical onesies. My mum had *buy* to both of us the same one, with a pattern of orange bears. And because they were the same size and we didn't like sharing, she wrote our names on each one. That way we didn't have to argue about which one was *whom*.'

I grumbled under my breath, thinking how stupid I was for not having that idea myself. I was an only child, so my mum had never written my name on my clothes, except when I was in school and had to have my uniform labelled that way so that we didn't get confused.

Why hadn't I thought of it before?

I rushed to the laundry basket. The day before, when I had taken a shower before going down to Guildon Forest, I had left my dirty clothes with the girl's nightgown. I opened the basket and rummaged among the contents.

'Here it is,' I said.

Dave picked it up and flipped it over. He looked on the inside of the collar and the sleeves, but shook his head. A few seconds later he stopped to look at the washing label. And he frowned.

'And?' I urged him to say something.

'Yes, there's a name on it. But I can't read it,' he answered, handing the garment back to me.

I took it and made an effort to try reading the name that, definitely, was written on the label. After the washings it had blotted out quite a lot, leaving an almost illegible scribble.

'I think . . . it says . . .' I was saying to Dave while I racked my brain trying to read it. It wasn't easy, but not impossible. I went through a few names that came to mind, trying to find one that could match with the scribble. 'Have you ever heard the name "Yäel"?'

Dave shook his head.

'Yäel, her name is Yäel,' I concluded.

That was the only one that would match the lines and dots of the scribble.

'Should we call your mum's friend?' Dave suggested.

'Yes, I've got her number downstairs,' I told him.

I went down to the living room. I was so happy about our discovery that I couldn't contain myself. I grabbed the phone book by the telephone, where Mrs McGregor's number was. And just before I went back upstairs, I made sure the little girl was fine. But on this occasion, wanting to surprise her and see her reaction, I did it in a different way.

'Are you all right, Yäel?'

Simple and accurate.

The child turned around, very slowly, as if she didn't want to make a single noise. I was surprised at the look in her eyes. They were full of such intensity . . . Puzzled? Surprised? Wanting to know how I had come up with that name? I don't know. But they did surprise me: those weren't the eyes of a child.

The girl scanned me with that strange look. She didn't know what to say. Obviously, she wanted to know how I knew that name since she hadn't told me.

Could I know something about her?

If she hadn't told me, who had?

I don't think it occurred to her that I'd found it on her nightgown.

'Yes, I'm ok,' she muttered under her breath, but clear enough for me to have heard it from the stairs.

I went up to my bedroom, smiling. That was her name and now I could provide a more complete description of her to help us find her parents. So, I dialled the number on the telephone by the nightstand and pressed the call button.

'Hello, who is this?' I heard someone on the other end of the line.

This time it wasn't Mrs McGregor, but her husband.

'Hi, Will, it's Eva. Merry Christmas,' I said, raising my voice so that he could understand me. 'Is your wife at home?'

'No, dear, she's gone over to the lady at number five to have some tea. I'm alone here.'

'Well, that way you can have a bit of a rest,' I reminded him. In fact, I didn't need his wife. I asked him, 'Have you called your old police friend?'

And he told me that he had called that same morning, but his friend's shift at the police headquarters wasn't till late in the evening, since there wasn't much going on in town on days like that one. I told him we had discovered the child's name and that we'd thought it might help to find her parents.

'Sorry, did you say "Yäel"?' the man asked me, surprised.

'Yes, that's right. What is it?'

The man mumbled something incoherent.

'Oh, it's nothing, I just seem to think I've heard that name before,' he explained when I asked him what he meant. 'But . . . no . . . I don't know, I don't remember, to be honest. How are you all, anyway?'

'Uh, great, we're watching Christmas films, singing Christmas carols and we're quite jolly,' I answered him, trying not to laugh after seeing Dave's reaction.

Right after I asked Mr McGregor to give my telephone number to his friend at the police – so that he could contact me as soon as he knew anything – Dave and I went back to work with the script. I felt so much better and I could see the light at the end of the dark tunnel we'd seemed to be stuck in. But since we hadn't had time to ourselves for a long time ago, we quickly abandoned the script.

For a while, we talked about irrelevant stuff. We were so happy to have found a moment for just the two of us. But even though we didn't talk about our problems, they were still there. So, we tried to entertain ourselves by looking out the window. We breathed on the glass and made drawings in the mist. And, then, that peace we'd managed to create, free of troubles or puzzles, vanished as suddenly as it had come.

Truth be told, we loved gossiping as much as Mrs McGregor did.

'What did you *thought* about Stacey's outburst?' Dave asked me.

'So intense! I thought she was going to have a stroke.'

'And what about Yäel doing it on purpose?'

'I don't know. However long I think about it, I can't find any reason for her to break her those vials,' I muttered while misting the glass and starting another drawing.

'Stacey's right about what she said, though.'

'What do you mean?'

He hesitated for a moment. Then, 'The noise that the vials *do*. It wasn't as if they just fell: it sounded as if she had *crash* them against the floor.' He erased his drawing and misted the glass over again. 'I also don't see why the girl would have done it on purpose, but do you think that if they had just fallen, they would have *broke*?'

'Maybe; maybe not. But, why on earth would she want to break them?'

'And why is it that she only broke the insulin vials?' Dave emphasised, analysing that detail more closely. 'She could have broken just one of them. Or she could have *brake* the makeup.'

I gave him a grim look, trying to hold onto my good mood.

'Are you telling me that you agree with her?'

He laughed out loud and erased my drawing with the sleeve of his jumper.

'Even if we think badly about the child, she had no idea what those vials were for. She didn't even know what being a diabetic means. So, I don't think she's done it deliberately: she's not evil.'

'Did you, by any chance, not *seen* the look she threw to Stacey when she told her to go to bed?'

'Yes, I did, but it was me who took her to bed. What has that got to do with anything? She hasn't broken any of my stuff.'

He was quiet for a few seconds.

'Dave?'

'I believe that with you she's got something . . . special that she hasn't with any of us,' he confessed in a whisper.

'What do you mean?' I stopped drawing on the window to look at him. I didn't think the child had anything special with me. I was the only one to whom she had raised her voice. Not even when confronting Stacey, the night before, had she spoken with the same intensity that she had used with me.

'Well, for a start, she's in your house because you *pick* her up off the road . . . Not us . . . You did. She's been sleeping all this time with you.' I looked away: I didn't think it was something I ought to correct, since it wasn't his business that I had or hadn't slept with Daniel the night before. 'Whenever possible, she's by your side. She doesn't go to talk with Stacey or Daniel. And if she talks to me, like ever, it's because I'm with you.'

I began to believe maybe she did have something special with me. Perhaps she was seeing me as a mother? But no one asks their mother if she's going to kick them out of her house. That's what Yäel had asked me just a few minutes before in the living room.

'Well, and so what?' I asked him, assuming that he was half right. 'Having a different relationship with me doesn't mean that, because Stacey told her to go to bed, she would break anything of hers.'

Was that even true? I couldn't shake the thought from my head, producing a poignant echo among my other thoughts. It couldn't be that such a little girl could have an evil side. As I'd said, Yäel had no idea of what those vials were for. At least, not until I'd explained to her Stacey's problem and her need for insulin. It didn't make sense to accuse a little girl we'd picked up in the middle of a snowstorm of being deliberately spiteful.

'Oh, what *did* I know,' Dave snorted, not knowing how to defend his theory anymore. 'The only thing I know is that she doesn't *grows* any confidence in me.'

'Yeah, of course, as if you get along with everyone in this house.'

He gave me a mocking look and returned to mist his side of the window. 'And what about you?' he asked without looking at me, his tone serious.

I didn't say anything; I demisted my side of the window and looked outside. I stood there, watching how the snowflakes fell on the small roof under the window. I didn't want to talk about who I was getting along with or not, since I thought he was referring to Daniel. I never talked to Dave about him.

'I don't mean Daniel,' he let me know, reading my thoughts.

'Stacey, then? What's wrong with her?' I asked him, puzzled.

'That I don't think she's as much of a friend of yours as she *say* that she is.'

I frowned. I had never thought such a thing.

'Don't look at me like that: it's true. Stacey has always *envies* you,' the boy confirmed with a sharp voice. 'Maybe you haven't noticed, but I have. When we started "Prodigies" she used to dress so badly. Right after she *become* friends with you, she started dressing like you.' I gave him a sceptical look. 'Don't you believe me? You only need to have a look on *his* Instagram's pictures. If you wore heels, she put them on; once you put red lipstick on, she copied you a few days after; if you curled your hair, she would as well; if one day you decided to *wore* shorts, she would go and buy some the next day ... She's been copying you all along, as if she wants to be you. She *has envy* of you, believe me or not.'

'Really? And how do you know all this?' I poked him playfully in the shoulder. 'Do you have a crush on her?'

Dave put his fingers in his mouth and made an unpleasant grimace, as if he was going to vomit.

'Yes, of course, Stacey. No way,' he said, eyes wide. 'But I do know who she does fancy.' I didn't say anything; I waited for him to "surprise" me. 'She's got a crush on Daniel.'

'I know,' I informed him.

'What?'

'Yes, I know. In fact, it was her who encouraged me to accept going on a date with him. I know she was a bit jealous. But she told me that if he didn't look at her, at least he would go out with one of us.'

'You are pulling my *hair*, right?'

I shook my head, disappointing him. He would have thought that he was going to surprise me in the way he had when he told me Stacey envied me. I knew that she was jealous about my relationship with Daniel, but not about her envying me and wanting to be like me. And much less this idea that she wasn't really a friend to me. That was quite a different thing. Girls are jealous of other girls: life is just like that. But wanting to look just like me? Pretending to be my friend? What for?

'Dave, I think you're judging her without knowing her at all. If you wanted, you could even become her friend: I saw you two last night fighting over the last bits of popcorn, as if you had been friends all your life. She doesn't have a grudge against you as . . . as Daniel does. I know she can be irritating sometimes,' I said before he could argue, 'but she's a good girl. It's just that she hasn't got the best parents ever.'

'What do you mean?'

'I mean that her parents have always forced her to succeed,' I confided in a whisper. We had begun to raise our voices and in that house the walls seemed to be made of paper. 'On more than one occasion she's told me about it, over a good cry. I know what you think about her, but she's got feelings as well. She just has too much pressure on her shoulders. Her parents, especially her mum, have taken her to beauty contests since she was a child, and later on pushed her with acting classes. They wanted her to become someone. Sometimes, when she seems arrogant, she isn't: she acts the way her parents tell her to, and if she has to step over anyone to get on in life and make them happy, she will. But she isn't a bad girl.'

I had never told anyone that. And God knows that more than once I had wanted to defend her in front of someone. But she had told me that in confidence and I knew that Dave would not betray me.

He had never betrayed me with anything.

'If she *think* that she will be just like you, she is crazy. She can step over everyone, but never will get even close. Being an actor is in your blood. And, say what you want, when she *act* she *look* like she has milk instead of blood.'

'Well, we all get better with time. And we're all different. I'd love to be able to act as my . . . Fuck, I forgot to call my mum! She's going to kill me!'

But she didn't say anything. She had been busy with my grandparents, in a villa in the south of Spain, where she was spending Christmas. So, she didn't flinch when I called her so late. My family on my mum's side were all Spanish and very cheerful. They always had a reason to have a good party. During Christmas, all my family – about thirty or forty of them – gathered to eat together at my grandparents' house.

And as mum was busy, we exchanged good wishes and I summarised the events of the day. She was sad about my situation with Daniel, but she knew I was strong and that I was well accompanied with Dave.

She spoke with him for a while in Spanish. Even though I was born in Spain and I was raised there until I was seven, my Spanish had got rusty over time. We spoke English at home, so my mum always enjoyed any chance to speak to anyone in her mother tongue. And often they would both decide to take the piss and get me confused.

My mum had always been fond of Dave.

Once we'd finished the call and didn't feel like gossiping anymore, we went down to the living room with the child and took out some cards. At first, we struggled to find an easy game for the little girl, but in the end the three of us played together without a single argument.

On the plasma screen, the two women could see that moment. Julia wondered how it was possible that everything had ended in such a tragic way. Who would have foreseen that that trip was going to become international news? They were just four young adults and a child of who knew what age.

She stopped looking at the screen and flipped through her notes. She found she had scribbled more than one meaningless doodle in the margins, absorbed with the young girl's story. She went over some ideas she had underlined more than once, making them stand out from the rest.

During Eva's narration, Julia had tried every possible angle with her questions. She had tried to learn more about all the friends, find out details the audience would be interested in, and even that she herself was curious to know about. Gradually, she had been able to make the girl give depth to her story, a story which would captivate the viewers, not only with the facts, but with the past of the most famous youngsters in the world.

But the girl had been blunt when Julia had asked about her feelings for Dave. On the one hand, she was glad she'd got a clear answer. On the other, she was irritated.

She didn't want to spend hours and hours recording. She wanted to get to the point of it all, to get the young girl to tell her the most interesting bits of the story without omitting anything relevant. She didn't want to end up spending hours supervising the editing of the videos with her husband, having to cut out pieces so she could get a result that made sense within the limited screen time.

Throughout the interview, she was feeling a tingling inside her. It wasn't every job that gave her butterflies in her stomach. Just when she was doing something big. And this time, those butterflies were tickling her insides more strongly than ever.

Every now and then her mind flew out of the office, and a few seconds later she'd find herself smiling. She realised how inappropriate those sketches of happiness were. The young girl was telling her something dramatic and painful, and she smiled in return?

"Copy and paste," Julia told herself. She would correct it in the edit.

'Occasionally, we found out that Dave was cheating with the cards . . .' She became aware that the girl was still talking.

'Wait a second, Eva,' she interrupted her. 'Just so the audience doesn't get lost, since it's a rather complicated story, we should do a bit of a summary.'

'Alright,' the girl said.

'That Christmas morning,' Julia spoke with that direct and confident voice of hers, somehow managing at the same time to keep her tone velvety, 'Daniel got close to fighting with Dave, after he'd broken the present you'd given to Dave. Daniel had just come in from outside with Stacey, who separated all of you and imposed some order.'

'Yes, that's right.'

'All of a sudden, you heard the child breaking the insulin vials that Stacey had in her bedroom. And before leaving the house, an upset Stacey insinuated that the little girl had done it on purpose. Later on . . .' she had another look through her notes, in which she had plotted out the events step by step, 'you asked Daniel for a break in your relationship.'

'Mm . . . hmm.'

'In the afternoon, with the help of your friend, Dave Campos, you discovered the child's name in her nightgown, the name you believed would help you find her family. And when you and Dave were able to have a moment alone, he began to open your eyes to the child when he said he had some sympathy with Stacey's hypothesis. Isn't that right?'

The girl doubted the answer to that question. She took a drink of water and tried to reply as best as she could.

'It's not like he opened my eyes. Although I didn't say it out loud, I knew something wasn't right about that child. After not saying a word for a long time, all of a sudden, she decides to speak? She was getting mad at Stacey and not with me? She broke her insulin vials right afterwards, whether she did that on purpose or not?' She shook her head, still not understanding. 'Of course, I knew for myself that the little girl was hiding things.'

'But . . .' the woman prompted.

'But,' the girl went on, after taking a deep breath, 'she was a child. If it was now, knowing what I know, after all . . . I wouldn't be so indulgent with her. But even when Dave tried to make me see something he wasn't even able to understand himself, more than anything I tried to protect her.'

'But protect her from what?'

8. "Just a damned accident"

That was only the beginning.
 Some people might be able to ignore an everyday event like a child breaking something. But not the person whose things had been broken.

Stacey hadn't said anything against Yäel since she'd come back from her walk with Daisy. She had devoted herself to being pleasant to everyone and behaving as if nothing had happened. At lunch she ate quietly, ignoring Yäel's glares. And even though she maintained that unusual, cold tone towards Daniel, a casual observer might have said she looked happy.

But I knew her better than she thought I did. I knew that, behind that mask of indifference, she was replaying what had happened over and over in her mind. Maybe it was the sparkle in her eyes or her forced smiles. The fact was, she needed some time to process what had happened and to put her thoughts in order. It wasn't going to be long before she decided to open her mouth.

And it happened that same night.

Dave, Yäel and I had been playing cards for what seemed an eternity. An eternity of peace and tranquillity in which assumptions and ungrounded accusations had no place. Time flew by and the rumbling of our stomachs was the only thing that brought us back to reality.

On the stairs appeared Stacey and Daniel. They walked down without talking to each other, their faces serious.

I knew the moment had come.

'Tidy up the table, we're going to prepare dinner, sweetie,' I told Yäel.

She nodded and, polite and helpful, began to collect the cards that lay next to Johnny. Every few seconds, she put the teddy's ear close to her lips and whispered something to him, carrying him with her as she moved around the table.

After observing her natural and childlike behaviour for a few seconds, I headed for the kitchen with the others. I turned on the oven and pulled out a chicken from the fridge.

'I'm waiting,' I said to Stacey.

They all had been watching me gather the ingredients to complement the chicken. All of them stood in silence. Stacey had opened a bottle of water and drunk half of it, taking long, noisy gulps.

'I know you all believe me and know that that brat has broken my vials on purpose,' she began calmly, cold as ice, her arms crossed. 'I'm your friend, and I know that you'll all give me your support over someone you don't even know at all. I know I can always count on you. Even though–'

'What?' I cut in abruptly. She had begun to talk faster and faster, using that sarcastic tone of hers that got on my nerves. 'What's your point?'

'I don't want her in this house,' she summarised succinctly.

I looked back at her. For a moment, a measly moment, I believed she was going to burst out laughing. But those words weren't a joke. She had meant each and every one of them.

'What did you say?'

'I don't want her in this house.'

'I thought it was *my* house,' I reminded her provocatively.

'And that means you get to decide for all of us how and with whom we spend our days, right?'

'Mmm . . . Let me think . . .' I said, with a mocking tone. 'Yes, it does, actually.'

She grabbed the bottle of water, unscrewed the lid and took another bad-tempered gulp.

I could hear her breathing becoming harsh and strained. Often, Stacey looked more like a child than a young adult, even though she was the oldest of the four of us. When things didn't go as planned, she would throw a tantrum, so angry she struggled even to breathe.

'Look, Stacey, I don't care if you want her in this house or not: we have no alternative.'

'We could leave her right where we found her.'

Her reply made no sense, but its deep coldness made me shudder. I laughed, focused on the cooking.

'I don't know what you're laughing about. For all we know, her parents have abandoned her, I wouldn't be surprised . . . We just know she talks when she wants, and to whoever she wants,' she pointed out, watching me intently, 'and we have no idea where she's from, or why she was in the middle of the road. And her way of thanking us is to start breaking my stuff –'

'So, you still think she did it on purpose, then?' Dave asked, curious.

'Yes,' she confirmed.

I looked at Dave, my expression telling him what I needed to without words. I wasn't going to allow accusations or frivolous hypotheses. I washed my hands and turned to the girl.

'Do you, or do you not have more insulin? Yes, you do. So, stop going on about whether she did it on purpose, because you're not going to fucking die. It was just a damned accident, alright? She's a kid, not a rabid dog. Don't ever say again we should leave her where we found her. Perhaps we should leave *you* in the middle of nowhere and see what you think about it!'

My words had come out more harshly than I'd intended, and I stopped for a second to breathe. I needed to calm down and count to ten before I said anything I'd regret.

'Someone could call us tomorrow and let us know her family has been found,' I continued, trying to sound more positive. 'And, as suddenly as we found her, we'll get rid of –'

'And what if that doesn't happen?' Daniel asked without looking at me, just staring out of the window.

Cries of Blood

The continuous snowflakes floating down behind the glass didn't offer a great omen for the next day. So far, the snowstorm had got worse with each second that passed. Our biggest problem wasn't the child, but how we were going to get out of that place. At that rate, we would find ourselves confined to the house for days, or even a week.

'Thank you, Daniel,' I followed his gaze to the window, but didn't mention my own doubts. 'Well, then we'll have to take the risk and get her to the nearest town. Mr McGregor has an old friend he's going to call this evening and let him know about our situation with Yäel.'

'Yäel?' Stacey repeated slowly, as if unsure whether she'd heard right.

'We *find* the name in her nightgown.' Dave explained succinctly.

I waited a few seconds to let them welcome the good news. At least we knew something about the little one, and the police could take that into account. And I could only pray that, at any moment, the landline would ring and bring a breakthrough.

'The thing is, tomorrow is our last full day in the house – if the weather lets us leave, of course,' I pointed out, not wanting to dwell on that detail. 'Let's try and spend the time we have left here in peace, ok? I'm the first one to wish we hadn't found Yäel: I was hoping to spend some days away from the world, relaxing and having fun with my best friends . . .'

Friends who would no longer be friends.

Friendships that were crumbling without us even noticing.

And that was only the beginning.

'So you didn't notice that the child was listening to you all?' Julia asked, pointing to the plasma screen.

Eva turned her head in the direction of the presenter's finger. She could see in the security camera's footage how the little girl had quietly crept closer to the kitchen. She saw herself raising her arms while talking to Stacey, not noticing that the child had stopped tidying up the dining table and was spying on them from behind the chairs.

'No – to be honest, I was too busy dealing with my friends, the ones who weren't being very helpful,' the young girl defended herself.

'Could that conversation have been what precipitated the events that followed?' the woman proposed, taking a pen to her mouth, biting its lid.

Eva looked back at her. 'Maybe; maybe not.'

Julia took a long and deep breath, looking over her notes without reading them.

'I think I speak for all the audience when I ask the next question: how did everything start?'

The girl forced a smile; she had to control her emotions in front of the cameras. She took another sip from her glass of water, her vocal cords strained and irritated from so much talking.

'Before I say anything else, I should tell you what happened later that evening.'

After having dinner and washing the dishes, we all felt tired and didn't want to watch TV. We weren't in the mood to keep talking about what we would do about the child.

Why did everything have to be so difficult?

Just days earlier we'd been so happy and excited to take a few weeks off from the show. We'd been working for five months without a break. Makeup and dress rehearsals; meetings with the executive producers and directors, in which we went over and over how our characters were going to be in the new season: plots, conflicts, dramas, comedy; hundreds of hours each week at the set or on location, sweating under studio lights or shivering in the cold and rain . . . Of course we were excited.

Dave, who wasn't happy about spending more time around either Stacey or Daniel, had spent days planning what we'd do when we reached my house in Guildon Forest. He'd come up with thousands of possibilities. He'd even planned to make a short film; besides wanting to become an actor, he loved writing short stories.

We'd often made amateur short films before, the four of us sometimes joined by other members of the cast. In some of them, Dave would just be the director, whilst in others he also gave himself a leading role. We used to upload the films on YouTube, more than once facing reprimands from the producers of our show. But we tried to make them outside work, whenever we had time off – which wasn't very often.

For the first time in the year and a half since we'd started working on the "Prodigies" series, we had a holiday. Far away from everyone, without a single person telling us what to do and when we could or couldn't do it. We had waited long enough for that moment. And now, instead of carrying out all our plans, we were arguing and fighting all the time, unable to enjoy ourselves and suffering through long, irritating silences.

Even though my relationship with Daniel had more ups and downs than I'd have liked, I cared about him and we often had a great time together. Then there was Dave, my best friend, whom I respected and admired for his spirit, his determination to overcome the difficulties in his life. And last but not least, there was Stacey, who – despite everything – was my friend, the person I'd spent hours filming with, even laughing at our own shadows.

But that trip had changed all that, from the moment we had set foot in the car. There was no more laughter, except for when I was alone with Dave. But our relationship was too special. I knew we would always have each other, no matter what happened. But the rest of the time with the other two was becoming painful.

I tried to write all that down in my diary. I believed it would help me see our situation more clearly, like it had in the past; but this time, all it did was confuse me even more, creating new doubts in my mind.

What would I do if the snowstorm didn't stop?

We didn't have much food left and the village was too far for us to get to on foot. The car was useless unless the weather improved; in those conditions, I wouldn't even suggest that Daniel drove. He'd already moaned enough about bumping the car.

'What are you doing?' Yäel asked from next to me in the bed, curious and without taking her eyes off me.

It had been a while since I'd been so engrossed in writing down the events of my life. Until that night, I had never written a single page whilst in the same room as another person. Or at least, not with that person being wide awake.

The first night she'd stayed in my room, Yäel had been sleeping in the bed while I sat in the armchair to write my diary. Her presence hadn't bothered me then. And tonight, so absorbed in all my doubts, problems, puzzles and headaches, I had hardly felt her next to me. My thoughts had blotted out the sound of the air going in and out of her lungs. The smooth sliding of the pen on the diary's sheets had transported me to a parallel world, where time didn't matter, nor the heat under the duvet, nor even the light bathing shadows over the page as the pen moved up and down. I was in my own world.

'I'm writing my diary,' I answered her, covering their pages with my hand, feeling my thoughts unprotected for a moment.

In almost everything I had written that night, the child had a central role. She was the one to blame for the awkward situation in which we were living. The four of us had gone on holiday for a few days and, after being forced to pick her up, nothing was going as we had planned.

Next to her under the duvet, I felt like I was betraying her. My relationship with her was okay, after all. We had laughed, talked – just only about my life – and, so far, I had no personal reason to be angry with her. Yet no one would have thought that if they'd read what I had just written about her in those pages. I was blaming her for the change in Stacey, for breaking the girl's insulin vials, for being an extra responsibility that none of us really wanted, for becoming an unexpected and extra mouth to feed; and for not even letting me enjoy writing my diary, that moment that should have been mine and nobody else's. I could try to see myself as a mother, responsible for her child. But she wasn't my child, not at all.

'What is a diary?'

I closed the book and replaced the lid on my pen.

'It's . . . it is where someone writes their most private thoughts daily.'

'Every day?'

'No, sometimes you can be tired and don't write anything at all,' I explained, covering myself with the duvet and getting comfortable on my side of the bed. 'Some days you can write more than others. Can you write?'

She hesitated. It looked as she doubted whether she should answer me.

'Not very well.'

'And can you read?'

She smiled for a split second, but long enough that I noticed.

'Yes, I'm better at reading. Give me your diary and I'll show you how–'

I clutched the diary between my fingers, turning them into iron claws, protecting it from her. I couldn't help it.

In an instant, I could feel how the thin line of the only thing that gave me freedom in the world was breaking. When you are famous, you have no secrets. They emerge from under the rocks and everyone knows them. You can write whatever you want in a second, upload it on the Internet and someone, on the other side of the planet, will find it.

That diary was only mine. I could have secrets, say or think whatever I wished, and no one would ever find out.

'No,' refused the part of my heart I could not tame. I saw her startled expression. I tried to clear my throat and said, calmer now, 'No, sweetie. I've said that a diary is where someone writes his or her most private thoughts, which means that this one is also private. It wouldn't be a diary if more than one person read it, but a book.'

Yäel gave a sigh, wished me a good night and turned over in bed, showing me her back. After stowing the diary under my pillow, I did the same. I wished her sweet dreams and turned off the lamp on the nightstand.

More than once, I thought what a luxury it would have been not to have woken up that morning. I didn't start off on the right foot. I had slept badly and I was irritated. Every now and then I had woken shivering, finding myself uncovered by the duvet.

At dawn I realised I was alone in the bed and, unlike the previous morning and without knowing why, I felt relieved.

I stretched under the feather duvet and allowed myself the treat of another five minutes. I was on holiday, after all. Besides, I didn't have the slightest desire to go downstairs and face another day.

Something inside me was telling me something bad was going to happen. I felt it in my stomach, like a knot. So many things had gone wrong since we got there that now I felt it could only get worse. Perhaps, someone else would have thought the opposite: that the day would be wonderful and peace would finally take over in the house. But I couldn't shake that bad feeling.

I remained sheltered in the bed in the foetal position. I thought I was safe. I planned to stay there for as long as possible.

Then, eyes closed, I began to realise something. When you close your eyes, your other senses become more acute. I could feel something was out of place. I had no idea what it was. My throat felt drier than normal. After a long night of silent gasps, I hadn't yet drunk from the bottle of water by the nightstand. The room was as cold as the day before; I could feel it when one of my feet ventured unprotected from under the duvet. The bed sheets smelled of lavender and I couldn't perceive any other odd smell. My fingers played between the sheets, not noticing anything unusual in the softness and delicacy of the silk.

No, it was nothing to do with any of that. But what then? What was it that was calling my attention?

It dawned on me.

Silence.

It wasn't the kind of silence you'd try to fill with awkward conversation. It was another kind of silence. A silence of calm, tranquillity. A silence of death.

I stuck my head out of the duvet, brushed the hair from my face and looked towards the window. Like a thunderbolt, I leaped out of bed and almost threw myself against the glass. My hard breathing turned it to mist, just as the previous evening when Dave and I had drawn on those windows.

I stood there in disbelief, my eyes wide.

The snowstorm had stopped.

If I had fully opened my eyes when I first awoke, I would have noticed the bright light coming through the windows. It seemed as if the sunshine had been building up behind the clouds, behind those monstrous clouds full of snow, the ones that had now simply vanished from the sky. And it was as if all that reserved light now shone out from the clear blue dome, with nothing left to prevent it.

How could I have thought that something bad was going to happen?

This could only be good news. If the weather remained that way, we would be able to get out of there the next day, but not before leaving Yaël wherever we had to. Finally, we could go back to London and restart our old lives.

No more kids breaking things.

No more people whining every two seconds.

No more hypotheses or accusations about irrelevant nonsense.

We could go back to our homes, where Daniel and Stacey at least had their families waiting for them. I would be able to enjoy some time alone with Dave at my house; my mother was in the south of Spain and wasn't coming back until a few days later, and Dave's family were in Madrid. It was what I needed: no one else around.

Happy and contented, I put on some jeans and a blouse. I went to the bathroom and washed my face. I looked at myself in the mirror and smiled at my reflection.

I had never been so happy about the weather. In London, I loved the rain. It relaxed me. But everyone dreams of enjoying a sunny day.

That morning's sun meant so much more.

Freedom.

With that sudden mood change, I went downstairs. There I found something I wasn't expecting at all. I stopped at the bottom of the stairs to observe the astonishing sight. Dave, with Yäel on his lap, and Stacey were covered up to their chins with two thick blankets while playing Monopoly. The three of them were shivering, but they had wide smiles on their faces.

What was going on there?

The previous day they'd all been at each other's throats, wouldn't speak to each other or give each other a chance to be friends. Now, all of a sudden, they were huddled together, playing a board game and looking happy?

I looked around for Daniel, but he hadn't come down yet.

'Good morning,' I greeted them, taking my last step down the stairs. 'Do you know there's something called a "fire"?'

They looked at the wood-burner and told me they had tried to burn some logs, but without success. I left the three of them there and got on with starting up the fire. I did it happily. I loved helping others, and besides, it was bitterly cold.

'Have you had anything for breakfast yet?'

They shook their heads.

Did they know how to do *anything?*

When I finished lighting the wood and making sure that no smoke was getting into the room, I went to the kitchen. I turned on the electric hob and placed a pan of milk on it. I grabbed a bag of porridge oats from one of the shelves and put enough for everyone into the pan with the milk. I even prepared an extra bowl for Daniel.

I looked out of the window, smiling to myself. The back of the house seemed so peaceful and solitary. The snow had piled up high during those last days. Some squirrels were running over the fence, jumping down to the ground and then back up the fence or a near tree. They were looking for something to eat. Perhaps their dray wasn't far from there. A few seconds later, they stopped, vigilant, turning their eyes silently from side to side. They twisted their heads, as if a sixth sense had warned them that someone was watching their every move. And then they spotted me through the window; but they ignored me, as if I wasn't important. I didn't represent any danger to them, and they went back to their search.

I stirred the porridge and turned off the hob when it got thick enough. I poured it into bowls and sprinkled a little sugar and cinnamon on top.

'Mmmm . . . Thanks,' the three of them warmed their hands against the steaming bowls.

'Where did you get the Monopoly?' I asked them, curious.

'It was among all the junk in the garage,' Stacey answered me between spoonfuls.

I sat on one end of the sofa and joined the game while I ate my own bowl of porridge. I appreciated the warmth going down my throat. And I was glad that we were all together – all of us except Daniel – and enjoying a bright and peaceful morning.

Daniel came down a few minutes later. He stared in amazement when he found the four of us playing, probably looking much the same as I had when I'd seen the others. He returned my gaze with a sheepish look when I told him I'd prepared him a bowl of porridge as well. He nodded without saying a word and went and fetched it from the kitchen.

'I can't believe it,' I growled when I went bankrupt, handing my last properties and bank notes to Dave. I got up and asked him for a cigarette, while he was bragging about knocking me out of the game and amassing his bundle of money.

Outside I zipped my coat all the way up and lit the cigarette.

It was a beautiful day. The sunlight had melted the icicles along the roof of the porch. A pair of birds chased each other across the blue sky, alighting on the branch of a pine tree and singing, then taking flight and swooping and soaring through the air once more.

The wind was also singing its own delightful melody, trilling through the branches of the trees. Its soft movement made little piles of snow fall to the ground, catching other branches on their way and shaking them in turn, creating a small white veil of flakes flying in the air.

I took a puff on the cigarette, enjoying that awful habit. I rarely smoked and, although I detested the smell of it on others, I savoured that moment, cigarette in hand, the birds singing, the rustling of the pine branches and the freshness of the air on my face.

Unknowingly, I was enjoying the last minutes of peace at that house.

The tranquillity was just a mirage. As certainly as I had sensed it when I woke up, it would not be a good day. The sunlight, the birds singing, the squirrels playing around the house . . . Everything was a farce, a distraction.

Daniel's voice pulled me back to reality.

'It's stopped snowing at last.'

'Yes, indeed. Finally, something to enjoy, right?' I said, giving him a sheepish look.

I didn't know what else to say. It hadn't been long enough to talk to him about our relationship: I would need a break far away from him to know if I missed him or not.

He lit a cigarette, saying nothing more.

I looked up to the treetops, searching for an escape from that awkward situation.

'Maybe we can all go for a walk later . . .' I whispered after a few minutes of silence, then instantly regretting the stupid comment. Was that even what I wanted? All of us going for a walk? Including Daniel? Perhaps, if Stacey had managed to sit down with Dave and Yaël to play peacefully, I could also leave my resentment aside. 'There's a small stream near here –'

'Yeah, maybe,' he interrupted me, his voice soft. He wasn't expecting me to start a conversation. He hadn't come out to talk.

I tried to clear my mind and not feel overwhelmed by the silence. I remembered that we needed to bring more logs from the back of the house so they could dry inside. Therefore, I got up and headed for the stairs. But when Daniel yelled at me to be careful on the steps, it was too late. One of them capsized under my weight and I fell into the snow, just as Stacey had done the previous day.

Even though the snow cushioned my fall, I groaned in pain as I felt my ankle twist over the wooden step.

'Are you ok?' Daniel exclaimed, running to my rescue.

He offered me a hand and lifted me up. I trembled as I put my weight on my twisted ankle and staggered, almost falling again. Daniel reached out and grabbed me just in time, and I let myself rest on his chest. I looked up into his eyes. They were bathed in the orange sunlight, turning them from pure blue to greenish brown. I took a deep breath.

'Yes, I feel alright,' I whispered.

Neither of us moved. I could feel his arms holding me tight against his body. We looked at each other and both felt the pain that had taken over our hearts. And I buried my head in his chest.

I didn't cry.

I didn't say a word.

Neither did he.

We remained in that position, enjoying the contact with each other as if nothing had come between us.

'I think I can walk,' I said a minute later. He let me go and I headed for the back of the house.

Daniel didn't follow me; he just lit another cigarette. When I reached the wood pile, I stopped and sat on the floor. My ankle was aching, but I knew the pain would go away soon: it would have been more painful if it had been anything serious.

I massaged the tender area and stayed sitting down for a minute. When the soreness began to ease, I stood up and took a few logs.

'Careful,' Daniel reminded me from his position by the front steps.

I saw that he had been having a look at the loose step. He had lifted and removed the wooden board, leaving a hole on its place. I took the logs inside.

'Come with me to the garage,' I called back to him. 'Maybe there's something there to fix that.'

He followed me in and, together, we looked around all the junk. Behind some piles he found a huge red toolbox. He took out several hammers and screwdrivers, then smiled while pulling at the end of a black cable. When he reached the other end, I saw it was attached to something that looked like a drill.

'Is that any good?' I asked him.

'It's a nail gun,' he explained, smiling. He could have said it was a weapon of mass destruction and I would have believed him; I had no idea about tools. 'But it hasn't got any nails left. Wait, no, there's a box full of them. Perfect.'

Next thing, he asked me for an extension lead. I dug one out and he went straight back outside.

'What's Daniel doing?' Stacey asked, raising her eyes from the Monopoly board.

'He's fixing the step. I almost cut my head open,' I said, taking the seat next to Dave.

And . . . God, what I would give now for Dave never to have said what he said then . . . But I had no idea of what was going to happen next . . .

'Why don't you go outside and help Daniel?' he suggested to the child.

She was watching Dave and Stacey playing, the only ones in the game who still had money. She was clearly bored, so she welcomed the idea with a smile and rushed from the sofa.

'Put on your coat and wellies,' I warned her before she went.

Yäel turned around, her teddy bear in her hand. She apologised with a funny look and put on the coat and wellingtons that sat next to the front door. Daisy scampered after her.

Once she'd closed the door, Dave snorted and said, 'Finally! Do you fancy a . . . ?'

' "Do you fancy a . . . ?" ' Julia repeated, watching on the plasma screen as Dave ran up the stairs.

Eva had abruptly interrupted her storytelling and averted her eyes. For some reason, she seemed to feel ashamed and didn't finish her sentence.

The plasma screen now showed the footage of two security cameras. One of them displayed Daniel, kneeling on the steps leading up to the front door, placing the board in its place. Next to him, the child stood smothered in a coat that obviously wasn't her size and which fell below her knees. In the other video, the two girls were waiting for Dave in the living room.

'Eva?' the presenter called her attention back to her.

Eva stared back and made a noncommittal gesture.

'If you don't say it, we'll see it anyway on the security cameras,' Julia warned her.

The girl frowned. Absurdly, she had not considered this detail. And now it was too late. Besides, she told herself, she had agreed to tell her story from beginning to end.

'I haven't come here to tell you how good we were,' the young girl said, fixing her remorseful eyes on the presenter's. 'We were just like any other young people . . . we wanted to have fun. I don't regret agreeing to Dave's suggestion.'

'And that suggestion was . . . ?' the woman murmured. She waited for a few seconds, wrote something in her notes and moved closer to the girl. 'Eva, I'm not here to judge you for what you did or what happened. You wanted to tell your story to hundreds of thousands of people,' she said pointing to the camera aimed at them, 'who are confused after all the lies that have been published about those days in Guildon Forest. No one is perfect.'

'He offered us some marijuana,' the girl declared.

Julia leaned back in her chair and could not restrain a smile. She looked straight at the camera.

'Well, if my memory doesn't fail me,' said the woman making a theatrical gesture towards the lens, 'it was Jesus who said that the person without sin should throw the first stone . . .'

The presenter pulled a funny face at the camera and then looked back at the girl, who was smiling, apparently reassured by the odd comment.

'I thought Dave must have suggested something much worse,' Julia went on, waving her hands as if none of this was the least bit important. 'Did you enjoy it at least?'

'Not really,' Eva denied the charge, wiping the smile from her face. She looked at the screen. 'As you can see from the footage, Dave came down a few seconds later and began rolling a joint–'

'But . . .'

'But we never even got to light it. Dave had the idea of asking Stacey to invite Daniel in, so that we could all be together for a bit. Not that we often smoked,' the girl hurried to point out, 'but now and then, if we were in a house far away from the press, or at a party . . . Sometimes we'd get carried away and just fool around. Whenever we'd smoked, it had been the four of us together.'

'So . . .'

Cries of Blood

'So, Stacey called Daniel and he came in, right after telling Yäel that he'd be straight back.'

The girl went quiet again. She gestured to the screen. Julia's husband unmuted the videos so they were able to hear what the two security cameras had recorded that day.

In the footage playing on the right-hand side of the screen, Julia saw Daniel enter the living room with Daisy and join the three others, among them Dave with what looked like a cigarette in his hand. But it was clear Daniel realised it wasn't a cigarette. He accepted the offer with raised eyebrows, apparently surprised that Dave had included him after what had happened between them.

Julia kept her eyes fixed on the screen. She was hoping to be able to find a good clip for the trailer . . . This interview would be dynamite: the love and hatred between the most famous stars in the world, their true and fake friendships, accusations around every corner, drug use . . .

'Ohhhh!' Julia jumped on her chair, frightened by a loud blast that came from the footage playing on the left of the screen. There she saw the extension lead, a cable running from it to the nail gun, which was held by a black shadow: the little girl in the oversized coat.

'No . . .'

The four of us jumped in shock. Even the dog pricked up her ears and turned her head towards the front door. We looked at each other. Dave sat with his eyes wide open.

'The child . . . The nail gun . . .' he babbled.

We all ran outside, bumping into each other, wanting to be the first out of the door. Despite my painful ankle I got there first, with Daisy running between my legs. I stopped in the doorway and had to close my eyes for a moment. The sun was higher now, reflecting against the snow. The light blinded me for a few seconds, and I rubbed my eyes with both hands.

Part of me didn't want to ever regain my eyesight. My mind took advantage of the situation and played tricks on me. It was as if time stopped and I could see the headlines in the papers, each one more gruesome than the last: "Actors from 'Prodigies' kill a child", "Missing girl found dead at Eva Domínguez's house", "Child dies at home of drug taking TV cast" . . .

When I regained my vision, time seemed to start again. Among the blurred figures I first recognised the shape of the child with her coat on, teddy bear in one hand and nail gun in the other.

'What's happened . . . ?' I stammered, straining my eyes to adjust to the light.

When the rest of the figures came into focus, I saw the little girl next to the car. We had arrived just in time to see it begin to tip forwards in the snow. I remember in precise detail how the front tyre, the one on our side, slowly deflated as the weight of the vehicle pressed the air out of it.

Daniel was the first to react. He pushed me to one side and jumped down the steps. He landed next to the child, removed the nail gun from her hands, looked at it then at the flat tyre, and slapped Yäel sharply across her face. She collapsed on the snow from the force of the blow and lay there, a hand pressed to her cheek, now red and bearing the clear imprints of fingers. It seemed as if the pain didn't hit her at first. Then she closed her eyes and cried thunderously.

'You moron!' Daniel shouted at her.

Daisy started barking at him, baring her teeth. I pounced on the boy, taking the nail gun away. I wanted to make sure he didn't do anything stupid.

'She's a child, Daniel!'

'Yeah, a fucking child that's just punctured the tyre!' he shouted at me, freeing himself from my arms.

He tried to pounce on Yäel, but Dave had taken her out of his reach, moving away from us while the little girl screamed in his arms. The dog kept barking at Daniel.

Cries of Blood

'You and your precious car!' I mocked him, grabbing Daisy by the collar, trying to get her away from him at the same time as reassuring her. 'Is that a reason to hit her?! She's just a child!'

'Stop fucking saying that "she's just a child"! Don't you see what she's done?!'

'Yes, punctured the tyre. I have eyes!'

'Not just *a* tyre! The only spare tyre left!' the boy bellowed, all self-control lost.

His words struck me fiercely. I remembered that just a few days earlier Daniel had got a flat tyre by "accident", being a twat with his brand-new car. So, he'd had to put on the spare from the boot. I'd been with him that day and we'd had one of our many arguments.

'And you just leave her alone with a nail gun?!' I was blind with anger, crushed by the consequences of his actions. But a child wasn't to blame for it. 'Only a fool leaves a nail gun with a little girl! Didn't you even think to unplug it?!'

'If your best friend here hadn't decided to start smoking weed, I wouldn't have had to think about anything!'

'Don't you even dare try to bring Dave into this,' I warned, pointing a finger at him. 'He's not to blame for you not having a brain.'

'And how did I know she was going to puncture the tyre?'

'Oh, yes, of course, as if that was the worst that could have happened! What do you think your beloved press would say about it? What would they write about Daniel Ferguson?' I mimicked the tone he'd used when he read the magazine articles at Mr McGregor's store. ' "The handsome redhead from Kent"? How about the stupid actor who's thick as a brick and leaves a nail gun with a little girl without unplugging it first?!'

He stared back at me, offended. But when he opened his mouth to answer, we heard Stacey's voice behind us. She hadn't moved from the front door. She didn't even seem concerned by the situation. Now she directed her words at me, her tone cold and deliberate.

'I'm sure it was just "a damned accident".'

'Excuse me?'

'Yeah, it's alright, "she's just a child", isn't she, Eva?'

'Don't start again with this.'

'Why shouldn't I? Should I be afraid?' she teased me, folding her arms across her chest. 'Perhaps you'll come to your senses when you realise that, without a car, we're now stuck in this house thanks to your lovely girl.'

I couldn't take it any longer. I felt helpless, not knowing what to say or do. Everything was being thrown at me and I had to defend myself for something I hadn't even done.

'Dave, take the girl. We're leaving!'

The boy froze, as if he didn't understand what I'd said. I ran towards the house. Stacey moved away from the door to let me pass. I grabbed my coat and Dave's and went outside again, giving Stacey and Daniel a murderous look as I went.

'We're leaving!' I said to Dave once again.

I took Yäel by the hand and walked to the gate. Dave put his coat on awkwardly and followed us, hurriedly. The dog ran after us, ignoring the commands of her owner. I shoved the gate open, making it screech and bang against the post as it closed again. I strode away from the house.

Behind us I heard Daniel shouting something, but I ignored him. I couldn't stop to listen to any more nonsense.

9. "Is this *lead* to your house?"

It is incredible how things can change from one second to the next. Moments earlier we had all been together. The wonderful weather had improved everyone's spirits. We had been playing Monopoly so peacefully, the four of us. Stacey hadn't had any objections to spending time with Yäel. I'd even believed Daniel and I'd had some kind of rapprochement . . .

But, once again, everything had gone wrong.

I tried to focus on walking, holding the child by the hand. It was a few minutes since we had left the house and no one was saying a word. Even Daisy, who dodged the fallen tree trunks with playful agility, hadn't dared to bark or whine at all. She just followed us as if it were her daily walk. I didn't wait for her when she stopped to do her business, but she ran through the snow and found us a few moments later.

I felt the anger growing in my heart, making it thump in my chest. But I knew I had to ignore it, take a deep breath, count to ten, twenty . . . or a thousand. I couldn't let myself get carried away on an impulse. Enough things had already been destroyed by our impulses on those holidays.

Dave kept asking me to walk more slowly. The child was stumbling, struggling to keep up with me as I almost dragged her by the hand. Her coat, two sizes too big, prevented her from moving quickly. But I ignored his pleas until we had gone far enough that Daniel or Stacey wouldn't hear what we said.

I let go of Yäel's hand, turned on my heel like a dog chasing its tail and sank onto the ground. I leaned against the trunk of a huge tree, feeling the snow wetting my trousers. I didn't care; I needed to clear my thoughts.

'Why? Why did you do it?' I asked the girl dejectedly.

I wasn't interested in knowing what had driven her to puncture the tyre, but she had to understand the seriousness of her actions.

'No . . . I . . .' she mumbled back, clutching the teddy bear closer to her chest.

I shook my head, unable to avoid shedding a few tears. After all that time, when the snowstorm was finally over and we had just one day before we left . . . And now we had no way out, however much we wished to leave.

Why did it have to happen to us?

Hadn't we had done enough picking her up from the road?

I felt I didn't want her near us anymore. The sooner her family was found, the better for all of us. Breaking the insulin vials was one thing, but bursting the tyre of Daniel's car was completely different.

'I didn't know that it was . . . I didn't want to . . .' the child stammered and turned away, intimidated by the fury in my eyes.

Dave came over and sat next to me. He put an arm around my shoulders.

'What *done*, it is done.'

'No, Dave, that's not good enough,' I said feeling tired. I moved closer to him and buried my head on his chest, shivering. 'What are we going to do now? How on earth are we supposed to get out of here?'

'Well, maybe your mum's friend could take us to the *more near* town and from there we could take a train or something . . .'

I wiped my tears with the sleeve of my coat and took a mouthful of cold air. Even though we had the sun above us, it was freezing cold. And although my trousers were now wet through from the snow, I didn't care. That was the least of our problems.

Dave couldn't see the problem with calling Mr McGregor to give us a lift to the train station. Why should we ask him to do that? We had driven all the way up there by car. We'd gone back and forth to the village without any problems. We had a vehicle . . . but now it was useless. If only I had foreseen the danger of having the child near the nail gun . . . But no, I didn't foresee it. None of us did.

'Look on the *good* side,' Dave said to me, lifting my face with his freezing hands so that my eyes met his. 'No one is hurt, right?'

I snorted and elbowed him playfully. 'Tell that to Stacey or Daniel and see what they say.'

'And what do I *cared* about what they say? They are assholes.'

'Hey, you think that Yäel broke the vials on purpose too,' I chided him.

'Well, yes, but not that she has *exploded* the wheel, if that is what Stacey was implying,' Dave defended himself. 'They are two totally different things. *At the end*, she is a kid and we have to thank God that she has not *opened* her head in *two*.'

I stood up and shook the snow from my trousers. I looked around and noticed that the child was playing with Daisy. They were running around the trees, chasing each other. I was grateful that nothing had happened to her. Not because we were famous and the press could find out about it, but because she was just a child. A child we didn't know anything about and who we had picked up on the road.

But if the four of us weren't okay with each other, how could we live with the little one among us?

I shook my head, exhausted, trying unsuccessfully to clear those thoughts from my mind. I offered a hand to Dave and helped him to his feet. He proposed going back to the house, but Yäel shook her head shyly, lifting one hand to her cheek. She didn't want to go back so soon and face Daniel again. I didn't want to go back either.

'No,' I kept my tone neutral, 'at least not for a bit. Let's go for a walk. I was looking forward to the snow stopping to fall so that we could go out.'

Dave didn't complain, but he shivered. There was no need to put into words my desire to delay our presence in the house for as long as possible. I'd had enough of all the drama the previous day after the two boys had almost come to blows. Daniel had raised his hand to someone then too, and I hadn't liked seeing that new side of him in the slightest.

It was why I'd told him we needed to take a break. What would happen now?

Stacey and Daniel were very good friends. In our absence, I guessed that she'd be trying to get him to see what she thought of as "reason". She would make him believe the little girl had punctured the tyre deliberately, as she claimed she had also broken the insulin vials. Stacey would take advantage of Daniel's temper and the fact that the two of us weren't getting along. I wouldn't be there to make him think objectively and to remind him that Yäel was only a child.

I was afraid. I wouldn't allow him to raise his hand to anyone else, and much less to a small girl. Maybe we all deserved a slap now and again; but it wasn't for us to hit the child. Yes, she deserved a punishment, but violence wasn't the answer. And even though I believed myself the most sensible one in the group, I was afraid that I didn't know how I would react if Daniel tried something like that again.

It was better that we didn't go back just yet.

Therefore, followed by Yäel, who avoided holding my gaze by hiding behind her teddy bear, we continued walking in the opposite direction to the house.

It had been so long since I'd last walked through that forest. Everything was different from how I remembered it. I presumed it was due to the snow as I'd never been there in wintertime. This time at least I could see perfectly thanks to the sun that filtered through the branches of the trees. But every time I had walked across that mountain before it had been either spring or summer. There were flowers and the ground was almost dry. This time everything was covered by a thick layer of snow.

The snow overtopped our boots and worked its way into our socks, so we had to take a detour wherever it had collected in deep drifts. As a result, we walked through areas I hardly remembered any more. We passed the stream I'd told Daniel about earlier that morning as we'd stood on the porch. It was frozen solid. The pebbles beneath the thick layer of ice looked like small silver balls. We walked across it and two minutes later found a clearing in the forest, surrounded by a group of tall rocks.

'I loved fairy tales when I was little,' I confessed to Dave, trying to loosen up the atmosphere. As soon as I'd set foot in the clearing and spotted the group of rocks, old memories had sprung suddenly to mind. 'My father used to tell me a beautiful story about fairies and their magic circles. Once when I was here,' I said standing in the centre of the clearing, pointing at my surroundings, 'I found a perfect circle of mushrooms. More than once after that I would sneak out and come here.'

'*For what?*' he asked me with feigned enthusiasm, mocking my odd memories.

'Who knows. I would put on my pretend fairy wings and start dancing, thinking I would attract the fairies and they would take me to their magical world,' I replied with a smile on my lips. 'Every time I went missing, my father knew where to find me. One time I fell asleep here. He woke me up, inside the mushroom circle, and took me back home. The next day I got really ill, feverish and coughing. I was lucky to get away without a good scolding from my mum . . . And even if I hadn't got ill, I knew that . . . that I had my father protecting me, treating me like a little princess.'

My smile faded and Dave came over and gave me a hug. For a moment I stood paralysed. That was one of the reasons I had asked Daniel for a break . . . And this was the second hug Dave had given me in less than ten minutes.

'I'm . . . sorry,' he murmured, feeling my body rigid, and started to move away.

I grabbed his arms and put them around my back, letting him know I didn't mind. We were friends, right?

We stood there, still. Somehow, I needed that contact. It made me feel less alone, which I then realised it had been a constant feeling. I put my head on his shoulder. I felt the warmth of his body and realised that, although he had been moaning about feeling cold, he was inexplicably hot; I, however, was freezing.

'Do you miss him? Your dad, I mean.'

'Yes, I miss him a lot.'

The statement came out of me instantaneously, almost as if I was happy to talk about that and nothing else. For some reason I had no qualms about talking about him with Dave. Nobody, not even my mother, had ever succeeded in making me open up about my feelings as Dave had. I'd always refused to talk about my father, pretending everything was fine. But Dave had a quality no one else had.

What could that quality be? Even today, I don't know. I just know he's the only person I've opened up to about those kinds of deep feelings. The only one who had ever understood and respected me from the beginning.

But I was afraid of what that meant.

Why couldn't I even mention my father's name in front of Daniel? He was supposed to be my boyfriend. Surely, I should be able to be more open with my partner than with a relative or friend.

But there I stood, far away from my boyfriend and hugging Dave. Pleased to have his warm cheek against my own, feeling our hearts beating almost in unison, our breath mingling. And I feared he felt something more than friendship for me.

Even so, I let myself enjoy that hug.

'I miss him quite a lot,' I said again, afraid of talking about something else.

'Have you *talk* about this with your mum?'

'No . . . I can't. Just remembering his name breaks my heart–'

'So why *you can* with me?'

Why? Why did he have to ask that question? I was already feeling guilty enough for only being able to open up with him, and for feeling so comfortable with his arms around me. I didn't want to think about the answer to that. I was happy as I was.

'Who cares,' I muttered and, changing the subject, I said instead, 'I'm sorry for bringing you here with us. You didn't want to–'

He squeezed me in his arms and gently rubbed my back.

'Sshhh . . . I like *be* with you, Eva; I didn't want to be alone for Christmas. So calm down, no matter how much bad *air* there is in the house, I know I'll always have –'

'What are you doing?' The child's voice came from behind us.

We jumped away from each other instantly and the breath caught in my throat. I had almost forgotten she was there. I turned and looked at her. She didn't avoid my eyes this time, but stared at me as if drawn by a force stronger than my own; and now it was I who tried to avoid her dark eyes.

'I'm sad,' was the only thing I could think of saying after an awkward silence.

'Why?'

For a few seconds I wasn't sure how to answer. I had no idea why I felt I needed to excuse myself. Had I even been doing anything wrong?

'Because of what you've done, Yäel,' I replied as fast as I could, trying to breathe normally again. 'I'm trying to protect you and you're just making it so difficult.'

She didn't avoid my gaze. She stood there in her wellies, Daisy licking the fingers of one hand. With the other she held Johnny by one of his arms, leaving his body to hang next to her legs, almost touching the snow.

'But I'm good,' she argued, pulling a face as if she had never hurt a fly.

I let out a derisive laugh. 'Oh, really? What about refusing to go to bed when we tell you to? Or what about not helping us find your family? Or breaking Stacey's insulin vials? Or puncturing the tyre?'

She didn't show any signs of regret. Actually, she simply returned my gaze impassively.

'You do realise that we're going to take you back to your house when the police find your family,' I continued, 'whether we can drive the car or not?'

'The police?' she whispered.

'Yes,' Dave confirmed. 'They know we have you and they're looking for your parents. And, any moment now, they'll call to tell us they have *find* them.'

She didn't say a word. She stood as still as a wax statue, letting the dog nip playfully at her fingers. But this time her expression wasn't quite so impassive . . . It was as if a doubt had crossed her frozen gaze.

'Are you all right?' I asked her, getting closer. 'You do miss your mummy, right?'

I felt stupid. Of course a child of her age would be missing her mother . . .

'Yes . . . I'm sorry I broke the tyre,' she said in a voice that didn't fit with her words.

Dave and I looked at each other frowning. This was the first time we had managed to get even a shy "yes" from the little one about her family, and yet there was something unusual in her voice. But she was a complete stranger to us, often surprising us with her looks, innocent sentences and questions. So we didn't dwell on the strangeness of her tone for long.

'Yäel, I don't want you to say sorry,' I said, speaking less harshly, 'but to stop doing bad things. Do you know what happens to kids who do bad things?'

'No.'

'They don't go to heaven nor ever get presents or treats,' Dave said seriously.

She hesitated for a split second and said something that, even now, I still have engraved on my memory.

'And what happens to adults who do bad things? Do they get punished? Where do they go?'

We both froze. There was something so strange about the way she'd said it; it's difficult to put into words. We were talking with a girl of . . . six, seven years old? Everyone knows kids talk in such an innocent way. And yet Yäel spoke with a voice that didn't seem to belong to a girl of her age. All at once, that young face seemed to mask a greater maturity than we had given her credit for.

It was just like the time I'd given her a painkiller and she'd refused to take it. As soon as I pulled the doctor card, she'd rushed to accept it, and left me open-mouthed after showing me she had swallowed it and didn't need a doctor anymore.

Rather than talking to a child, it was as if we were conversing with a grown-up woman inside a child's body. Dave and I looked at each other, one of those glances that said what we needed to without words.

'Who is doing bad things?' Dave asked her.

She raised one hand to her cheek, where I observed the marks from Daniel's fingers could still be seen.

'Adults,' she said seriously, taking her hand out of reach of the dog and wiping it on her coat. 'Everyone says I do bad things . . . But what about them?'

'Who are you talking about?' I asked her. At first, I'd thought she meant Daniel, and I wouldn't have blamed her for that. But somehow it seemed as if she wasn't talking about him after all.

She held my gaze for several seconds, then turned away. For a moment I believed I saw her smiling. Just for a split second, almost imperceptible; but that wasn't the first time I'd thought I'd seen her doing something like that. Her eyes, smiles, grown-up talk . . . They all seemed to hide something I couldn't quite understand.

'I'm cold. Let's keep walking,' she said all of a sudden, hopping around and playing with the dog.

Dave and I followed her, not understanding her behaviour at all.

Would we ever get her? Would she ever stop saying or doing those things that made her such a mystery?

Julia cleared her throat, bringing Eva's attention back to the office. She felt as if she had just woken from a nightmare. She felt tired. Her legs were aching from sitting for so long. And Eva noticed there wasn't light coming through the blinds anymore.

She wondered how long they had been doing the interview.

'So, the child didn't say anything else about her family?' Julia asked.

'No, she didn't.'

'And what exactly were those "things" you thought she was doing every now and then? "Her eyes, smiles, grown-up talk"?' the presenter asked her, quoting by heart the words that the girl had just told her.

Eva finished her glass of water and refilled it for the umpteenth time. 'I guess everyone will have their own interpretation,' she said after taking a sip. She looked at the presenter with weary eyes and noticed that she was focused on the footage from one of the security cameras, which was showing Daniel angrily kicking the car. 'At this point I don't think I need to say that the child wasn't normal. I was blind, unable to see the situation objectively. I was focusing on protecting her over and over again. I tried to integrate her into the group, although the guys weren't willing to accept her. And I didn't see her real face . . .'

Eva turned her own face to one side, just in time to prevent the camera aimed at her from catching the tear that rolled down her cheek.

She felt stupid. With every word with which she recalled those events, she dug her nails into the palm of her hand. She blamed herself for everything that had happened. Listening to herself, she feared that anyone who watched the interview would do the same. If she had noticed at the time all those little details she was now describing, perhaps she wouldn't have been in that room being interviewed now.

'She knew how to play her cards very well. She knew whom to get close to,' Eva apologised.

'When did you find out her game?' Julia asked, serious.

'I don't know if it's appropriate calling it a "game" . . . But it was a bit later when we saw the tip of the iceberg.'

We had continued walking through the woods, keeping moving to try and get warm. Neither Dave nor I wanted to go back to the house, even though he complained about the cold every now and then – he didn't really have on suitable trousers for such temperatures. So, we kept moving slowly through the trees, trying to enjoy the beauty of the surroundings as much as we could.

The girl was scurrying between the tree trunks, followed by Daisy. The dog searched for her whenever she tried to hide behind a tree and brought her a stick that Yaël would throw far away. From time to time the animal would go missing for a minute and then return with a long, heavy branch that she dragged forcefully through the snow.

'Oh, Daisy, you're so stupid,' Yaël scolded her, throwing the branch on the floor. 'That wasn't the one I threw for you. Come on, keep looking.'

Daisy went running back between the trees, sniffing around the snow and getting lost behind small bushes. In the end, the girl had to show her where the stick had landed. The dog recognised it and barked at her, jumping euphorically around her feet.

Dave went to play with the two of them; I just watched. He could throw the stick further than Yaël, although occasionally his aim was a bit off and it crashed into one of the nearby tree trunks. Then the dog returned it right away. Once, he happened to throw it quite far. The stick flew through the branches of the trees without touching any of them, twisting in the air. Daisy shot forward, chasing it with her eyes fixed on the sky.

When the dog reached it, she grabbed it between her teeth and stared right and then left.

'Daisy, pretty girl, come here,' Dave called her.

But the dog didn't pay any attention. She dropped the stick to one side, losing interest in it, and began walking deeper into the woods. Dave called her, but she ignored him and kept on walking. We could see the greyish-black fur on her backside contrasting against the bright white snow.

We followed her, but the girl and I stayed a bit behind. My ankle had been bothering me more than I wanted to admit. Dave had asked me to go back to the house, but I downplayed the pain.

The boy reached the dog and grabbed her by the collar.

'Where *did* you think you're going?' I heard him saying in the distance.

He remained there, looking around. I didn't know what he was looking at until we caught up with him.

A mountain path.

To the left we could make out the main road. The snow covered the surface, but it was clear this was a mountain path that crossed the forest just like the path we drove through to get to my house from the main road. I frowned, puzzled. I couldn't remember any other route higher up the mountain, just the one we had taken that first day.

'Is this *lead* to your house?' Dave asked me while holding Daisy, who wanted to follow the path in the opposite direction to the road.

'Not as far as I know,' I said, looking at the path that went deeper into the forest.

My house was in the other direction, so I didn't think for a moment that the path could lead there. Surely if that were the case, I would have known about it?

'The stream splits the mountain. If the path led to my house, there should be some kind of bridge, and I don't remember ever seeing anything like that.'

'So where does this go? All paths lead somewhere.'

'I want to go back to the house, I'm cold,' the child suddenly growled.

Dave and I looked at each other, reading each other's minds.

'But we're quite close. We can go and see where the path *go* and then go back . . .'

'No,' she refused.

'It's not that cold,' he argued.

'But I want to go back,' she insisted. Then she grabbed my hand and added, 'Besides, Eva's foot is painful.'

I didn't say anything. On the one hand, the child was right: my ankle was becoming more painful and I knew I should rest it for a while. On the other hand, the discovery of that path and the sudden willingness of the child to go back to the house were two elements that attracted my attention like a magnet. Moreover, Yaël hadn't asked me once about my ankle during that walk. She'd probably seen me limping at some point, when the pain had got stronger. But she hadn't deigned to ask me how I was.

Why was she refusing to investigate the path?

Why was she using my ankle as an excuse?

Why pretend it was too cold when she was wearing a thick coat and better boots than ours?

I knew right then that Dave and I would walk along that path later on. We would find out why it was there, near my house, and why I didn't remember it from all the years I'd spent in Guildon Forest. If Yaël didn't want to go, then she didn't have to come with us. And I saw in Dave's eyes some kind of understanding. He guessed what I was thinking and, without the child noticing, he gave a small nod.

But first, we had to go back to the house and leave the little one there. I even thought I'd treat myself, rest my ankle for a bit and put some ice on it. I knew it wasn't broken and it wouldn't take me long to recover. But I still needed to rest, even if it meant being under the same roof as Daniel and Stacey.

'Alright,' I said to the child, lightly squeezing her hand, 'let's go home then. With Daniel and Stacey.'

I spoke unemotionally, watching every gesture of the girl. I was surprised that she didn't say a word this time. As if she wasn't afraid of Daniel, as if nothing had happened. I almost thought I saw a glow of tranquillity in those dark eyes as she held my hand and jumped over the rocks and fallen tree trunks.

That look confused me, but at the same time it opened my eyes.

I could not trust her any longer. I decided to always keep her in my sight, to make sure I was able to analyse even the smallest detail of what she said and did. But I was no longer going to have any compassion for her.

It was as Dave had said to me: *"what done, it is done"* and there was no chance to change the past. And thinking about it rationally, it wasn't as if anyone had been injured. Stacey still had insulin, and although we were no longer able to get out of there the next day, she would have enough for a few more days. And the tyre could be replaced with a new one.

Dave, the child and I walked back to the house.

Shivering, we passed between the same prominent trees we'd seen before, walking over our own footprints in the snow. We crossed the frozen stream, the clearing surrounded by rocks where I used to play when I was a child, and the tree on which I had collapsed an hour before.

When we got to the house and I closed the gate behind us, I realised that Daniel had fixed the loose step. He was standing next to the car, watching the three of us with a neutral expression, almost indifferent. His face was greasy and oil-stained. He was holding the flat tyre, the deadly nail that had deflated it on display.

It was a brutal picture.

We had arrived from London without a single problem with the vehicle, and now it was completely useless. A simple tyre had led to our biggest fear. In an instant I realised that I hadn't been thinking rationally.

What did it matter about an *irrelevant* mountain path? The same one that, for whatever reason, Yäel had refused to go along?

Cries of Blood

At some level I now understood Daniel's reaction to the girl destroying our only way out of there. I understood what had driven him to violence again, making everything so unbearable that I had nothing left to do but escape from that house for a while, get away from all the negativity and the problems that seemed to emerge out of nowhere.

The realisation intensified every one of the questions and worries that plagued me then. Like not being able to go back home. Having to deal with the situation all by ourselves.

Who was going to help us?

When would we be able to get rid of the child?

Would things ever go back to the way they used to be?

I hated that situation and the feeling of helplessness. I couldn't understand how we'd reached that point, and what had changed us all so atrociously, to the extent that it felt as if we didn't know each other anymore. As if, instead of being friends together on holiday, we were just flatmates with our own independent lives.

I cooked some pasta with meat sauce and Stacey and Daniel left to eat in their bedrooms. As soon as he'd finished eating, Dave disappeared off to his room as well, saying he wanted a siesta. And in a flash, I found myself alone in the living room, watching cartoons on TV with the child, accompanied by all those worries.

Next to the fireplace, the coloured lights of the Christmas tree lent a dim glow to the surroundings. That rainbow splash fell over the metallic wrapping paper of the presents that lay at the base of the tree. And the light reflected in all directions, catching my attention.

It was amazing how this Christmas had been ruined in just a few hours. How the season spirit had vanished – if there had ever been any in the first place.

I wrote in my diary, trying to analyse everything that had happened in those hours. I placed some cushions under my sore foot, soothed by the comforting warmth that emanated from the fireplace and the multicoloured lights of the tree.

I was tired and sore, both physically and mentally. All my thoughts, doubts, fears, assumptions, the painful ankle and my loneliness overwhelmed me. And the only thing that comforted me was to write on those sheets of paper. I let my pen stamp all my worries in my beloved diary. I didn't know then that it would be the last time I would ever write in it.

I would not return to write a single word on its pages. Not shed even one drop of ink over its yellow sheets. I would not spray it with my favourite perfume, letting it age in my hands and absorb the moisture from my skin. The final pages would remain forever blank.

10. The diary and the call

Eva Domínguez, daughter of Spanish actress Olivia Domínguez and American director Liam Lawrence, has told us how the story that everyone has spoken so much about began. Two years ago, she decided to go to her home in the mountains, near the small village of Guildon Forest in the north of Scotland. With her, she took three of her colleagues from the world-famous TV series she was then filming, "Prodigies": her boyfriend, Daniel Ferguson; her friend and colleague Stacey Martin, and Stacey's puppy; and, her best friend, Dave Campos, who had been close to landing a lead in the show, but had instead been given a role as an extra, becoming one of the "prodigies" at the most famous school in the world.

'They drove all the way from London,' Julia continued, staring at the camera and using that professional and undaunted tone of hers, 'not expecting the rough weather to end up turning into a huge and horrifying snowstorm. They arrived at the village without any trouble; but before they reached the house, they almost ran over a child of six or seven years of age, who was standing in the middle of the road. The little girl, who was wearing only a nightgown and holding a teddy bear, would not speak a word about where she had come from or where her parents were. So, Eva decided to take her to her house, get her warm and, later on, get in touch with whoever was necessary to find her family.'

She left a dramatic pause, staring at the camera with those confident, green eyes. She let a few seconds go by to give future viewers time to choose their sides, and so that her summary wouldn't come across as long or tedious. She was a professional: she knew how to manipulate her audience.

All the while, she watched Eva's every movement, listening to the slow breathing that betrayed how exhausted she was after that long day.

'What Eva didn't know at that time were the consequences that would follow. Four young people, famous and talented, but somewhat impulsive and – like any other human being – flawed . . . and now with an unknown little girl around them. A girl who, even though she seemed innocent and content when she spoke to Eva, was gradually letting them see a less friendly face. It took some time – some people might think too long – for Eva to notice that something wasn't right. And a mountain path not far from her house, which she had no prior knowledge about, became the thing that forced her to open her eyes.'

The woman closed her notebook and grabbed Eva's diary. She flipped it around; she didn't examine it, but let it be captured by the camera lens, its yellow pages closed. Pages that harboured every detail of those events, a version of the story that had never been shared in public before. The same version she was now trying to summarise as quickly as possible.

'Unfortunately,' she continued, frowning and staring first at the camera and then at the diary in her hands, 'this is only the first part of the unheard version of events by Eva Domínguez, who will accompany us in the next and final part of this programme, here at the BBC. Don't forget to join us at the same time tomorrow for the end of this tragic true story. And though the setting of Guildon Forest might remind you of a tale by Charles Dickens, the ending is like nothing you'll find in any of his books.

'Internationally famous young men and women, fun, drugs, arguments, love and hatred, true friendships, and a girl whose identity will be discovered in the next episode, alongside what happened next. We'll uncover the truth behind all the lies that have been spread by people who weren't there, and we'll find out the true story of what happened two years ago in the small, Scottish village of Guildon Forest . . . Cut.'

Eva jumped at the sound of the camera's side screens closing.

She had been listening to the presenter's words, lost in her own thoughts. It seemed amazing to her how the woman had summed up, in just a few minutes, everything she had been telling her throughout that day and for the first time ever.

She almost felt unable to believe it was her own story. As Julia had said, this was only the beginning of her version of the events of two years ago.

She was upset at being in that room, participating in that programme. She was more than that horrible story. She was the daughter of Olivia Domínguez, Oscar-winning actress and critically acclaimed across the entire world. She had followed in her mum's steps and had received plaudits for her own work, both on the big and small screen. And then there was her late father, Liam, one of the most prominent film directors in Hollywood . . .

Why? she asked herself. Why did people have to remember her for that story? A story that didn't define her as a person or a professional? The same story that, although she needed to expose it to the public once and for all, had been the cause of more than one nightmare? Was she mistaken in unveiling those events that had tormented her two years ago? Should all that have remained as nothing more than a tragic and unfair misfortune of the past?

'Was it necessary, that comment about drugs?' she asked once she'd made sure that the red light of the cameras had vanished.

'It's called journalism.' Julia smiled as she gathered her things and rose from the chair. 'Besides, you're the one who brought it up.'

'But not for you to use it against me,' the girl protested, getting up in turn.

'Don't you see, Eva? No one's going to say a single word about whether you wanted to smoke a bit of marijuana: nobody cares. It's no more than an anecdote or a headline to attract the people who love a hint of scandal.'

'You're wrong: they'll remember it perfectly and they'll think of me as a drug addict,' the girl contradicted her. 'All I'm going to get is more false headlines.'

Julia gave her a bitter smile, upset by the hurt in Eva's words.

'Smoking some weed doesn't mean you're a drug addict, honey. Those people have already added to their bank accounts a tasty slice by writing headlines at your expense. This is the moment,' Julia grabbed Eva by the shoulders, 'the moment to shut their mouths and show the whole world they've been lying, show it so clearly that the only thing they'll have left to do is to try and redeem themselves for all their poisonous words. Unless, of course,' she went on, her tone changing from fervent to cold and impersonal, 'you decide to let them off the hook. Let them carry on calling themselves journalists, when all they really are is a group of trashy, unscrupulous storytellers.'

Eva looked down at her hands. She stared at the tips of her fingers, the nails bitten almost raw.

'If you wish, after the programme is aired, I'll help you take them to court. No one should go spreading around stuff like that without any truth or evidence behind it.'

Eva nodded ambiguously. She appreciated Julia's support: more than once it had been hard to keep her head held high and not to let her voice break into tears. But she reminded herself why she had accepted Julia's offer; why she had chosen her, from all the journalists who'd approached her for her story.

Julia was a professional in the news business, with an almost supernatural power. More than once she had found her way onto lists of the most influential figures on the planet. And the dozens of contracts with different TV channels across the world was testament to her reputation.

Eva decided not to oppose her. She would let Julia handle things the way she thought best. After all, Eva was just an actress; Julia would have her reasons for her methods.

She said goodbye to the presenter and her husband without saying anything more about her doubts. She let Julia know that she would go around to the office, now converted into a mini TV studio, at the same time the next day. Then she left, waving away their offers to escort her to the door.

The sound of the metal door closing behind her reverberated in the marble corridor. The young girl walked with weary steps to the lift, pressed the button and, when the screen at the top indicated that it had arrived, she entered the spacious interior. The doors closed noiselessly. Eva let her body sag against one of the walls.

She felt unable to fight her disquiet any longer. She held her hands to her forehead while taking deep, ragged breaths, carried away by her emotions. This time at least she was away from anyone's gaze. She felt her hands trembling and pressed them together in her lap, her chest heaving. When she felt the tremors begin to subside, she reached into her handbag. She searched through her things for a bottle of antidepressants and swallowed a pill.

Half a minute later, she got up, straightened her coat and readjusted her handbag on her shoulder. She pulled back the hair covering her face, looked at her reflection in the lift's mirrored wall, and pressed the button for the ground floor.

Words came out of nowhere, describing every sensation and thought. Julia didn't need to press the play button to remember any of the words she'd heard throughout that day. The darkness and silence of the night helped clear her thoughts and focus on her writing. She recalled each and every moment with ease, remembering every nuance of the story.

It was just a few minutes since Sam, her husband, had brought her a plate of green asparagus, fruit and freshly brewed tea on a tray decorated with a Union Jack. But although she had thanked him, she'd ignored it. She couldn't afford distractions. A writer should get carried away by her ideas – or in this case, the young girl's words – when they were still fresh in her mind. If she didn't commit them to paper now, they would be forgotten, and Julia knew she'd be left with an unpleasant feeling of guilt. So, she had to concentrate, no matter how long it would take.

She had spent the last two hours writing what she was sure would someday be her most successful literary work. It didn't matter that it was a book based on facts she would simultaneously expose to the world in a prime-time TV programme. Julia was an intelligent woman and knew what details had to be kept aside for the book that would undoubtedly break sales records. The excitement and passion that was possessing every part of her body and mind would bring her glory. She could almost taste the success and recognition of her "Fucking boom!"

When she finished writing she looked at the time, saved the file as "Guildon Forest's case" and turned off the laptop. She glanced down at the plate of asparagus, now cold and dry, and left her office by a side door.

She went home, pleased as always at how easy it was to go to and from her office. She put the plate in the microwave to warm while she prepared a fresh cup of tea. At the same time, she shot glances at Eva's diary, the only thing she had taken from her office apart from the tray of food.

'I'm going to read for a bit, alright?' she informed Sam, who had already gone to bed, shirtless, and was watching a programme on the TV that hung on the bedroom wall.

'Why don't you leave it until tomorrow and get in here with me?' he proposed with a wicked tone.

But Sam knew that tonight, as so many times, his proposal would be in vain. For Julia had an uncontrolled eagerness for the success of each and every one of her projects, which always absorbed most of her time. Sam had tried talking to her about it, warning her that her obsessive attitude towards work could damage their marriage.

But he didn't want to step in this time. It was clear to him that this new project wouldn't take her long to finish and, besides, she had taken a two-year sabbatical in which she had fully devoted herself to their marriage. He had enjoyed the company of his wife for a good while now, and she deserved to satisfy her ambition after having kept it locked away for so long.

Therefore, Julia went back to the kitchen, took the plate out of the microwave, finished preparing her tea with milk and sugar, and went to the living room. There she ate quickly, looking down at the street through the window, trying to disconnect for a few minutes.

She had a dilemma. She had a job that needed to be done to perfection. The job that she felt from the depths of her heart would be her "Fucking boom!" And it would give her not only the two-part TV programme, but her next book.

But she had far too much information. She'd read about so many hoaxes and rumours in the media. All of them had created prejudices and preconceptions about the events – and most probably they were all wrong.

She just wanted to enjoy this opportunity, treat the complex and unique story objectively. And maybe . . .

It was clear she had an advantage over the other journalists who had been cruelly enriching themselves with the young actress's story. Only she, Julia Stevenson, had what two years earlier the law enforcement agencies of Scotland had held in their hands – the unique and irreplaceable diary of the girl.

This was the same diary in which Eva had written each and every one of her thoughts, feelings and problems. It told the story of how a girl of her age and social position faced reality, and the vicissitudes of life beyond the paparazzi's flashing cameras.

She couldn't wait to read it.

When she finished her dinner, she sat down on one of the designer armchairs in the living room. She turned on a small side lamp, got comfortable nestled against some cushions and covered herself with a cream-coloured, hand knitted blanket. She grabbed her cup of tea and stared at the cover of the diary.

It was dark brown, the colour of earth, with delicate flourishes across the front and back. She opened it and began to read paragraph after paragraph of Eva Domínguez's life.

The open and personal nature of what she saw shocked the presenter.

The first days Eva had written about dealt with day to day life on the set of "Prodigies". She described the early days of the TV series, how at first nobody would have bet a penny on its success, but how it soon began to gather awards in different countries. She detailed how it grew bigger and bigger, reaching new parts of the world as its fame grew with every new award.

She spoke about how she got on with her co-stars and the rest of the team. But the thing that caught Julia's attention was that, on almost every page, Dave, the Spanish actor originally from Madrid, had an even more prominent role than she had expected.

Page by page, Eva described the first days of their friendship and how it had grown day by day. Stories of their small adventures, between one shoot and another, or their plans outside the set. Visits to Eva's house, introductions to her mother, and how Olivia had quickly grown fond of the young extra.

Further on, Julia read about the beginnings of Eva's romance with Daniel. The advice from her friend, Stacey, pushing her to accept a date. The insistence and passion of the young actor that had seen her carried away by the moment, acting against her own preferences and lifestyle. The constant jealousy and small episodes to which the young girl gave such relevance on those yellow sheets that, even after all this time, their memory seemed to linger like scent on the paper.

She discovered that the young girl had been faithful to her experiences and, not having reviewed her diary, the words had nevertheless been engraved by fire in her memory. She even recognised a few of the sentences, word for word, that the girl had made immortal in her diary.

Nearly two hours went by while the woman took small sips of her tea and devoured the pages of the diary with graceful speed. Her eyes swept over the girl's delicate calligraphy, as if reading from a book she already knew well. It was like someone hearing a song for the first time and guessing the lyrics that came next. Until she reached the final pages.

There was still room for its author to record more of her experiences, but those last written pages were dated with the last day of the story the girl had devoted herself to telling. The same day that she had been recently talking about with Julia. The woman flicked through the pages after that day, but they were all blank; not even a casual squiggle, letter or number on them.

She prepared another cup of tea and retreated back under the blanket. Taking small sips, she read those last pages:

Dear diary:

I'm afraid today has been quite a strange day. I would even call it mental.

I woke up alone in bed, freezing cold due to the dreadful snowstorm that's been taking over Scotland these past few days. I felt like I wanted to keep sleeping and spend days wrapped up beneath the soft sheets of my bed. I didn't want to face another day in this madhouse. I didn't want to have to deal with stupid theories about Yäel, which is the name of the little girl that I have been writing about. It was thanks to Dave that I discovered her name. He proposed the idea that perhaps, as in his childhood, her name might be written on her nightgown.

Anyhow, I didn't want to hear any more nonsense from Stacey. Since she came back from walking Daisy through the forest, she has been acting very strangely. [. . .]

All of a sudden, I realised there was something strange in the air . . . The fucking storm had vanished! I couldn't help but feel a sudden happiness at finally seeing the sun in the sky. There it was in all its glory, giving me back the beautiful views around my mum's house, right in the woods of Guildon Forest.

I went downstairs and found something I was not expecting in the slightest: Stacey and Dave playing Monopoly with Yäel?! What the hell was going on there? All those arguments and mood swings and now they were behaving as if nothing had happened, as if they were all just as peaceful as nuns! [. . .]

But when Dave had the stupid idea to smoke some weed, that imbecile Daniel left the little girl unattended with the nail gun. And the result, dear diary, was a flat tyre on his car. An accident that wouldn't have been such a big deal if it wasn't for the stupidity of Daniel, who had also had a puncture on one of the tyres before and hadn't remembered to buy a new spare. So that was it for the car we came here in, and the same one we'd intended to use to get out of this place.

Why?! Why have these things always got to happen to me?!

Daniel got so mad and slapped the girl on the face. She fell on the floor crying out loudly with pain. I argued with him, defending the child for the umpteenth time, since it doesn't seem anyone is willing to do so. After all, she is just a child. A child like any other, who breaks things without thinking or meaning to do it. I couldn't take it any longer: I grabbed our coats and left for the forest with Dave and the little one. I needed to get away from there, clear my head, get things off my chest without Daniel or Stacey around to see or hear me. Not until we were far away enough from the house did I try to talk to Yäel. [. . .]

Dave, as always, calmed me down with his sweet words. [. . .]

Why can't Daniel be like him? Dave has all the qualities I would like to see in him: kind, peaceful, intelligent, controlled ambition, not a DIVA, a life that has made him so sweet and lovely. No, Daniel has to be a conceited twat, hypocritical, bossy, cocky, violent . . . I can't stand him any more: I don't want him anywhere near me. I don't care about what mum will say, he's not the guy I want to spend my life with. Not while he keeps behaving the way he has been lately. Only a guy like Dave could make me happy. But he is my friend . . .

I don't know, today in the forest, while we forced ourselves to walk and tried to relax about all of our problems, I had a weird feeling. Dave happened to hug me on two occasions, with less than five minutes between them. Is that what friends do? Do friends feel so peaceful and comfortable the way that I, at least, felt? Sometimes, I'd love to know what's going on in Dave's head. I'd like to read his thoughts and know how he really feels about me. Because today I haven't been quite sure about him. I felt as if the only thing he wanted was to be next to me...

But I also felt that way! I wanted him next to me, reassuring and protecting me! He's the only person with whom I can talk about my beloved father... [...]

The issue that I have now is bigger than I'd like to admit: I do not trust Yäel. But at the same time, my ego prevents me admitting that to my friends. And I know that if I confess it to Dave, all I'll get will be him talking for hours about every little detail. I don't want any of them to tell me "I told you so". [...]

It's all because of a weird and perhaps stupid moment in the forest during our walk. We had been walking far away from the house when Daisy, Stacey's puppy, discovered a new mountain path. I had no idea of its existence. And the problem isn't that I can't remember it, since the mountain is quite big and it's impossible for me to know it like the back of my hand. No. The problem lies in the fact that it doesn't lead to my house. As I said to Dave, there's a small stream between the house and the path, so the path would have to cross over it. For that reason, there should be some kind of bridge. And if I'm sure of something, it's that there's no such bridge that crosses the stream.

So, I came to the conclusion, like Dave, that no path exists in the forest for no reason. That path has to lead somewhere! Or is it *that the snowstorm has disturbed me too much? But when we found it, Yäel got nervous and wanted to go back to the house right away. She gave stupid excuses to get us to return without investigating where it went.*

I definitely can't trust her. And truth be told, I don't want her around us.

[. . .]

I'll have to call Mr McGregor and ask him to give us a lift in the morning to the nearest town, and we'll leave Yäel at the police station with his friend. None of us wants to stay trapped in this place, and we have to take the opportunity of the snowstorm having stopped for the time being.

So, I'm going to rest for a bit next to the comfy warmth of the fireplace and, when my damned ankle stops hurting a bit, I'll take Dave with me. We're going to find out where that new path leads. And tomorrow will be another day.

I'll write you some more tomorrow,

Eva Domínguez :)

Julia turned the page, as if her eyes had failed her before, but the next pages remained blank. No one had written anything in that diary in the last two years, and no one would ever do so again.

She suffered a horrible anxiety that fuelled her desire to know what happened next. She couldn't be left like that. She felt as if she had been watching a film and, in the last ten minutes, the player had burst into flames. She couldn't wait for the next day when Eva would go back to her office to shoot the second part of the interview. But with an effort of will, she succeeded in overcoming the ferocious need to watch the rest of the footage from the security cameras.

What really mattered weren't the images they would display, but the feelings those cameras could not capture. Feelings that the girl had lied about. Yes, she had lied of her own free will.

When Julia had explicitly asked her whether she liked Dave, she had said no, emphatically, without even blinking. And the woman had believed her. Her solemn face had convinced her and made her cross off that question, doubt, allusion, from all her notes.

But what Eva had said during the interview and what she had written in that diary didn't seem to match at all.

Had she really liked Dave as more than just a friend? Had Daniel been right with his continuous jealousy? Had she lied to everyone with the performance of the century? But most importantly, as a tiny little voice said inside her head, why would Eva have lied when she had handed over her own diary? Did she by any chance not remember her words? Did she not stop to think that Julia was going to end up reading each and every one of them? Or was all of it some kind of misunderstanding?

Annoyed with the young girl and with her eyelids drooping in exhaustion, Julia decided to switch off the lamp and to go to bed. The next day, she would get all the answers she needed.

No one messed with Julia Stevenson.

Not very far from there, Eva was back in her suite at The Ritz Hotel. It was a few minutes since she had finished her dinner, which a cheerful man from the room service had brought to her room.

She hadn't been in the best of moods after the first part of the interview with Julia. And she didn't have any interest in almost being followed around by any of the other staff members: always so helpful, nice and polite, with permanent smiles at the corners of their mouths.

She had preferred to keep her bad mood to herself. She didn't want anyone to see her like that.

That day had been harder than she was willing to admit. With all those repressed memories that she had been forced to remember . . . But, even knowing that it wasn't going to be easy, it was what she needed.

Even so, lying in bed on the softest sheets she had ever encountered, the young girl couldn't fall asleep.

The bedroom was practically pitch black. Only a faint light sneaked in from behind the white curtains.

She didn't want to take any pills. At least not that night. Her doctor had recommended taking them only when they were most necessary, since they were quite strong, and she shouldn't become dependent on them. More importantly, they occasionally gave her horrendous nightmares. And she sensed that this night would be one of those occasions.

Consequently, she had been lying on top of the bed, still wearing the cream coloured dress, staring up at the ceiling.

It was what she used to do in her room at her mother's house, in London, where she had stuck dozens of little stars on the ceiling. When the lights were off, they glowed in the dark, showing a whole universe just for her.

But she wasn't at her mother's house. She wanted to be there, but she couldn't. Neither could she stop mulling over that last week, time and time again.

It had been two years since she had fled from everything and everyone, hiding as best as she could in the south of Spain, giving only brief news to her family and friends. For that reason, her mother had been immensely excited when she found out Eva was finally returning to the city.

She had suffered a thousand hells, worrying for her beloved daughter. Not knowing where or how she was. With just the dozen or so text messages Eva had deigned to send her, trying to reassure her that she was resting and that a psychiatrist was seeing her.

Now her mother was immersed in shooting an independent film with a director who, apparently, was promising to be the next-next-next James Cameron. Therefore, Eva didn't want to worry her. She didn't want her mother seeing her in this condition. Both had already gone through too much.

And Eva still had to go through one last step before she'd feel prepared.

A few days earlier the girl had sent her mother a message, asking her for a certain telephone number.

The exact same number that she had previously held in her hands. The same one she had carried inside one of the pockets of her handbag, handwritten on paper, feeling it grow heavier with each passing day.

She had dialled it on more than one occasion in the past and someone would pick up the phone instantly. But she would go silent, not knowing what to say, until whoever was on the other end of the line would hang up the phone.

One day, in the middle of a panic attack, Eva had set the paper on fire. She saw it burning with pleasure, afraid of seeing it intact one more time.

But a long time had passed since then, and with the decisions that she had lately taken, her psychiatrist was sure it was the moment for Eva to face her fears.

At the thought of it the girl felt once again that same panic attack that filled her whole body, making her shiver from head to toe. Her head began to spin, she straightened up and felt a sudden, overwhelming heat that wouldn't let her breathe. The heating was on all day in there, making the hotel a pleasant place to stay. But she preferred the cold, as long as it wasn't too extreme.

She grabbed her handbag and coat and left the room. She walked over the red, peach, green and blue carpet that ran throughout the whole hotel, until she reached some stairs. She ran down them and almost fled through the doors, followed by surprised looks from the concierges at reception, who at that time of the night had barely anything to do.

'Good evening, Miss,' the two doormen dressed immaculately in black greeted her. 'Are you going to require the Rolls-Ro–?'

But she cut them off sharply with a shake of her head and kept walking. She turned left and rounded a corner, passing under an arch with the illuminated letters of the hotel.

She stopped for a few seconds next to one of the square, grey stone columns that divided the pavement from the road. And she took a deep breath under the black hanging lamps in the passageway that Julia Roberts and Hugh Grant had walked through in a scene of "Notting Hill". Eva had watched that film so many times, over and over; but on this occasion she had a very different perception of the place.

There were lots of people walking by, mostly youngsters returning home after a night at the movies or drinking beer with friends in the park. None of them noticed Eva, with her smart outfit and tense face, nervous, struggling between breaths.

She didn't look at anyone either.

Once she felt the oxygen flooding her lungs, she began walking again, heading straight to Green Park, where the gates remained open. When she came out of the covered passageway, she didn't notice the raindrops. She walked quickly towards the park, away from the hotel and its heat.

Fresh air. The night's coolness. The darkness sullied by the streetlights. Water falling down her forehead, bringing her back to reality, as if she had just come out of a dream. It was what she needed. Freedom. To see all kinds of people still sitting on the grass at the park. They were scattered over a clearing beyond the gates.

A main walkway, with the occasional individual cycling along it, separated the park from the hotel and the rest of majestic buildings that could be glimpsed behind a tall fence. The walkway was sheltered under the canopy of tall trees with huge trunks, between which a not-so-shy squirrel was scurrying.

Eva ducked under one of the black metal rails and sat at the foot of one of those trees, letting the rain that seeped through the leafy foliage bathe her face.

Sitting on the floor, enjoying the fresh air and the cold night in the park, she watched how people began to disperse as the rain fell.

London was a city where citizens never knew what to wear. If someone wore a coat, it would be a sunny day; if they didn't wear a coat, it would turn cold; if someone was carrying an umbrella, no matter how long or short, it would never rain; but if someone didn't carry one, it would most certainly start raining cats and dogs. Eva allowed herself a shy smile while staring at the people who ran to the Tube station or searched for the shelter of the trees. In a few seconds, there wasn't a single group gathered on the grass, as the rain began to pick up strength and fall with more ferocity.

Minutes later, Eva was still sitting, hugging her legs close to her chest. She let the rain run down her skin, indifferent.

It seemed as if she was the only soul alive in the park. And it was then that she realised that she was feeling lonely. She didn't want to be alone; she wanted to be happy again and be around her friends, laughing, telling jokes, making plans to stay out for dinner . . . She hated feeling so disgruntled. It was that bipolarity that at times made her want to be surrounded by people, and at others made her wish to be all by herself. She wanted to feel again like any other ordinary girl out there.

And, perhaps, she could manage that if . . .

'It's time,' she whispered, and took out her mobile phone.

She searched through her mother's messages. She had a list of long and tedious messages she had barely bothered to read. And among one of the last ones she found what she was looking for. She tapped the telephone number written in the message and the phone asked her if she wanted to call that number.

Cries of Blood

Between the trees, a few metres away, she thought she heard a few fallen leaves rustling. She turned her head, but all she saw was a couple under an umbrella, followed by a little girl with dark hair. There was no one else around. Everyone had disappeared under the veil of heavy rain. She stared back at her phone and pressed the call option on the screen.

When she placed the handset to her ear, she heard an intermittent beep for a couple of seconds.

'Good evening, Liz Rowe speaking, how can I help?' She heard a woman's voice saying, her tone sweet despite the time.

Eva didn't remain quiet this time; she was determined.

'Good evening, Liz, I know how late it is, but I was wondering if I could talk with room twenty-three,' she said, keeping her own voice soft and calm.

'I'm sorry, but you'll have to call again tomorrow morning, in opening hours,' said the woman, somewhat abruptly this time.

Eva took a deep breath, blaming herself for not having called sooner. But she had to try, even if it meant that she had to use her own gimmicks.

'Oh, excuse me, I haven't introduced myself. I'm Eva Domínguez, a friend of the resident at room twenty-three. If I'm not mistaken, you have been receiving large quantities of money under my name–'

'Oh, yes, of course, Eva . . .' The line went silent for a moment. 'Your mother has been calling almost every day. What a lovely woman,' she said, returning to her sweet voice from the beginning of the call. She was the one in charge of the institution, and every month without fail she received envelopes from Eva with cheques for generous amounts. 'We've been long waiting for you to call.'

'I know and I'm sorry that it's taken me this long, but I need to talk with the resident in room–'

The woman hurried to ensure her that she would go around to room twenty-three and find out if it wasn't too late for the call. Eva deeply appreciated her help. As a rule, she knew, lights were turned off about eight in the evening and all the residents should be sleeping at that time of night.

She waited, sitting under the tree, feeling the rain soaking her hair. She loved the sensation of the drops trickling down her body, leaking through her clothes, feeling their coolness. But she didn't have to wait long:

'Eva? Are you still there?'

'Yes, I'm here.'

'There's no problem. I'm going to put you through to the room, alright?'

'Yes, thank you very much, Liz,' the girl thanked her, smiling.

At the other end of the line, classical music was playing. And half a second later someone picked up the phone and just said, 'Eva?'

Eva closed her eyes, letting the tears run down her cheeks to blend with the raindrops. So much time had passed since she had heard that voice . . . It struck her as very changed, playfully childlike and deeper than she remembered. Hearing her name made her feel defeated by the pain.

'Yes, it's me . . .' she could only say back.

'Where are you? Are you going to come and see me soon?' The voice sounded childlike, innocent and mournful, but with a perfect, clear British accent. 'I miss you so much, Eva. I want to see you, but you never come to visit me. And no one lets me go and see you . . .'

'I know, sweetie, but I'm quite busy . . .' she lied without knowing what other excuse she could give. 'But I promise that I'll come to visit you very soon.'

'How soon?' demanded the voice, with some excitement.

Eva wiped her tears with the sleeve of her coat and didn't know what to say. She just sat there, under the tree branches, watching the rain fall. She felt the grass beneath her, dry except for the few raindrops that rested on the small leaves like tiny diamonds illuminated by the lamp posts. She found herself pulling small handfuls of grass with stiff fingers.

'I don't know, but soon.'

'You're lying to me,' she heard the accusation.

'No, I'm not lying . . . I just don't know if I'm able to see you, not after . . . you know, everything.'

At the other end of the line, the other person didn't say anything back. She could only hear the heavy and faltering breathing against the phone.

'Please, say something,' Eva pleaded in a sob. 'I too have missed you a lot. There's not a day that I don't think about you . . . I'm sorry, sorry that you are where you are . . . It's my fault, if only I hadn't been so stupid, perhaps, right now we could have been with each other.'

She let the silence be broken only by the music the rain was creating over her head, between the leaves and the branches of the tree.

'Swear it,' the voice demanded after a few seconds. 'Swear to me that you're not lying. Promise me that you're going to come and see me soon, because I'm scared of this place. The halls are empty throughout the day. And no one, except the doctors, comes to see me . . . Your mum came one day and she couldn't tell me when you were going to come. So promise me that you're coming this week!'

Eva swallowed.

The call wasn't going too badly. She knew what she was facing. The changes in that voice were obvious, but what she feared the most was the physical aspect of the individual. She didn't feel strong enough to be there, in room twenty-three, staring at eyes she wouldn't be able to recognise. Eyes that had gone through a lot more than she had during those long and painful two years.

Would she have enough courage to stare into those eyes?

Would they reflect the guilt that could be guessed at in hers? A guilt that had plagued her relentlessly for so long?

Could she really keep avoiding that meeting?

For how long?

It's time, she told herself once again.

'I swear . . . As soon as I can, before the week is over, I'll come and see you.'

11. "Neither the good are so good, nor the bad so bad"

I woke with a start to the landline's shrill ringtone.
When I'd finished writing my diary, I laid down on the cushions, covered myself with a blanket and basked in the pleasant warmth that emanated from the fireplace. And I had fallen asleep.

I stretched, feeling the remnants of a happy dream slipping away, and got up to answer the call. My ankle felt a bit better than before. I walked towards the side table, next to the sofa, where the telephone was. Yäel lay there, placidly clutching her teddy bear. She must have been asleep too, for she stared back at me with a disoriented look, eyes tired.

'Keep sleeping, sweetie,' I whispered to her while picking up the phone. 'Hello, who is this?'

'Is this Eva Domínguez?' asked a deep and serious voice.

'Yes, that's me. Who are you?' I asked, sleepy.

'Good afternoon, I'm Officer Tom Farlane. I received a call this morning from Will McGregor, who made me aware that three days ago you found a little girl on the road into Guildon Forest.'

I confirmed it, excited to finally receive that call. For a moment, I even thought they had found the child's family. But it wasn't the case.

'No, I'm afraid we haven't received any call about the disappearance of a child,' the officer said gravely. 'In fact, we haven't had anyone missing within a thirty-mile radius for months. I've got in contact with all the police stations in Scotland and there's no news about a missing child within the last couple of years. We've contacted Social Services and forwarded all the details that Mr McGregor has given us.'

'So, what can we do?' I whispered furiously, going into the kitchen so that Yäel wouldn't hear me.

The child had gone back to sleep – or at least I thought she had. I realise now I don't know what really happened. Nothing from that point on made any sense.

'I'm afraid you'll have to wait for Social Services to come to the house. But with the road conditions the way they are, I'm not sure when that will be. They'll get in contact with you when the snowploughs clear the road to Guildon Forest. I'm sorry for any inconvenience, but after the snowstorm things are going somewhat slowly across the whole country.'

I said nothing; I could just imagine what the others were going to say when they found out we'd have to keep the child with us for even longer.

'I'm sorry, officer, but we can't stay at this house any longer,' I said firmly, my tone expressing clearly that I didn't have any intention of staying in the house with that child a moment longer. 'We were supposed to leave tomorrow and now we have a flat tyre, thanks to the little girl.' I emphasised those last two words.

The officer huffed and I heard a noise on the line.

'I'm afraid I can't do anything else for you. You'll have to get in touch with your car insurance and they'll let you know when they can get someone out there to help you. However, there's something I wanted to ask you,' he lowered his voice, as if he too had to be careful about someone else hearing him. 'It's about the girl's name.'

'Yes?'

'Will McGregor said you'd found her name on the nightgown she was wearing when you discovered her in the middle of the road. And he told me you thought her name was Yäel, is that right?' the man asked me, stressing the child's name.

'Yes, well, maybe that's not exactly right. It was hard to make out the label. Why are you asking?' I didn't understand his interest in the name if he wasn't going to do anything about the situation.

'Well . . .' Except for some creaking and a door closing, there was a long silence at the other end of the phone. 'What I'm about to tell you, it has to stay between the two of us.' I agreed. 'Around three years ago, one of our colleagues at the police station got fired. I can't discuss the reasons; they're meant to be kept confidential.'

'But, wait a moment – what has that got to do with the child?'

'The thing is, that man lost his job and had to retire before his time,' the officer continued, ignoring my question. 'The amount he received from his pension wasn't enough to meet his mortgage and other bills and he had to sell his house. And it was then that he left town.

'Supposedly he moved in somewhere very close to where you are right now,' the man said after a few seconds of eerie silence. 'I can't say for sure, since his friends and colleagues lost contact with him. But, despite the time that's passed, I still remember he was married to a woman . . . Well, let's say she picked the wrong man. She'd just got divorced from some other guy when she met him, and she ended up marrying him. It was a big mistake.'

I frowned, confused. What had all this got to do with the child? Could these people be her parents?

'I never heard that they had a girl, although the woman had had a daughter with her previous partner. But she would be in her mid-thirties or early forties by now. So, it can't be their child,' the police officer concluded.

'So why are you telling me about this man and his wife?'

There was another long silence, during which I could hear only his distant breathing. When he spoke again, his voice was uneasy. 'Because his wife's name was Yäel.'

Now it was me who didn't say a word.

'I don't know what to tell you, but McGregor told me the name sounded familiar. And he wasn't sure where he'd heard it before,' he confessed, reminding me my own conversation with Mr McGregor. 'But I've never met anyone with that name except for the wife of our old colleague. I don't think there's any possibility that it's a plain coincidence; that would really be some coincidence, right?'

'I think you should know something,' I confessed in a whisper, going upstairs. 'Hang on a second.'

I knocked on Dave's door, but he didn't answer. I went into the bedroom and found him asleep. I reached out and gently shook him by the shoulder. He woke grumbling and saw me with the phone in my hand.

'I'm sorry, officer, I didn't want the child to hear me.' Dave raised his eyebrows, silently asking what was going on. 'The thing is, today we went for a walk through the forest and, by chance, we found a mountain path I had no idea existed. My parents have been coming to this house for years, and I've never heard them say there was someone else living around here.'

'What *happening*?' Dave mumbled, rubbing his eyes with his fists.

I put the phone onto speaker and we both heard what Tom Farlane asked next. 'Have you found out where it leads?'

'No,' I said.

'Then I recommend you to do so. Perhaps that girl belongs to whoever lives there. I doubt it; but you never know. The coincidence of the names is strange. I'm going to give you my personal telephone number. You can reach me on it at any time. Do you have anything to write it down with?'

I looked for a pen and paper on the dressing table and wrote down the officer's number. I told him I would go out that same afternoon to find out where the path led and that I would call him as soon as I knew.

Then I hung up the phone and, as best I could, summarised the conversation for Dave, who was still drowsy. When he'd wiped the sleep from his eyes and I'd finally got him to understand what I was trying to tell him, we decided to get ready and head straight out into the forest.

And, for the hundredth time in those few days, everything turned against us.

I went to the bathroom to take a quick shower. After that long morning with its arguments, slappings, people pushing others, my twisted ankle, a long walk in the forest and that mysterious path, my head was spinning. I sat on the floor of the shower for a while, mulling over the conversation with Tom Farlane.

Could that couple he had told me about be Yäel's family? And if so, why had she refused to follow the path? Or was all of that about the names just pure coincidence? Could some people really have lived for so long on the other side of the stream without my family ever having known about them?

When I got out of the shower, I told Dave to wrap up warm, since night was falling and the temperatures would drop drastically. He went to his room, put on an extra jumper and grabbed his coat. I took a shoulder bag and my own coat and met him on the landing. We knocked on Daniel's and Stacey's doors, but no one answered.

We pushed open their doors, but neither of them were there. 'How weird. Where can they be?' I asked Dave.

I hadn't heard them go out, but perhaps I wouldn't have done over the noise of the shower.

'Me *either* . . .' Dave began to say.

Both of us froze.

From downstairs we heard the hysterical screams of the child, turning our blood to ice in our veins. We looked at each other and shouted in unison: 'Daniel!'

We ran along the landing and down the stairs. We arrived to see Daniel holding the girl and shaking her furiously. Daisy was barking frantically and trying to bite him.

'What are you doing?! Stop it! Daniel!!'

I pushed him, forcing him to release the child, who was crying uncontrollably. Stacey appeared behind us and ran to Daniel, holding him back.

'What the hell is going on?' I burst out, pushing the dog to one side while I wiped the tears from Yäel's face.

She rushed to pick up her teddy bear and squeezed it tightly against her chest. The puppy stood by her side, licking her hand. I looked straight at Daniel and asked him for an explanation.

'Nothing. Nothing is going on!' But he wouldn't meet my eyes.

'What do you mean, nothing? So, you just happen to be grabbing and shaking the child for no reason?' I said, beside myself with fury. I didn't trust the girl, but I wasn't going to tolerate that kind of behaviour. I didn't want any more violence.

'Nothing's happened. Leave me alone!'

'No, I'm not going to leave you alone, Daniel. What the fuck is wrong with you?'

I felt someone pull the back of my coat and turned around. I saw the child smiling, although she was still shaking. I didn't have time to analyse the reason for that smile. My head was full of what I'd just seen and I couldn't process anything else.

'I caught them doing something bad,' the girl said, turning a mischievous look on Daniel and Stacey.

I looked at them too, not understanding.

'Doing what?'

'Shut up!' Daniel warned the child, pointing at her with one finger.

But she didn't tremble with fear; she spoke with a voice that was so calm it made the hairs rise on the back of my neck.

'They were kissing . . . Daniel and Stacey are now boyfriend and girlfriend.'

'What . . . ?' I began to say, turning my head from Daniel to the child and back again.

But I couldn't finish the sentence. I ran out of air in my lungs, overwhelmed by the girl's serious words. They paralysed my body and mind. I couldn't think or do anything for seconds that felt like years.

And that dark smile of the child wasn't helping at all.

I stopped looking at her and fixed my eyes on Daniel. Then I looked at Stacey, who was covering her face with her hands. I understood that the child was telling the truth. If not, why else would Daniel tell her to be quiet? And why would Stacey cover her face, now as red as her hair?

'Tell me it's not true,' I mumbled.

He avoided my eyes, embarrassed. And suddenly I saw the situation all too clearly. 'Since when? Since when, Daniel?'

Stacey removed her hands from her face and looked at me. I could see her pain and embarrassment at being caught that way. She was ashamed of having betrayed our friendship, kissing the guy who was supposed to be my boyfriend.

Apparently, she wasn't as good a friend of mine as I'd thought. It was just as Dave had said.

'I'm so sorry, Eva.'

'I don't want to listen to you. I don't want to know anything about you. You're just another whore–'

'O.K. that's enough.' Daniel said, pushing Stacey behind him.

I looked at him with hatred, rage, disgust.

'You . . . You don't tell me what I should or shouldn't do, Daniel. I've told you that more than once.'

'I've done nothing wrong. Yes, I kissed her,' he shouted, looking at the child first and then at me. 'And? Wasn't it you who wanted a break?'

I clasped my head in my hands, not believing what I was hearing.

'A break! A fucking break!' I spat at him, raising my voice and getting closer. Dave grabbed my arm and I turned and shouted at him: 'Don't! I'm not like him . . . I am not like you, Daniel. You make me sick! You've been cheating on me all this time. You disgust me . . .'

I closed my eyes, hoping that when I opened them again, I'd be far away from there. Away from that scene. Far from both of them: the girl I'd thought was my friend, and the boy I'd imagined was my faithful boyfriend.

'So I ask you for a break! That doesn't mean you get to go around kissing the first bitch that comes in sight . . . Where do you think we are? In an episode of "Friends"? No, Daniel, we live in the real world. I think you've watched too many films. And I can't believe you're giving me that excuse . . . What about before the break?'

He didn't answer.

Instead we all heard laughter that cut through the silence, slashing it into pieces.

The four of us looked at each other, not understanding. We turned together and saw the child near the chimney, next to the cushions and blanket where I had fallen asleep earlier. From her throat came a devilish laugh that chilled me to the bone. Even the puppy tilted her head to one side and pricked up her ears, not knowing what was happening.

'What are you laughing about?' I asked her rudely.

She sat on the cushions, her teddy bear by her side, and continued to laugh.

'I pity the four of you,' she said, struggling to contain that horrible laughter. 'You shout at each other, hurt each other, and never agree on anything . . . And you blame me for breaking some vials I didn't even know were important . . .'

'What are you saying?' Dave asked.

The child looked at him calmly. The flickering light of the fire lit up her face and gave her eyes a strange gleam.

'Neither the good are so good, nor the bad so bad.'

She held my dairy in her hands.

'What?' Daniel whispered, not recognising what it was. He knew I kept a diary – he'd even seen me writing in it once – but I'd never let him read it, just as I hadn't let Yäel read it the night before.

'Yes, Daniel. Maybe Eva wants to explain it to you . . .'

I felt Daniel's penetrating look on my back, asking for an explanation. But I couldn't speak. I was thinking how stupid I'd been for not putting the diary away. I'd forgotten all about it after the unexpected call from the police officer.

Now Yäel was holding it in her hands. She opened it and flicked through the pages, firing up a rage inside me that stopped me from moving or thinking. I didn't know how worried I should be.

' "Why can't Daniel be like him . . . Kind, peaceful, intelligent, controlled ambition... Only a guy like Dave could make me happy . . ." '

'That's enough!' I screamed and ran to take the diary from her hands.

'Is that what you think? Is that why you wanted a break: to write in your diary how much you love this asshole?!' Daniel shouted at me while angrily pointing at Dave.

'And what does it matter to you! You're the one who goes around kissing filthy whores!'

We yelled horrible things at each other. Yäel watched all of us from her station in front of the fireplace, laughing every now and then, getting us even madder and making the argument even worse. Never mind that any of us told her to keep quiet. She just kept laughing and smiling from her corner. Meanwhile, the dog barked at the four of us whenever we raised our voices.

'Dave, put on your boots. We're leaving,' I told him when I'd had enough of it all.

'Oh, yeah, Dave, run after her like a lapdog,' Daniel said.

But Dave didn't pay any attention to him. He rushed to get his boots and left the house after me. Daniel came behind us. I could hear the crunch of his angry footsteps on the snow and I turned around, scared. After all I'd seen, I half expected him to go and beat up Dave. But he only said one thing.

'Where do you think you're going?'

'For your information, I'm going to find out if the child's family lives on the other side of the forest.'

'I think you're forgetting to take your beloved kid with you.'

I screamed in frustration. But I had to explain to him – even though I didn't feel like it – all about the unknown mountain path, the man and the woman with the same name as the little girl.

'And why is it that the two of us have to stay here with her while you two go out?'

'Because, besides Yäel, we're the only ones who know where the path is. And to be frank,' I said, grabbing Dave by the arm provocatively, 'we don't want to be under the same roof as you two.'

The London Eye could be seen through the slats of the blinds, spinning slowly in the distance. Looking back at Julia, Eva saw the passion in her eyes. She could read her expression easily; and she knew the next question the presenter was going to ask.

'Reading your diary, especially those last sentences that Yäel started to recite by heart,' the woman began, reviewing her own impressions in her notebook, 'one gets the feeling that you did in fact like Dave as more than a friend. Yesterday I asked you a simple question, Eva, and I'm sorry if I have to ask it once again. But the last pages of your diary,' she said holding the book in both hands, 'give anyone reading them a lot to think about.

'You've come here, to give this interview, to tell the true story of what happened that Christmas two years ago . . . Did you or didn't you like Dave as more than a friend?'

Eva had turned her head towards the window and was looking at the glorious white roulette wheel on the horizon, where hundreds of people went to view London. Even though her eyes were far away from the office, she was listening to the woman: word by word, syllable by syllable. But she had already explained how she had felt two years ago.

'As I told you: no. I know what I wrote. If you want, I can repeat every single word by memory,' said the young girl, tired of having to defend herself on a subject that was nobody's business; but she knew this was show business, and she didn't flinch. 'I can understand that people might imagine something different from what I wrote then. But I don't lie; I don't get anything by doing so. I'm nothing like all the journalists who have gone around publishing lies about me.'

'So, can you swear that you never loved him?'

Eva hesitated for a couple of seconds. Then she looked at the screen, now frozen, where the images of the day corresponding to her story had been reproduced. And she stared at the boy standing behind her own figure. Of course she liked him: he had been the best friend she had ever had in her entire life. No one had ever understood or treated her the way he had.

'Liked him, yes; loved him, no. They are two very different feelings, Julia. I've always liked Dave, and I will until the end of my days; but I never loved him . . . And even if I had, it doesn't matter, because he would never have returned those feelings.'

Julia's eyes shone brightly for a few seconds.

Eva knew the presenter had her right where she wanted her, but somehow sensed that the woman wouldn't continue down the same road. Throughout the interview Julia's questions had twisted and turned. Once she got the answer she was waiting for, she moved on to another topic.

It was the way she did things.

Besides, over the previous day, Eva had seen how the presenter recapped the story in the way that suited her. She asked her questions in a sweet tone, but they were as direct and deadly as arrows of fire. She'd made Eva relate details of her story she hadn't wanted to tell, details she hadn't even thought about before.

But Eva had known what she was getting into.

She had worked in television for years, winning her first acting role at just ten years of age. She knew she had to be careful with people like Julia. And more especially with Julia herself: she'd heard the stories about the way she operated.

She was a woman, like Eva, however in that business she was a goddess; or perhaps it would be better to say a demon. She had destroyed the image of more than one celebrity with just a sentence from her lips.

Nevertheless, it wasn't difficult to distinguish the two sides to the woman. Once the improvised studio lights were on, the playful lioness that wouldn't hurt a fly would turn into a beast with fiery eyes, furious and dangerous. She even treated her own husband, Sam, differently.

So, whenever she thought she saw the demon lurking, Eva gave in gracefully. She would smile sweetly and give the answer the woman wanted, taking care to phrase it carefully to stay faithful to her own story.

Eva had already gone through enough. She needed Julia by her side, protecting her. And in a way, she had grown fond of her.

'Are you listening to me?' she heard the woman asking, suddenly, as if waking her from a dream.

'No, I'm sorry. What were you saying?'

'I asked you what happened next?'

'I can tell you what I lived in the forest, but not what happened in the house. Thank God the security cameras recorded it all. Why don't you take a look for yourself?' Eva asked, pointing at the plasma screen.

12. "What do you want from us?"

Julia accepted the young girl's proposal with a nod. She put the diary to one side, shuffled her notes theatrically and looked straight at the camera.

'While we have been listening to Eva's version of the events, you at home have been able to watch some short clips from those never-before-seen videos. As Eva has said, she went with Dave to the woods around Guildon Forest, so she can't tell us about the events in the house at that time. But we have the unseen footage from the house and, as soon as production can play it,' she said, looking fleetingly at her husband behind the camera, 'we'll watch what happened in the living room.

'It has never been said what really happened in those moments. We have a hysterical Daniel, whose car tyre had been punctured by Yäel – accidentally? – hours before; an embarrassed Stacey, who had been betraying her friend for who knows how long; and a child, Yäel, the one who . . . well, I wouldn't know how to describe her at this point in the story. After having behaved very affectionately towards Eva, her attitude began to make Eva distrust her. And that argument . . . I believe I speak for everyone now when I say that laughter was both surprising and disturbing, something we will never be able to forget; and that evil, public reading of the deepest feelings that Eva described in the last pages she ever wrote in her diary.'

Julia took a deep breath after her long speech. 'Get ready, because without further ado, here are those moments.'

She grabbed her pen in her right hand, playing with it. She didn't know exactly what to expect from the footage – especially after seeing how Eva had looked away from the screens, as if she could not endure watching them one more time.

She was proud of her tenacious and persistent work in that interview, but not about that fleeting image of the girl, looking lost as she stared away from the plasma screen. That image demolished the tall, strong wall that separated Julia the lady next-door from the all-powerful Julia Stevenson, presenter and television star, acclaimed writer . . .

Her tough attitude had taken her to the top, overcoming all the barriers that had stood in her way; for in that world only the strongest survived. How else could have she obtained those important and revealing details from the girl during the interview?

She wasn't to be blamed for the harrowing ordeal the young girl had lived through, but . . . had she been harsher than necessary with her? Should she have lowered her voice and not let the wild and uncontrollable side of *Julia Stevenson* take over? Either way, she told herself, she had already delved enough into all the characters. Next time she would be kinder to the girl.

She shook the doubts from her mind and returned her eyes to the plasma screen. There, camera four filled the whole screen, and she was able to see and hear what the two youngsters were saying, just as if she were there.

'Why did you have to kiss me?' Daniel was asking Stacey, his back to the camera.

The camera was positioned right over the front door. It had captured the boy's back, Stacey sitting on the sofa with her hands covering her face, and the child sitting in front of the fireplace, listening to the conversation while stroking the dog's thick fur.

'Didn't you notice the TV was on the cartoon channel?'

'Of course, that's the easiest thing to notice now, isn't it? Like I was the only one who hadn't realised,' Stacey retorted, taking her hands angrily from her face. 'If you were a real man, we wouldn't have had to notice anything.'

'What do you mean by that?'

'I mean that you're an asshole!' she shouted at him, getting off the sofa and pointing at him furiously.

'Excuse me?'

'Do you really not realise you've not only been playing with Eva, but also with me?'

'I haven't played with anyone who didn't want to play.'

Stacey did not accept those words. 'What are you trying to say? Did Eva want to play? Did she even know who she was dealing with? And what do you think I am? An inflatable doll without any feelings?'

With each word, she took a step closer to Daniel. He didn't reply and Julia, in her office, wished he would turn around so she could see his reaction to those hard but accurate points.

'I don't know how I let myself get carried away with your lies. All the promises you made me over and over again, promising me you were going to leave her, that I was the one you really wanted, that you were only with her because of her fame,' the girl broke into tears, her voice choking in sobs.

He couldn't help but go to her and give her a hug.

'And it was all true, Stacey. Of course I had every intention of leaving her. You are my one and only girl. I've never lied to you. But I love her too.'

She slipped from Daniel's arms and slapped him hard. 'You make me sick,' she said, just as Eva had said minutes before. 'You've never known how to treat a woman, and you never will.'

'What about you? Do you even know how to treat your own friends?' he rounded on her cruelly. 'Let me remind you I wasn't the only one hiding our relationship from Eva. You were supposed to be her friend and you never told her anything.'

'Because you said you were going to do it! You lied to both of us every single day! How do you think I felt every time I went to work and saw Eva? Do you know what's that like, to look straight in her eyes and think about what we were doing behind her back? Do you understand how it felt not to know if she'd already found out about it all? Every day I got up and went to the set and almost expected Eva would come up to me and split my head in two. And even that would have been better than seeing the two of you snogging in every corner, not caring whether I saw you or not.'

This time Daniel didn't answer. He sat on the sofa and put his hands over his head. The pressure he was under was palpable. He had just admitted that he loved Eva, for whatever reason; but he also loved the young redhead, there was no doubt of that.

'I'm sorry . . .' he babbled. 'You know it wasn't easy at all. If I had told her I was with you, both of us could have been fired. Her mother is one of the producers. What do you think she would have done when she found out?'

Now it was Stacey who didn't say anything. She turned to face the window, leaving her face visible to the camera.

'Then you shouldn't have started anything with me. You should have thought that through before choosing her in the first place. What does she have that I don't? Is it that her family is richer than mine? Is she prettier than me?' She threw a litany of angry questions at the boy without even looking at him. Daniel didn't dare to open his mouth. What could he say to fix the situation? 'If you really cared so much about your job, you could have been smarter and put an end to your relationship after one of your arguments. God knows you had enough of them! If you loved her as you say you do, you wouldn't be arguing with her all the time. But no . . . you always fix it with her and now both of us are screwed. Tell me, what do you think is going to happen when we go back to London?' she finished, dropping onto the sofa next to him, leaving a gap between them.

Now only the soft crackle of the logs in the fireplace could be heard in the footage. The two of them sat on the sofa, looking in different directions.

'Now you can live in peace,' Yäel said, as though someone had asked her.

Daniel turned to face her, tired of the situation.

'Sorry? Don't put your nose where it doesn't concern you. You're just a fucking brat.'

But she made no sign of feeling hurt. Instead she smiled and said, 'Maybe . . . But I've read many things in your *girlfriend*'s diary.'

The little girl's sarcastic tone of voice when she said "girlfriend" enraged Daniel. He picked up a cushion and threw it straight at her, but he missed and struck Stacey's dog, who got up and showed him her teeth.

'Daniel!' Stacey shouted at him.

'What?! I don't give a shit anymore. If she wants to talk that way to the bitch of her mother, she can do, but I'm not having her doing it with me!'

The child, who had got up and taken Daisy by the collar to calm her down, had ignored Daniel's violent reaction. But as soon as he insulted her mother, her face contorted in a rictus of pain.

'Leave my mum alone . . . It's not my fault you lie to each other . . .' Her pain was suddenly replaced by a smile. 'Besides, Eva is the one who should apologise to you. I've read so much about Dave in her diary . . . "I love him so much", "he is so handsome", "he kisses much better than Daniel . . ."'

Stacey grabbed Daniel's arms at the last second. He had moved as if to throw himself at the little girl, and the dog began barking at him. Daisy pulled herself clear of the girl's hands and Stacey struggled to hold onto both Daniel and the puppy at the same time.

'What do you want from us? What the hell do you want?' he was shouting.

'Yäel, go to your room . . . I said go to your room!' Stacey shouted at the child when she began to protest.

And Stacey stayed there, with Daniel and her puppy, one kicking the furniture, feeling impotent, and the other one now barking even more.

About two minutes went by in the video, the actor still clearly angry after the child's words. And Julia, sitting in her office, was writing her personal notes like a madwoman, but still attentive to every detail of the footage.

She couldn't believe the words that had come out of the child's mouth.

She had read that diary, the same one that now rested on one side of her seat. And she knew, for the first time in those two days, that the girl was lying.

Eva could have written more things than normal in her diary about her day-to-day life with Dave. But if Julia was certain about anything, it was that she had never kissed him; at least, not in any episode that Eva had recorded on any of those pages. And, although she wouldn't be surprised if Eva had in fact omitted such a thing from her daily entries, those statements struck her hard.

What kind of child said things like that?

The woman underscored that question in her notebook and continued watching the rest of the video.

Daniel was screaming now, ignoring Stacey's pleas. She was trying to calm down Daisy, but to no avail. In the end, she grabbed the dog in her arms as best she could and carried her upstairs.

'I can't believe it! It can't be true!' Daniel was shouting, alone in the living room. 'Why the hell does this hateful kid care about our lives? I wish I'd driven the car over her! What a fucking weight we'd have taken from round our necks . . . !'

He continued ranting all alone in the living room, until all of a sudden he fell silent.

He circled the sofas several times, machinating over something. His facial expression had changed. He was no longer frowning or grimacing; now he looked from side to side with wide eyes. He stood next to the phone and picked up the phone book. He opened it and flipped through page after page until he stopped at one.

'What are you doing with the phone?' Stacey, now alone, asked him from her position on the stairs.

'I'm going to call those friends of Eva's mum.'

He dialled a number, explaining to Stacey as he did so that Eva had told him about a mountain path in the forest, and a woman whose name was the same as the child's.

'Good afternoon, Mrs McGregor, it's Daniel . . . Yes, Eva's *boyfriend* . . . I was wondering if you knew anything about a woman called Yäel? . . . Apparently, she might live on the other side of the forest . . . What did you say? . . . Then your husband has remembered? . . . Could you say that again?' the boy asked her, covering his free ear with a finger. 'Sorry, can't hear you properly, could you raise your voice? . . . What? . . . Hello?'

A few seconds later, he smashed the phone against its base.

'Are you going to tell me what she said?' Stacey asked after a couple of seconds had gone by in silence.

'I don't know, something really strange . . . I couldn't hear very well. She said something about cats . . . or I don't know what.'

And he flew towards the garage door.

Back in the studio Julia made a hand gesture, and Sam switched the footage on the plasma screen to show all four security cameras once more. Now two of them were playing their footage. In the living room, the girl was standing still, apparently not knowing what to do or say; in the garage, where the dim light didn't show much, Daniel stumbled over piles of junk until he succeeded in grabbing and pulling something from among the rubbish. It was an old bicycle.

The woman needed no explanation from Eva to know who it belonged to. She had already described how they had encountered it before, among the boxes in the garage. Nor did she now show any sign of acknowledging the madness of the boy taking the bike. He didn't seem to have any qualms about grabbing it.

'Where are you going with that bike?' Stacey asked him.

'I'm going to pay a visit to the old lady,' he answered, putting on his coat. A moment later he walked out of the front door, slamming it behind him.

As I had predicted, temperatures dropped drastically out in the forest. And it didn't matter how many layers we'd put on: the cold quickly sank into our bones.

We walked briskly through the snow, practically feeling our way, swallowed by the sudden darkness of the night, leaving behind clumsy footprints. Only the moonlight, high in the dark sky, allowed us to see where we were placing our feet. Sometimes a cloud flew between the moon and us, and we returned to groping our way in the pitch black.

We didn't say a word for a good while.

We focused on walking the same route we'd taken a few hours earlier. And once again, we crossed the clearing where I used to play when I was a child, past the frozen stream, and between the trees where Dave, Yäel and the puppy had been playing.

We walked until we reached that mountain path.

I looked to the left, where we could guess the tarmac of the road lay under the snow, and where not a single car passed by. Still in silence, we took our first steps towards the depths of the mountain.

I was furious at everything: the list was endless. So, I focused on moving as quickly as I could to keep myself warm. I needed to clear my head, to try to forget that argument with Daniel.

The boy's screams and Stacey's betrayal echoed in my head like a shout in a deep cave. They tormented me, and I could feel the pounding of my heart in my chest. I couldn't stop myself mulling over the whole thing again and again.

Why did we have to end up this way?

How could it be that everything was turning from bad to worse?

Weren't we going to be able to enjoy a moment of peace?

Behind me, Dave was also quiet. I knew him well enough to know the helplessness he was suffering after not being able to get in between Daniel and me, holding back the words he'd wanted to say.

Yes, in a way, he was a coward. He was never able to stand up for himself against those who picked on him. And even though he could understand what we were saying very well, he struggled with his English and it was difficult for him to talk if he was nervous.

On the other hand, I knew his main reason for not saying anything was that he respected me. That argument was Daniel's and mine, not his. But he had definitely heard the child's poisonous words about what I had – or hadn't – written in my diary.

That was certainly his business.

And, as anyone could have foreseen, it didn't take long for that silence to be broken.

'Is it true?' the boy asked me, his teeth chattering in the cold.

I played dumb.

'I don't think I have to remind you what she said,' he told me, grabbing my arm to make me stop. 'Have you *write* those things in your diary?'

I stared back at him, trying to discern his eyes in the semi-darkness. I could just make out how his face showed the signs of the many different emotions he was feeling at once. And I knew then that I couldn't answer him.

I started walking again.

'Yes, it's true,' I admitted. 'I wrote them.'

He tried to keep pace with me.

'Then have I been the reason you *ask* him for a break?'

'Please, Dave, let it be. I've already had enough of this with Daniel for now us keep talking about the same thing,' I growled at him.

And he didn't argue. He remained quiet for a bit; but he'd always been able to say what he thought to me. I always gave him time to think how to express himself in English.

'No, Eva, I can't. Not after these last days,' he admitted, annoyed. 'I came here because you *insist*.'

'So now you're blaming me for getting you into all this?' I asked him incredulously.

'No, that is not what I want to say. Listen to me,' he shouted at me, grabbing me again to make me slow my steps. 'Eva, I can't pretend like nothing had *happen* when you write in your diary those things about me, or how you *compares* me with your boyfriend . . . or ex, whatever you want to call him. I can't just put it *asides* . . . Because I feel the same way.'

I stopped abruptly and he bumped into me hard. We grabbed each other to avoid falling over in the snow; however, we let go immediately.

'What did you say?' I asked him in a neutral tone.

He lowered his head and pressed his arms to his body, shivering. I could read on his face that he had instantly regretted his words. That *thing* that allowed us to understand each other so clearly, without words, betrayed him.

'No . . . I didn't want to *said* that . . .'

I waited until he raised his eyes to me again.

'Yes, you wanted to say that, Dave. But I don't understand why you're thinking about these things. We're friends, right?' I asked him, profoundly doubting it.

It seemed like I didn't really know anyone anymore.

In just four days I had discovered that I didn't know my own friends at all. Every second, it seemed, they did something that took me by surprise. It was as if my whole life had turned one hundred and eighty degrees. And with it, my friends as well.

How could I not have realised that Daniel was cheating on me? How on earth had I let Stacey pretend to be my best friend? I had never seen any sign of what was going on. And, even then, standing there in the forest, I didn't know the details. It wasn't until later, when I watched the videos and forced myself to believe it, that I finally opened my eyes.

But Dave . . . the person with whom I had shared so much. So many talks, films, walks, calls . . . All the times he had been to my home, talking to my mum . . . Did he really feel something for me? He had hugged me, cheered me up, supported me, made me smile during the bad times . . . Was all that because he cared for me as more than just a friend? Was that possible?

I shook my head and turned away from him, continuing along the path.

A little further on I spoke again. 'I didn't ask Daniel for a break because of you, Dave. And after everything I know now, I don't regret it. He's not the man I want to spend my life with, and he never will be. We are so different.'

I focused again on the path. I didn't want to talk about Daniel anymore. It was breaking my heart and, besides, he was a waste of the cold air that filled my lungs.

I strode on, trying to ignore the searing spasms of pain in my ankle. But the dozens of times I tripped over fallen tree branches and rocks hidden under the snow weren't helping at all.

Minutes later, Dave remembered the mobile phone he still had in his pocket. We didn't get any signal in the area, so he hadn't used it. But now he pulled it out and switched it on, pleased to be able to put it to use, even if it was just to light our way along the gloomy track.

'Do you think that man and his wife could live at the end of this path?' I asked him pointing to the dark and sinuous passage between the trees, trying to lighten the atmosphere.

'Maybe. It's the only thing that *make* sense: if the child isn't from the village and there is no other town for miles, there must be a house somewhere. Either it belongs to *those* couple or to someone else. Sorry,' he apologised as the light from the phone turned off for a moment. He turned it on again and we proceeded slowly through the freezing forest. 'The question is not whether someone else is living here,' the boy pointed out, 'but who would leave a child of Yäel's *ages* alone and in the middle of the road? So far away from anybody . . . Lucky we passed by when we did.'

With those words in our minds we walked further along the path, deeper and deeper into the forest. We walked closer together now, the distance between us closing with every step we took.

In the bleak darkness of the forest, we began to feel as if we were being watched. It was as if we were in a horror film, every small noise giving us the creeps: the crunching of the snow beneath our boots, the wind howling between the treetops, an owl hooting, making us turn our heads in its direction.

Not that we were in a dangerous area. Over the years, virtually all the wild animals had disappeared, leaving a deer here or a Scottish wildcat there, the occasional fox going about its business. And yet, on more than one occasion, Dave and I grabbed each other's hands, startled by the sudden snap of a branch behind us.

But nothing came to meet us.

We walked for a couple of minutes more until Dave squeezed my hand hard. He switched off the light on his phone and the two of us stood still.

'Do you see what I see?' he whispered, faint clouds of steam forming with each word.

I nodded. I could also see what attracted Dave's attention.

A light.

Barely more than a yellow glow at the end of the tunnel the trees formed over the path. But it was there, drawing us forwards to where it was coming from.

So our feet began to crunch again on the thick layer of snow.

I couldn't really believe that someone was in fact living there. Or that Mrs McGregor hadn't mentioned it – if she knew, that is. One way or another, I was just hoping we were finally going to find Yäel's family.

I couldn't wait any longer to get rid of her.

I smiled, excited, thinking that by the next day we would be free. We would find a way to get back to London. And we wouldn't have to see each other's faces again for a while. I doubted how long I could stay under the same roof with Daniel and Stacey.

I knew myself too well to the extent of being afraid of what I could possibly do or say.

I had had it already with all those awkward silences. Those arguments and sudden mood changes, the atmosphere worsening day after day. I couldn't bear one more day in that house, I was sure of that. I needed to be back at home – maybe not with Dave anymore; but at least back at home, where I could call the rest of my real friends, watch Christmas films and not having to cook for people I didn't even want to see.

And with those false expectations, we reached the place where the light was shining out.

'It can't be,' I muttered, almost inaudibly.

Dave held my hand more firmly.

The two of us, feet buried in the snow, stood very still. And now we could see the light clearly, blinding against the pure darkness of the night.

A house.

A freaking house in the middle of the forest, just like mine.

A house I had no recollection of.

A house where Yäel's family could be living.

Was that possible? Could the child's parents be inside? Three nights after we'd found her, never giving any sign of wanting to get their daughter back?

Not even a single call to the police?

13. "Don't you want to be pretty?"

I couldn't have been there before in my life, that was for sure. I would never have forgotten about that house, its single storey built of dark stone.

Next to the building there was a small vegetable patch. The fence that had once surrounded it lay on the ground. We could see only a few clumps of weeds protruding from the snow.

The house didn't look any better. At the corners, some of the dark and dirty stone had fallen away. The roof looked as if it were ready to collapse at any moment. At the front, from a window with yellowish curtains and glass cracked by the cold, the light shone through.

How could anyone live in such conditions? I had never suffered from hunger nor lacked for anything. My parents had amassed a great fortune and I had always lived surrounded by luxury. I knew that hundreds of thousands of people weren't so lucky. But I still couldn't understand how anyone could live in a house like that.

Cut off from the world, out of the sight of everyone.

If Yäel really came from that house, I told myself, I'd feel sorry for her. I wouldn't wish anybody to live in a place like that, surrounded by the solitude of the mountain and the forest, so far away from the village. Almost abandoned to their fate.

But could Yäel really have lived there? Didn't she go to school?

She had told me herself that she could write, and obviously she could read perfectly well. If she was attending school, it would have to be away from Guildon Forest; there was no school there. But even so, she would have had to pass through the village to get anywhere, so Mrs McGregor should have seen her before . . .

Nothing made sense.

'Should we knock on the door?' Dave proposed.

I nodded.

Cries of Blood

We took a few steps towards the gloomy house, holding hands, not prepared to separate for a single second. When we got to the front door, just a battered wooden board fitted poorly into its frame, I knocked on it with my fist.

We could hear someone speaking on the other side.

We waited a few seconds with the freezing wind rushing between our arms and legs, blowing my hair around my face.

'Hello?' I raised my voice.

But no one answered. The voice we were hearing continued with its litany.

'Knock again,' the boy urged me, shivering.

And so I did.

But this time the door creaked under my knuckles. Frightened, we saw the door staggering on its hinges with the force of my hand. It wasn't locked.

A faint beam of light shone out as the door swayed open.

'Hello?' I asked again. No one seemed to hear me, so I pushed the door open further. 'My name's Eva, and I'm staying at my parents' house, just a few minutes from here. Can somebody hear me?'

I looked at Dave, who urged me to go inside. I pushed the shabby board inwards, fearful that the homeowners would think I was a thief, and went inside with Dave.

Behind us the long shadows of our bodies lay on the snow, away from the house. When we stepped over the threshold, the light blinded us. We covered our faces with our frozen hands and our pupils narrowed, stung by the yellow light after the darkness of our long walk.

'What the . . . ?' I heard Dave saying next to me.

I slowly removed my fingers from my face. I blinked until my eyes adjusted to the lighting . . .

'Oh, my –' I said.

The house was in chaos. The front door opened into a small hall, which led to the living room. There was no door and we could see straight through to the room beyond.

Dark green sofas showed deep cuts here and there. Foam was sticking out from the countless slashes in the fabric. There were half empty cushions, their feathers scattered on the ground, and books with their pages torn and strewn across the room.

The walls were painted a blood-red colour, but in many places the paint had peeled away, leaving behind a greenish mould that had grown in the damp. On one of the walls there was a shelf made from broken wooden boards. A television sat in the middle of a cabinet: it was from this, we now discovered, that the voice we had heard from outside was coming.

'*Are* there someone . . . here?' Dave stammered, tightening his grip on my hand so much that I had to shake him off. 'Sorry.'

I took some steps towards the centre of the living room. There was no one there, but it was clear that hadn't been the case for long.

On top of a small table there was an old record player. The needle was in the air, hanging over the vinyl record that was still spinning.

To our right, we saw a closed door. This one was made of dark coloured wood, with frosted glass at the top. On the other side another light was on, releasing a fragile, bluish beam into the room.

'Where are you going?' Dave whispered, holding my arm.

'There must be someone here,' I answered him, removing his hand from my coat.

I approached the door and, after a moment's hesitation, I opened it . . .

If I'd been surprised by the exterior and the condition of the living room, I was even more shocked when I saw the state of the kitchen. The doors of every cupboard were hanging loose on their hinges, looking as if they might fall off completely at any minute.

There were broken plates on the surfaces, food still clinging to them. One of the shelves, which seemed to have been used to store jars of spices, had collapsed onto the counter, creating a mess of powder and broken glass. In the sink there was a huge stack of dirty plates, flies buzzing around them.

Retching at the smell, Dave rushed to the sink to turn off the tap. It had been left running, the water filling the sink and flowing over the sides. The floor was practically flooded and Dave's boots splashed through the water as he crossed the kitchen.

'There can't be anyone here,' he said, covering his nose.

An unbearable stench was coming from the fridge, its door left wide open.

Inside, there was only a small plate of cheese – or what had once been cheese – and a bottle of fermented milk.

'No,' I said, frowning. 'Maybe not right now, but someone's been living here. Nobody leaves the house lights on and disappears just like that. Besides, the door was open. Maybe they've gone out for something.'

'For what?'

'How would I know? The TV was on. Perhaps we should just wait for someone to come back home.'

Dave tried to persuade me to do the opposite. He didn't want to know who was living in such a house. No one in their right mind, he argued, would leave their rubbish overflowing the bins and all those broken objects spread across the floor.

'Remember,' I told him, 'the woman Officer Farlane told me about could be living here. A woman whose name is the same as the child's.'

Dave didn't protest; he left the kitchen and went back to the living room.

'Let's wait then.'

Eva paused in her narration and took a drink. Julia had asked her to stop for a couple of seconds while she caught up with her note taking.

'Did you find anything that drew your attention, or at least more than the rest of it?' Julia asked, once she had finished writing in her notebook.

'Yes, we did,' Eva assured her, her voice bitter at the memory. 'We tried to get comfortable where we could, waiting for someone to come back. Five minutes went by, then fifteen. I got up and began to inspect the house.

'It was then, without needing the owners to come back, that I discovered that the police officer, Tom Farlane, was right about it all. That man and his wife, Yäel, really did live there.

'I was searching the wardrobes in their bedroom when I found the old man's police uniform. It was worn and faded by the years. And yet he had hung it on a hanger, perfectly ironed and placed between his everyday clothes.'

'But three years had passed since he'd left the force,' the woman reminded her.

Eva, annoyed by the constant interruptions of the presenter, ignored her and continued with her story. 'That man, as I found out later, had lost his job because of his drinking. However,' the girl pointed out, 'he still loved policing – even though what followed made me think it was the wrong profession for a man like him.'

In the meantime, Dave, despite his fears that the man would enter the house and find us rummaging through all his stuff, had been checking the living room thoroughly. As I was about to move to the next room, he called me to go back to the living room.

'What's wrong?' I asked him, short of breath.

'Come here! Look what I have *find*.'

He was holding what at first sight I took to be a book. But after a good look, I discovered what it really was. He had found a photo album.

I got closer and the pictures it held took me by surprise.

The child, Yäel, was in them!

I read the inscriptions under each picture, written with the careful calligraphy of someone who cared about the task. Each one gave a brief explanation of who the photo showed, and when and where it had been taken.

"Sarah planting tomatoes," one of them said, the photo above showing the child kneeling next to the vegetable patch; "Sarah playing with Kitty," read another, showing the child holding a honey-coloured cat in her arms; "Sarah and Johnny sleeping," read a third, showing the child wearing a white nightgown, fast asleep as she hugged her teddy bear.

Sarah.

Her name wasn't Yäel, it was Sarah.

'Are you sure it's the same girl?' Dave asked me stupidly.

I punched him on the arm. Of course it was the same girl. The same one that was now at my house; the one we had picked up from the road with that same teddy bear; the one with whom we had been living during those last few days.

'Then why did she *said* her name was Yäel?'

'Well, she never actually said that,' I corrected him. I had to be fair to her, even though I'd been thinking exactly the same thing. 'She just went with the flow when we called her by that name.'

But I didn't have time to think about it any longer, since when I flipped the pages on the photo album I found something even more bizarre.

A woman was in some of the pictures, alone. Beneath them were the same brief explanations mentioning her name, Yäel. In others, she was next to a man; but his head had been completely cut off. Someone had taken their time to make imperfect circles, cutting out the photographs where his face should have been. Not a single picture had escaped. From the first one to the last, wherever the head of the so-called "George" should have been, there was just an empty space.

'Who could have done this?' Dave gasped, staring at the pictures.

'I suppose the same person who's done all of this,' I pointed to the destruction in the living room. 'What I don't get is why this couple, if they've lived here with the girl long enough to have a photo album, they haven't reported her disappearance.'

'They seem to have disappeared as well,' Dave said. He had relaxed, no longer expecting anyone to come through the front door at any second.

I remained sat on the sofa, feeling the springs pointing into my body under the half empty cushions. My head was spinning. I was so tired of having to think about all these puzzles.

I looked from one side of the room to the other and something caught my attention.

There were videotapes spread on the floor. The old-fashioned, black VHS type. I got up and went closer to find the child's name, Sarah, on all of them. I looked up at the TV, which was airing a documentary about sea life. There was an old video recorder on the shelf beneath it. I picked up one of the videotapes and slid it in.

'Can you see a remote control anywhere?' I asked Dave, who turned around on the sofa to look for it.

We didn't need it, however; a few seconds later, the TV screen turned black and the letters "V", "H" and "S" appeared in the top left corner. Here was the child again, somewhat younger than she was now.

I pressed the fast forwards button on the old film player. They were home made videos, showing the child innocently playing with her teddy bear, the cat from the pictures often around too. I put on tape after tape, passing from one to the next, looking for something without knowing what it was.

And then I found it.

The screen was covered in a veil of white and black flickering snow, accompanied by an annoying noise. The next thing that came on screen took us unprepared.

The man was holding the camera looking down, letting us see his bare feet as he walked around the house, not quite in a straight line. He went into a room, the child's bedroom, where he raised the camera and focused it on the girl, who was drawing on a sheet of paper. She was half naked, wearing just shorts. And the man began to talk. He could barely say two words together, clearly under the influence of alcohol while . . .

A painful memory crossed Eva's eyes, and she closed them abruptly. She raised one hand to her cheek to wipe away her tears. Julia just watched her, letting the silence take over the room.

The woman offered her a tissue and Eva accepted gratefully. Julia sat down again, resting her back against the chair and crossing her legs. She wrote a few lines in her notebook but didn't say a word for a while.

'If you'd like to stop,' Julia began, her voice mellow and calm, 'we can take a break.'

'No,' the girl refused brusquely, her tone sharper than she had intended. 'It's hard to remember something you have been determined to forget, to erase from your memory . . . That bastard molested the girl. And maybe Sarah doesn't deserve anything good after . . . everything that happened. But that's something no child should ever have to go through.'

'Do you think those acts are what made her behave in the way she did later? Could it be,' Julia looked at the camera as she continued, 'that the abuse did irreparable harm to the child? To that girl with no family that, until now, we have known as Yäel, but we now know was really called Sarah? A child who was that man's granddaughter – that's right, isn't it? She was the granddaughter of his wife, Yäel, whom she had married not so long before. And he had been fired from the Scottish police just a few years earlier.'

The girl didn't nod, but neither did she contradict Julia.

The presenter was being very cautious now. Soon, her words would be broadcast on televisions all around the world. She had to be careful about what she said, as this was a very delicate topic to be discussing on TV. Moreover, the police had confiscated those videos two years before, so she was counting on Eva's faltering description.

But she wasn't going to make her dwell on the subject anymore.

'Shall we watch what was going on at the same time in your house?' Julia proposed, forcing a smile despite the discomfort of the situation.

Eva nodded, keeping her eyes shut.

Eva had asked them to stop filming so she could tell them about the rest of the footage. Julia asked her husband to start the camera rolling again, then turned to the lens and spoke solemnly.

'I'd like to inform everyone at home that the scenes you are about to watch, as you will realise, aren't the original footage from the video cameras in the house. Due to the nature of the acts depicted, a group of professional actors will recreate the events that occurred in that living room.' She gave a short pause and pretended to read something from her notes. 'I'd like to remind you all that, at this point in the events, Daniel had left the house on the old bicycle belonging to Liam Lawrence, the late American film director and Eva's father. So Stacey, the child and the puppy were alone in the house.'

She waved her hand as the footage recommenced.

The plasma screen showed the living room, full screen. There Stacey could be seen trying in vain to revive the fire in the wood-burner. She opened the door and threw in some logs, but all that happened was that smoke billowed into the room. The fire alarm detector began to beep loudly.

Stacey hurried to open the front door and windows. She picked up a magazine and, standing on a chair, fanned away the smoke from the fire detector as fast as she could. In a matter of seconds, the room became silent again. The girl coughed loudly, trying to breathe in the fresh, clean air from outside.

'Where did Daniel go?' the child could be heard from the stairs. She came down the steps and observed the scene, apparently unmoved.

'What do you care?' Stacey snapped at her.

She brushed her hair from her face, went to the kitchen, washed her hands and returned to the living room. For a while, she said nothing; she ignored the child and covered herself with a blanket. But she couldn't control herself for long.

'With a bit of luck, we'll get rid of you soon.'

'Oh, really?'

'Yes, really, you insolent brat,' Stacey spat with a Machiavellian smile. 'As soon as we find your parents, we're going to tell them all the mischief you've done and you're going to get into real trouble. If you think Daniel slapped you hard, get ready for the spanking your daddy will give you.'

The child just smiled back at her. She sat down near Stacey, hugging her teddy bear and stroking his ears.

'Oh, Johnny, this girl has no idea of anything,' the child told the bear, placing him on her lap and moving his head so it looked as if he was shaking his head. 'She doesn't know that I don't have a daddy or a mummy.'

Stacey, who had tried hard to ignore her, turned in her direction. She stared at the girl, frowning, the surprise by the statement clear on her face.

Julia was surprised too: the child had flatly refused to talk about her family or personal life before. She had always changed the subject, instead asking the others about their own lives.

What had made her start talking about her family now?

Could she, perhaps, have sensed that her identity was gradually being unveiled? Could she have known that Daniel had gone out to talk to Mrs McGregor, the one who seemed to know something about her? Or could she have guessed that Dave and Eva had followed the same path she had refused to walk along earlier that day?

Whatever the answer, neither Julia nor Eva would ever know. There were things that none of them would ever find out, and that would torment them forever.

'What do you mean by not having a daddy or a mummy?' Julia heard Stacey ask Sarah.

'My daddy was using cocaine and died years ago,' the child said, in a matter of fact way. 'And my mummy died in a car accident.'

Stacey looked horrified. Was she now feeling sympathy towards the girl?

'My grandma has taken care of me since I can remember,' the small creature finished saying.

'Well . . . Then your grandma is going to spank your bottom, because you've been a very naughty girl,' Stacey reprimanded her. 'I'm sure you'll regret being so bad and learn to respect other people's belongings.'

And, *for the first time ever*, the child left her teddy bear sitting alone on the sofa. It was something that neither Stacey nor Julia – who was now following the footage with avid eyes, almost unblinking – overlooked.

'What are you going to do?' Stacey asked her, staring at the teddy bear.

She didn't look at Sarah, who walked around the sofa and stood behind her. Stacey didn't have time to turn and see what the child was about to do.

'What I should have done long ago.' And as fast as lightning, she grabbed the small lamp on the side table by Stacey, raised it in the air and smashed it against the back of the girl's neck.

Stacey fell unconscious to the floor, letting out only a muffled groan as she crashed into the carpet.

Julia jumped in her seat. She looked across at Eva, who was still not looking at the screen, unable to hide the pain on her face. When Julia looked back at the screen, the child was grabbing Stacey by the ankles, dragging her towards the garage door.

The view changed to the footage from the security camera in the garage, allowing Julia to see how Sarah eagerly pulled the young actress down the stairs.

Cries of Blood

The presenter narrowed her eyes with every thud of Stacey's head and arms against the steps.

Once the child had dragged her to a clear area in the middle of the room, not without effort, she left her there, inert. She began searching through the boxes and smiled when she found a few pieces of rope with which she tied up the girl.

Sarah left the garage but was back a minute later, her arms full of Stacey's belongings. She opened every bottle and jar and spread their contents around the actress, one by one. She picked up a small brush, rubbed it with makeup and passed it over the girl's face.

Stacey seemed to smell the products and began to regain consciousness.

When her face was covered in a mix of colours, she awoke fully and groaned in pain. She found herself tied from head to toe, pain reflected in her face.

'What . . . what . . . what are . . . you doing?' She could hardly speak, breathless.

Sarah, her back to the camera, said, 'Don't you want to be pretty?'

'Why are you doing this? You are evil . . . Let me go . . . please . . .'

And Stacey began to cry uncontrollably, while the child passed the makeup brush all over her face. Sarah stopped for a second, looked at her and stroked her hair with something that looked almost like tenderness.

'I'm not naughty. You adults are the naughty ones. I just want the best for all of you –'

Suddenly she stood up and rushed up the stairs from the garage. Sam didn't have time to switch to the footage of the security camera from the living room. The puppy could be heard barking off-camera as she heard her owner's cries of distress.

A minute later, the little girl came back down the stairs, a tiny briefcase in her hands. Stacey was trying to loosen her ropes, but her aching body didn't have the strength to escape.

'What . . . what are you doing?! Why have you taken that?!' the girl yelled, twisting from side to side. 'Stop! Yäel!'

At first, the child's back was to the camera, so Julia couldn't see whatever it was she had taken from the briefcase. By the time she was able to glimpse the object in the child's hand, it was too late for any commentary.

Sarah raised an insulin syringe in one fist. In the other she held the last of the insulin vials. Stacey was trembling violently now. The girl smashed the vial against the floor with all her strength. It shattered on the tiles.

'Now, I do know what this is for,' she growled, her voice deep and demonic. 'And this is how it sounds when someone smashes it against the floor on purpose.'

'Why?! Why are you doing this?! Let me go! Please!' Stacey wept, spitting drops of makeup from her lips.

'No one touches JOHNNY!' the child shouted at her.

She filled the syringe with the liquid makeup that was spread in a puddle over the floor and raised it in the air.

'What are you doing?! No . . . ! No . . . ! Nooooooo!!'

It happened fast.

The needle stuck deep in Stacey's flesh, right in her neck. The child pressed down on the syringe and discharged the liquid it contained into the actress's body.

Julia put her hands over her mouth, letting her notes drop and scatter across the floor as she watched Stacey writhe in agony.

Seconds later, the young girl lay still on the floor of the garage . . . lifeless.

The child seemed to lose interest. She left her lying there, and climbed the stairs back to the living room. But she didn't close the door behind her. She still had things to do.

Julia watched the screen, terrified by what she had just witnessed. She saw Sarah, the little girl who had once seemed so innocent but who had just dispatched Stacey in such a brutal way, pick up her wellington boots and take them down to the garage. She plugged something Julia couldn't see properly into the wall and then shut the door.

How could such a thing have happened?

What reasons could have led her to commit such a brutal murder?

She was just a child!

Sarah, looking completely relaxed, went to the sofa where the teddy bear was waiting for her.

'Very bad, Johnny. Do I have to do everything?' she reprimanded the bear. From upstairs came the sound of Daisy's constant barks.

She held the teddy to her ear and moved his head from side to side, as if he were telling her something.

'I don't know . . . Are you sure?' she asked the bear and held him close to her ear once more.

The next thing she did was leave the teddy in his previous position and after she went to the kitchen. When she came back to the living room, the camera captured what she was holding in one hand.

It was a frying pan, so heavy that she was struggling to carry it. But she took it up the stairs, carried by a force that seemed almost supernatural.

Shortly after the puppy's barks were replaced by a low growl, then silence. When the child came back, she was dragging the inert body of the little dog, whose white front was now dyed dark red. She left her next to her owner in the middle of the garage.

Julia couldn't believe what she had seen. For the first time, she understood the suffering the young Eva Domínguez had concealed all this time. Was it any wonder she had fled and hidden from the media after what had happened?

She hadn't been fair to the girl. And she regretted more than one of her pointed remarks.

14. "I'll be back in a minute"

It's hard to believe that one's life can be taken away so easily. But it's even harder to feel the way I've felt for the last two years.

I have never been able to get those images out of my head. Hundreds of times I have woken up in the middle of a nightmare, reliving those moments again and again. So many times I have suffered Stacey's grief and pain in my own flesh, waking from my dreams to find, with a lacerating guilt, that I was still alive.

I'd lie there in bed, wherever I was, feeling guilty for not having realised what was going on, for being tricked so easily. But, above all, for being the one who was able to wake up from those nightmares.

I couldn't do anything for Stacey.

So many words remained unsaid. The laughter we'd once shared was muted by the memory of the last harsh words we'd said to each other. And I will never know if maybe, over time, we could have forgiven each other.

Could we have turned that page and become friends once again? Even though that page had been engraved with fire in my heart?

Perhaps, if I hadn't gone with Dave to that house on the other side of the mountain, Stacey would still be here. Who knows?

But I did go.

Although I didn't know it then, those videotapes we'd found in the house were tricking me. Their harsh images clouded my eyes, and I quickly removed the tape from the machine. I couldn't think clearly, and they made me forget the resentment I had begun feeling towards Yäel . . . Towards Sarah.

I listened to the wind whipping the front door against its frame and could only think about the vile things that man had done to the child.

Who in their right mind could behave that way?

'And all this time we have only . . . ' Dave trailed off, overwhelmed by the images we'd seen.

I couldn't say a word. I was feeling stupid for having doubted the girl. All those half smiles, the words she had said and what she had done . . . Was she traumatised by being raised in such a horrendous environment? After living under the same roof as that bastard? Surely, she was the one who really needed help.

But we had insisted that she had broken Stacey's vials on purpose for some dark reason. Stacey had thrown her teddy bear against a wall. The same teddy that was her only nice memory of the hard childhood she had endured. And then Daniel had slapped her when she had punctured one of the car tyres.

'God, we are so horrible. How could we have thought so badly of the girl?' I whispered, not knowing how wrong I was.

'Do you think she *mean* . . . this when she talked about adults doing bad things?' Dave asked me, analysing that moment in the forest with Sarah.

'I have no doubt at all,' I replied.

I threw one of the videotapes against the wall and slumped against the sofa cushions. Dave sat next to me, still holding the photo album. I took it from him and flipped through the pictures slowly.

It was incredible what that child had had to live through. And seeing her in the pictures looking so happy next to the real Yäel made me cry. In some of the photos, I recognised that happy smile that she had sometimes showed when she had been around me. That little face of an innocent girl who expected nothing from life except to play and fill her tummy with sweets.

And that made me think about something else.

'What about Yäel? The real one,' I clarified, looking at Dave.

'What's up with her?'

'How could she allow such abominable behaviour? She seems to have loved Sarah. You just need to look at all these pictures, at how much care she's taken to organise and label them,' I said, looking at the album in my hands.

I felt confused looking at that collection of photos. All of them happy, except the man; I understood then why he didn't have a face in any of them. Ordinary situations, like the girl planting tomatoes, playing with her kitten, drawing in her room, dressed as a witch . . .

'I don't think the woman knew,' Dave said. 'Otherwise don't you think she would had *leave* the house or reported him to the police?'

'Officer Farlane didn't tell me anything about this. He didn't even have any idea they had a child with them,' I pointed out, recalling the conversation with the police officer. 'But, then, why didn't she run away? Why didn't she take the girl with her and leave that bastard?'

Dave just looked around, his surroundings seeming to intrigue him.

'Do you think a woman would let him *lived* in a shit hole like this?'

'What do you mean?'

'I don't know, look at the state this place is in. I doubt the woman had *some* influence in the house. By the looks of it, this man is twisted.'

'Then why didn't she leave him?'

Dave got up and looked at me wide eyed.

'Do you see a woman in this house?' he asked, waving his arms at the room.

No, there was no woman to be seen. And I doubted that any woman could have lived in those conditions. But something was bugging me.

'Do you think they have left?' Dave didn't seem to understand my reasons for asking. 'Do you think anybody could live with just mouldy cheese and stale milk in the fridge?'

'So where *is* the girl come from?'

With every passing second, that question was getting harder and harder to answer.

If someone lived there, it couldn't have been long since they had left. We had found the child just three nights before. And it seemed to make sense that she had been living there. How else could we explain her appearing wearing just a nightgown and holding a teddy bear?

Cries of Blood

And once again, another big question arose. 'Where is Yäel and her husband?' I said, racking my brains. 'I don't think she would have left the child alone in the forest, no matter how bad things were. And much less in the middle of a snowstorm. This makes no sense, Dave.'

He began to pace around the living room, not bothering to dodge the objects spread across the floor. It felt as if we were in one of those films where everything seems impossible, and then all the questions are resolved in a simple and crazy way at the end of it. But neither Dave nor I could see any logical answer to what was going on there.

We felt terrified, sitting in that house straight out of a horror film. A house where a little girl had lived until we had found her.

Whatever had happened there, and whatever reason had led her to appear in the middle of the road days before, I now understood why she had been silent at first. It was normal that she hadn't spoken for a while. And it was normal too that she had been a bit weird with her answers. The girl needed serious help.

Or at least, that's what I thought then.

Not far away from where we sat, she had just murdered our friend and her puppy. And we could only think about her innocence, and her tough past. We hadn't understood the real, dark game she was playing.

Eva took a long, deep drink from her glass of water. She wiped the tears from her cheek and put her fingertips to her mouth. But she took them away again instantly, since she had no nails left to bite.

The presenter, meanwhile, was outside on the balcony. She had drawn the blinds, opened a sliding door and disappeared a moment later.

Julia had never used to smoke, but the scenes from the security cameras at the house in Guildon Forest had affected her, and now she needed a cigarette.

When Eva had first resumed her narration, Julia had been distant. She didn't seem to be there. Her face, Eva could see, had changed. She no longer had that sweet and interested smile. She was no longer taking notes as she had before. She just listened to her words, as if Eva were talking on a radio channel that no one paid much attention to. Julia couldn't take her green eyes from the plasma screen, where she was watching how the child, two years ago, had cleaned any trace of the puppy's blood from the stairs.

She didn't even show any emotion when Sarah had changed her clothes and hidden the bloodstained ones under the sofa, and later taken her time to brush out the plaits Eva had made in her hair the day before.

None of those things changed the expression on her face.

So, Eva had continued with her retelling of the events she lived through in the house near her own, on that mountain in the north of Scotland. She didn't know if Julia was really listening to her, or if she should stop and ask her if she was alright.

In a way, she knew that anybody who heard her words or watched those videos would end up in the same state as Julia.

Eva had not fled to the south of Spain because it pleased her. She had not left behind her life, her family and friends because she wanted to: it had been the most traumatic experience of her life. Her story was difficult to tell and to make others, including herself, believe it; but fortunately, she had the footage recorded by the security cameras as proof.

It would take Julia time to process those scenes, so Eva kept telling her version of what she had seen and lived, until the woman looked her in the eyes and she knew that it was time for her to stop.

'I need a cigarette . . . Sam?' she called her husband.

Sam, who didn't look any better than Julia, threw her a pack of cigarettes. And as she stood on the balcony, he turned off the cameras, lights, plasma screen and the microphones that the two of them wore under their dresses. Then he disappeared through the side door out of the office.

Eva did not know what to do or say. She tried to relax in her red chair. She looked out of the window again, towards the London Eye. And she wished she were far away from there. Away from that uncomfortable situation, from the kind of silence that had given her so many headaches in the past.

'Are you ok?' she asked Julia.

She had waited for the woman to finish her cigarette and say something. But when she'd finished and threw it over the balustrade, she lit a new one. And one more after that.

'I can't understand how you've been able to live all this time with all of this inside your head,' Julia spoke from the balcony.

'Well, I've done my best. I had no other option but to live with it and try to move on with my life. But the continuous lies in the press, all those headlines and the pictures of me in the newspapers–'

'I understand,' Julia said, taking a last puff on her cigarette.

She closed the sliding door behind her and stood there, seeming not to know what to do or say. She went over to her desk and sat down. She didn't say a word.

Eva saw that her face was emotionless. She sat in silence, looking around her office without really seeing anything.

'I'm sorry for all I have done.'

'What do you mean?' Eva asked her, not understanding.

'Well, you know, the way I hounded you. My trips to Spain, trying to find you. All of those headlines caught my attention. I spoke to my old boss and we reached an agreement for a future TV special . . . This one . . . So, I began looking for you.'

She gave a reticent look at the young girl and raked her shaky hands through her blonde hair.

'I went to your grandparents' house, in Almería,' she continued, 'thinking that you would be staying there. I had spoken with your mother a few days before, since I had interviewed her for one of my programmes in the past. We weren't friends; we had just seen each other more than once since then. She answered some of my questions, and I learned enough to understand that you were in the south of Spain. And, after some research, I found out where your grandparents lived.

'That's how I ended up at their house,' Julia continued, while the girl listened intently. 'My Spanish is horrible, so my conversation with them was pretty pathetic. Nevertheless, I got them to tell me that you were nearby. I asked around, and several people swore they'd seen you. And then one day, entirely by chance, I saw you myself.

'I went to a beautiful beach that day. I don't remember the name. Something about "los muertos".'

Eva's eyes widened. She knew exactly which beach Julia was talking about: she had often gone with her family to Playa de los Muertos, the Beach of the Dead. And she remembered pictures of her appearing in the newspapers across the continent, taken while she was there.

'Yes, Eva, I'm sorry: I couldn't help myself. I saw you so relaxed, that I couldn't believe it. I learned that it was a nudist beach, although you were one of the few people wearing a bikini that day. At first, I thought it was a mirage, that it couldn't be you. But then I looked more closely and saw that it was you . . . I took some pictures and then I showed them to my boss.'

Eva didn't say anything. What was there to say?

On the one hand, she knew that Julia had only been doing her job in finding her, and that she'd done it well. But on the other hand, she couldn't understand *why* she had done it. Right after those pictures were published, the international press invaded her grandparents' street, following them to the market and wherever else they went. And Eva had fled from the hotel where she was staying, not knowing who had betrayed her.

Despite her gifts, letters and solicitous calls, Eva had not realised that it was Julia who was to blame for the press who had searched for her like hungry hyenas.

Now she knew.

'It's ok,' Eva said, however. She saw the surprise in the woman's face and added, 'After all, if it wasn't you someone else would have done it. When that happened, I finally realised that this story would follow me all my life unless I confronted it. That's why I accepted your offer, Julia.

'People wonder what happened in that house. And it doesn't matter who you are or where you're from: people are nosy by nature. We all prefer to ignore our own problems and spend our time talking about other people's. But hardly anyone ever thinks about the pain they are causing.'

She fell silent for a moment, got up from her seat and went over to the window.

'Have you ever heard of "Chinese whispers"? It's a kid's game where children sit in a circle or line, the first one whispers a word or a sentence into the ear of the next boy or girl, and so on.' Julia nodded and looked at her confused. 'It's got different names all around the world. But it's the same game. When the round finishes, the last person to listen to the word or sentence says what he or she thinks they've heard. But the result is always much different to what was said originally. And that's how people have distorted this story, one by one; they have been passing along what they believe they've heard, and for every day that has passed, the story has been transformed into something completely untrue.

'One day I was in a shop at my grandparents' village,' Eva recalled, 'when a couple of women from the area recognised me. They knew my family well. However, they'd never bothered to ask them what had happened. Instead, they listened to the stories other people were telling about me. And I managed to hear what they were whispering to each other, how I had been arrested by the British police for killing a child.'

The plasma screen was playing the security videos from the living room again.

Sitting on the sofa, with her teddy bear, was Sarah. She looked calm, as if nothing had happened.

Julia watched how the child played with the teddy, talking to him and placing the bear's mouth to her ear. She made up her own conversation with him. She would answer him and pretend that the teddy was talking to her.

A few minutes later, still unmoved by what she had done, she stopped. Something or someone was making a strange noise outside. A noise that, closer to the front door, the camera's microphone succeeded in picking up.

It was Daniel, who entered the house looking forlorn.

His hair was covered with snow. He was limping and there were several tears in his trousers. He left the bicycle by the door. The chain was hanging down, swinging next to the rear wheel.

Daniel stopped a few steps in, realising the little girl was looking straight at him from the sofa, saying nothing. It seemed as if he was trying to ignore her as he went to the fireplace.

'For fuck's sake,' he could be heard saying as he opened the front of the wood-burner and threw more logs inside.

His hands were stiff from the cold, almost blue. But he was able to light the fire again.

He sat near the glass door, staring at the back of the child's head. He was looking at her with suspicious eyes. Whatever Mrs McGregor had told him, it hadn't been good.

Once his hands had recovered their natural colour and the snow on his hair had melted away, Daniel went upstairs.

Sarah had resolutely ignored him and kept playing with her teddy. This time, her conversation with the bear was muted. Words didn't come out of her mouth, but her expression was eloquent. When she heard the boy going slowly up the stairs, she turned her head to watch him disappear.

A tiny smile, but big enough for the camera to perceive it, lifted the corners of her lips. And she remained there in absolute silence, enjoying the crackling of the fire, looking towards the stairs.

A minute later, she began to play again. Daniel was coming down the steps.

'Where are Stacey and the dog?'

It wasn't a question; it was a demand. Daniel's voice sounded threatening.

'They went out for a walk,' the little girl answered, not taking her eyes off Johnny.

On the other side of the mountain, Dave and I were arguing about why two adults would have left a little girl alone in the forest, in the middle of a horrendous snowstorm.

'Ok, let's just say that Yäel was still living in the house and that she hadn't *take* away the girl with her,' Dave was saying, eager to solve the enigma. 'Maybe she did not know that *his* husband was abusing Sarah.'

'With all these videotapes around in the living room?' I objected.

'Then she *know* everything and allowed it? No, Eva, she couldn't have known; or at least, she didn't want to say anything about it. Maybe he was not the only one who was out of his mind,' the boy suggested.

'That's not the problem, Dave,' I protested. 'The question is, where are they? Why have they left the house, leaving the TV and the lights on? Assuming that they left not long ago and that they're supposed to be back soon, why haven't they reported the child missing? It's obvious the woman loves her. I don't think they would have abandoned her to her fate.'

'Why is it that they are not back? It is too late to plant tomatoes at this time of night,' the boy joked, trying and failing to imitate an English accent.

I smiled for the first time in a long while. 'I don't know Dave . . . I have no idea!'

However we tried, we couldn't put two and two together. We were going in circles like fools, repeating ourselves.

I looked at the room, practically destroyed except for the TV. It was the only thing that had escaped the hands of whoever had made all that mess.

'I think we should go back to my house,' I said in a low voice. I was tired, freezing cold and my ankle was bothering me.

'Yes, you are right. But I plan to interrogate that girl. There'll be no more of her *hide* her name or her parents' whereabouts,' Dave said angrily.

I grabbed my shoulder bag from next to the sofa and turned off the TV. I zipped my coat all the way up; I hadn't taken it off as it was nearly as cold inside as out.

'God, Dave, it's really dark,' I said, looking out of the window.

Night had fully fallen on the mountain without us noticing. I didn't even know how long we had been inside. Dave had run out of battery on his phone, so we would have to walk blindly through the forest. And although the moon was shining, I doubted we were going to be able to find our way easily without a torch.

Dave began opening drawers around the house, but he didn't find anything that would help us see in the dark. He disappeared out of the living room for half a minute and came back with a big, round, silver object in his hands.

'What's that?'

He didn't answer, just pressed a button on the object and the next thing I knew a powerful light was blinding me.

'I think it *work*,' Dave joked, holding the flashlight towards me.

I smiled again. Only he could make me smile even in a situation like that.

Cries of Blood

But I got serious again at the thought of going back with that child. Although she had lived through tough experiences, she had been a pain in the ass. And I was still determined to go home the next day.

But of course, that plan was doomed to failure.

As we were about one step from the front door, we heard a noise coming from the kitchen. A thud.

'What was that?' Dave shouted, scared, grabbing me by the arm.

I shook him off. I was scared too, but he looked like a frightened schoolgirl.

I approached the kitchen slowly. I didn't know what could have made that noise. There were only the two of us in the house.

Or was there someone else after all?

The thought of it gave me goose bumps. My heart was pounding, sending the blood rushing through my body. Every nerve was taut.

'Eva? Where are you going . . . ? Let's get out of here,' Dave was whispering behind me.

But I ignored him. And I believe that's why I'm alive today.

I went into the kitchen to discover it just as we had left it. But before I came back out, we again heard the noise that had attracted our attention, this time louder and longer.

It was coming from behind a door we had failed to notice before, covered by a curtain. I drew it back and saw that water seeped under the door. I grabbed the handle and . . .

It happened in a flash.

Whatever was making the noise, suddenly stopped.

I glanced back at Dave then twisted the handle.

'I don't think we should go in,' he mumbled.

'Oh, shut up and give me that, little girl,' I reprimanded him, taking the flashlight from his hands.

I opened the door and discovered stairs leading down to a basement. And I also discovered why the house hadn't flooded.

The water that swamped the kitchen floor had seeped under the door, running down the steps, and making my tentative feet splash through the puddles that had formed.

I went down the steps one by one, a feeling of dread inside me.

Dave followed behind, holding onto the strap of my shoulder bag, scared to death. I knew he hated dark, enclosed spaces, and the state the house was in wasn't helping his nerves.

After a dozen steps, I stopped, suddenly realising my boots were under water. The flashlight helped us see that the water had flooded the basement high enough to reach our hips, so we didn't go down any further.

A fetid, musty smell hung in the air.

And there was something else. Something that struck me with its corrupted stench as soon as I took that last step down the stairs.

One second.

That was how long it took me to see everything.

The light from the flashlight burnt the air engulfed in the dark. I swept it from side to side, lighting up the flooded basement. And at the far end . . .

The most horrible thing I had ever seen in my entire life.

Daniel had prepared a hot cup of tea and was taking small sips. He didn't seem to care that it was almost scalding. He suppressed several shudders of pain, but he kept drinking.

He tried to ignore the child as long as he could, instead glancing sadly at the Christmas tree with the still unopened presents under its branches. But some primitive instinct wouldn't let him trust Sarah. He kept throwing murderous looks in her direction. And after ten minutes and another cup of hot tea, he couldn't restrain himself anymore.

'Where are Stacey and Daisy?' he asked again, raising his voice.

Sarah jumped in her seat and turned around. She shrugged and got up from the sofa. In her hands she held Johnny tightly.

'They went for a walk,' she said, not very convincing now.

'I don't believe you.'

'It's the truth.'

'Liar! Where are they? I don't think Stacey would leave you home alone. You might disgust her, but she would never do that,' the boy said vehemently. He added, 'And much less after all you've done.'

The girl didn't answer him. She had her back to the camera.

'Don't you look at me like that!' Daniel snapped at her, moving towards her menacingly. 'I don't believe you at all.'

'Why?' the girl's voice was trembling, her tone innocent.

'You tell me,' he said. 'Maybe you could start by telling me your real name.'

'My name's Yäel–'

'Liar! That's not your name!' the boy shouted, losing control. He glared at her, waiting for her to say something else. But she didn't say a word, just stood right where she was without moving an inch.

Daniel tried to calm down. He seemed to be thinking about something before he said, 'If you don't want to talk, that's fine. When Eva and Dave come back from their walk, they'll probably have your family with them.'

Then, the girl let her arms to fall on her sides, placing her teddy bear on the glass coffee table. It made a louder noise than one would expect.

'Where have they gone?' she asked.

Daniel looked at her with a wide smile.

'You know where. The path you refused to walk along earlier,' he added, his voice deliberately harsh.

The girl sat back down again, her back to Daniel. She placed Johnny on her lap and smiled.

'Oh, that one. So have they gone to my house, then?' She asked the question as if it was the most normal thing in the world.

'Is that where you live? On the other side of the forest?'

'You tell me, Daniel. It seems you know more than you're saying.'

The boy noticed the child's adult tone. 'So help me, you're not going to spend another moment in this house.'

He grabbed his coat and put it back on quickly. He took his scarf and gloves. Then he handed the girl her coat and looked around for her boots.

Julia guessed what the girl was about to say a moment before she said it.

'If you're looking for my wellies, they're down in the garage.'

'Go on then, what are you waiting for? Go and get them,' he shouted.

'I'm scared. Could you come down with me?'

But the girl's frightened tone didn't fool Julia. She knew what was going through the child's mind.

Daniel opened the door, turned on the light and began walking down the steps to the garage.

Meanwhile, Sarah rushed back to where she had left Johnny on the sofa.

'I'll be back in a minute,' she said.

The plasma screen now showed the footage from the garage. In there the fluorescent light flickered softly.

And it was not long before Julia covered her mouth with her hands, suffocating a scream.

It happened fast.

As soon as the ceiling light illuminated the room, Daniel froze between the boxes of junk. He'd been searching for the girl's wellington boots in the dark. But what he wasn't expecting to find was a trail of blood on the floor. A trail that led his eyes to the two inert lumps in the centre of the room.

A tangle of red hair covered in blood contrasted with white fur. The frosted figure of the young girl lay next to her dog. Stacey's face, covered in the mixture of makeup, had frozen, contorted in pain and suffering.

When Daniel tried to turn around, it was far too late . . .

Cries of Blood

His face twisted in a grimace of pain. Something was piercing his back like ice, fast and lacerating. He groaned, the noise of a wounded animal.

He fell to the floor, trying to reach his back with his hands. On his knees, he turned to find the child in front of him. In her hands she held the nail gun.

'You will never be able to hurt anyone again, Daniel,' she said, and raised it in the air.

Another cruel nail in his chest.

The boy rolled on the floor, his own blood mingling with the trail of the dog's. His body shook in spasms and his arms trembled furiously. A primitive howl came from his throat.

The noise made Julia's hair stand on end. She covered her eyes and stopped looking at the screen, where the child shot over ten more nails into the boy. And his howls began to fade.

When she opened her eyes again, she watched the little girl closing the garage door. Then she put on her boots and sat next to the teddy bear.

'I told you I was going to be back in a minute, don't tell me off,' she told Johnny. 'But I'm afraid you'll have to be brave . . . Yes, I have to leave you here . . . I promise I'll be back for you soon . . . I promise, I won't leave you alone for too long . . . I don't know, Johnny . . . As soon as it's over, we'll go . . . '

She got up and started to walk towards the door. But she turned again and picked up the teddy bear.

'Don't you think you've forgotten something? I need it, Johnny.' She looked at the bear sharply for an instant and then smiled. 'Thank you, you're always good to me.' She kissed him on the cheek and flipped him over.

Her back was to the camera, so at first Julia couldn't see what she was doing. A second later, she watched the girl throw the bear onto the sofa and turn around.

It was then that Julia understood.

The child had taken something from inside the teddy bear, something that had been hidden from the others the whole time. The same thing that, a minute earlier, had made the teddy thud hard against the glass coffee table. The same thing that, days before, had made a heavier sound as it crashed against the wall when Stacey had thrown it after Sarah had broken her insulin vials.

She strained to see what the girl was holding in her hands. When Sarah was close enough to the door and the camera, at last she was able to make it out.

The child was holding a gun.

Not a nail gun. A real one.

15. "Cries of blood"

We both gagged at the sight; but we weren't able to move. We just stood there, our feet in the freezing water.

I remember that moment, unfortunately, as if it were yesterday. The horror was indescribable; I felt as if I were going to stay in that basement for the rest of my life. As if I would never have the strength to walk, talk, feel, love, smile again.

It was very cold. We were at the threshold of what looked like hell. A different hell from the one we were used to hearing or reading about, closer than we had ever imagined. There were no winged demons surrounded by fire here. Instead it was a place of icy cold, a cold that was both physical and emotional.

Death.

That horrifying face nobody wants to see but that, right then, we were forced to look at directly. At least I had the comfort of not being alone. I could feel Dave next to me. He was seeing the same thing I was.

The light of the flashlight remained cruelly fixed on a corpse.

We found out later that the body belonged to the real Yaël. Then, all we knew was that it had been left tied to a chair, slightly upright, held by a mouldy rope coiled around it.

The woman was dressed in a simple dress with a pattern of blue flowers. Or at least that's what I remember. Maybe it was another colour. Maybe it didn't have flowers at all.

But I do remember other gruesome details.

Dave and I saw with horror how the head hung backwards, the neck cut from side to side. It was like being in an autopsy class for forensic students, a class we hadn't signed up for. And yet we stood there staring, seeing how the blood had coagulated around the neck. How the arteries dangled from her flesh, filled with worms that wriggled in the light of the flashlight.

The body, in an advanced state of decomposition, was at the far end of the room. The wall behind it was spattered with blood and small lumps of something slimy.

That can't be, I thought at first.

The woman had surely been murdered by those deep cuts to her neck, made by a furious hand. How could it be that the wall had ended up covered with splashes of blood? What were those slimy things that had slid from the top all the way to the surface of the water?

It was then that I saw a rat. It was on a shelf unit, near a small window. It had succeeded in climbing up the side of the furniture to the top and was running away from the beam of the flashlight I had trained on it. Above the level of the water protruded a metal bin with a pile of books and other objects scattered on it. The rat must have knocked them from the shelf to the bin.

I guessed that must had been the noise we had heard.

'Oh, my God,' Dave gasped.

He had stopped grabbing me, but still gripped the strap of my shoulder bag between his fingers. Only the constant retching caused by the scene in the basement made him let go and place his hands over his face.

The stench made it impossible for us not to cover our noses.

'Let's get out of here,' he said.

'Wait,' I told him. I had moved the flashlight from the woman's body to the rat, which had escaped through the window. And although God knew all I wanted was to get out of there, there was still something drawing my attention.

All that blood over the wall had to have come from somewhere. But it couldn't have been from the woman's neck; I saw now that her dress was almost unstained by any blood.

I moved the flashlight, directing the beam across the other walls and the water.

And there against the wall, nearby to the woman's body, was the husband.

Somehow, his face wasn't as shocking as hers. His skin was a bluish hue, and he was wearing an expression of . . .

Horror?

Surprise?

Panic?

Pain?

Whatever his last feeling had been, his expression had frozen in a hideous grin. A trickle of blood had run down his swollen face, and in the centre of his forehead there was a hole. The last drops of blood had slowly coagulated around it. His eyes were still open.

I will never forget those eyes. Blue irises, but with veins as red as the blood all over his face. Cruel eyes filled with fury.

'Who–?'

'What–?'

'How–?'

When I rested the light on the body, we saw another rat on the man's lap. It jumped off as the light hit it, surrounded by a swarm of flies. It landed on a pile of rubbish and nimbly ran up the shelf unit. It didn't give us another glance, but ran through the broken windowpanes near the ceiling.

My hands shook violently as I tried to steady the light over the two bodies. I could see the bloodied knife, with which the man had sliced the woman's neck, shining between the nervous beams of light like a small diamond drawing all my attention.

'Eva . . . please . . . let's get out of here,' Dave stammered, pulling at my arm.

I felt the basement vanished beneath my feet. Dave pulled me out, while I could only groan and retch. He took me to the living room, but I couldn't see anything. I had the image of the two corpses stuck on my retinas. And I knew then that I would never forget their faces.

'Give me the *number telephone* . . . Give me the number. Eva, give me the *number telephone*,' I heard Dave shouting at me, shaking me from side to side, trying to wake me from that nightmare.

I looked at him confused, not knowing what he meant. Dave was the only one who had a phone on him and it was out of battery. He knew that. Who was he expecting to call? But he kept shaking me, pausing now and then to cough to one side.

'Eva, please, give me the police officer's number,' Dave repeated.

And finally, I remembered officer Tom Farlane.

He had told me to call him at any time, and I had promised I'd do so as soon as I found anything. He was the only one who could do anything about what had happened in that house of terror. So, I rummaged through my bag to find the number, still trembling from head to toe.

I found it and handed it to Dave, who ran to one side of the living room, where there was a telephone on the floor. It was disconnected and Dave, trembling too, plugged the cable into the socket and picked up the handset.

'It *work*,' he said, not believing our luck.

I went to the kitchen, not really knowing what I was doing. I scanned the dirty plates and found what until that moment I hadn't realised I was looking for: a long, bright and almost clean knife, shining amongst the cutlery. I rushed to fetch it and went back to the living room.

Dave stared at me, startled. He looked me up and down and fixed his eyes on the knife I was holding tight in my hand.

'What are you doing with–?'

'Daniel and Stacey are with that girl,' I shouted. He looked back at me, not understanding. 'Dave, there's no one here. And that man has been shot in the forehead.'

He understood then, with no need for more words.

There was no other explanation for what we had seen. The man's brains were spread all over the basement wall. A man who had only a knife like the one I was holding in my hands. Not a gun. And if he'd ever had a gun, why would he have cut his wife's throat?

No, the girl had shot him.

How did it happen?

That's a story that was buried the day the couple gave their last death rattles. No one but the girl would ever know what had really happened in that basement.

'What are you waiting for? Call!' I shouted at Dave, who picked up the officer's telephone number and began dialling it. 'Not the police; call my house!'

He stammered something unintelligible. I told him to calm down and breathe. When he had half-controlled himself, he explained he didn't know my house telephone number, so I gave it to him. He dialled it and placed the phone to his ear, shaking.

'They don't pick up,' he told me with frightened eyes.

We finally knew Sarah's secrets. We knew where and with whom she had lived, and that their dead bodies now lay in the basement of her house. She had nothing more to conceal; at least, not from us.

'Keep calling until they pick up the phone! Stay here; I'm going back to the house. If they don't pick up, call Tom Farlane and ask him to come immediately.'

I ran out the door, with the flashlight illuminating every step I took on the snow. I could still see the corpses' faces between each flash of the light. I forced myself to concentrate. I ignored my painful ankle. I had no time for distractions or rest.

I ran as fast as I could. I didn't care about falling more than once, stumbling over the treacherous, hidden branches or sliding off over stones covered in snow. I kept running. That was the only thing I could do.

I had no idea what awaited me at the house. I could only hope that Daniel and Stacey were ok. I thought I would never forgive myself for having left them alone with the girl if something bad had happened to them.

And that's exactly how it turned out.

I have never forgiven myself for leaving them alone. But maybe that was what saved my life.

That girl had been playing with us. Intentionally or not, she had set us all against each other. We would never have argued that much if she hadn't been there. And perhaps I would never have found out about Daniel's infidelity; but I would have preferred that to what happened.

Now I can say that the girl didn't break Stacey's insulin vials on purpose – at least not the first ones, because she didn't have a clue what they were. If she'd broken Stacey's makeup instead, it wouldn't have had such a dramatic result.

However, no matter how bright she was, she shouldn't have punctured the car tyre. She had practically revealed herself to us. But today I think I understand her reasons.

She had been spying on us. She had heard our conversation in the kitchen. She knew that it was meant to be our last night in my mother's house and that we were about to find a way to get out of there and get rid of her.

But Sarah wasn't interested in us leaving.

Her deranged mind was enjoying making us argue with each other. Whatever had happened in the basement of her house, it had left its mark on her. Even though she had acted like an innocent little girl around me, that wasn't what she was now. She would never again be a little girl, much less innocent.

But my mind was blocked. I couldn't think how to tie up the loose ends. Instead, I was busy praying for my two "friends" to be in one piece. I was forcing myself onwards, desperate to get to the house as fast as possible.

Then, after one or two minutes running between the trees, I stumbled for the last time. The flashlight fell near me, still working, and the knife slipped from my hands and landed a few steps beyond where I had fallen.

Cries of Blood

I couldn't get up. My ankle was burning like a demon under my trousers. I had felt the pain and heard the faint, unpleasant cracking noise as I ran, but I hadn't cared. I had been obsessed with reaching the house: Daniel and Stacey were more important than my damned ankle.

But now I lay there gasping. With the snow under my body, the cold overtook me. I couldn't move. My arms, neck, legs, chest . . . my whole body was tired, tensed, aching; and yet I almost couldn't feel it through the chill of the snow.

A beam of light from the flashlight shone on the bracelet on my wrist, the one Dave had given me. And I thought of him. God knew what I would have done if it had been him in the house with the little girl.

'Eva, stand up,' I told myself.

I forced myself to get up. I couldn't let anything happen to my friends. No matter how dishonest they had been with me, nothing bad could happen to them. We would have time to talk about all of this like adults. I couldn't afford to lose two more people. Not after going through a dark time with my dad's death.

My dad.

I felt as if his voice spoke into my ear. I know it may sound ridiculous, but that's how it happened. I remembered his voice, so loving and sweet. He had always had a smile for me, even during the last days of his life. Now, he helped me to get up, despite the lacerating pain I was feeling. It wasn't only my ankle that was hurting, but my entire body. I grabbed the knife, hobbled towards the flashlight and . . .

Then I heard it.

A noise, reverberating among the treetops. It froze me more effectively than all the snow on the mountain. I opened my eyes wide, looking about me in all directions.

A few seconds passed, but there was not another sound. The owl that had frightened us before had stopped hooting. There were no more creaking branches or snow falling from the top of the trees, loosened by the wind. There wasn't even a breeze to whistle between the treetops. It was as if everything had frozen. As if we had all agreed to wait in silence.

And I heard it again. A gunshot, coming from behind me. It was as if it had landed just a few feet away from me. But even in my sudden panic, I knew that nothing had touched me. That shot had come from a long way off.

I turned quickly, understanding the situation at once. I didn't need any more time to know that the shot had come from the place I'd just left: the home of Sarah and her grandparents. That house that until that night I'd had no knowledge of.

'Dave!' I screamed with every ounce of air that filled my lungs.

I clutched the knife, cutting myself with its sharp edge. But I didn't care. My body renewed itself by a supernatural force. It didn't matter that I ached, that I was tired and cold. Whatever had happened in that house, Dave was facing it alone.

I had left him alone.

I started running again. I followed my footprints, one after another, making my way back to the house. I hadn't got far, so it didn't take me long; but those seconds seemed like decades. Seconds in which Dave's life could be at risk. And when I saw the house at the end of that path, it seemed to approach me instead of the other way around.

I was blind with panic. I felt divided, as if I had to take care of all my friends. After all, they were in this because of me. I had made them come to Guildon Forest, and now Daniel and Stacey were at the other side of the forest, while Dave was in that gloomy house. I hadn't doubted for a moment that I should go to help him.

It wasn't a choice.

That gunshot couldn't be ignored.

Was there any chance that Dave had found the weapon with which the man had been murdered in the basement? Had he picked it up and, by accident, taken a shot? Not just once, but twice?

Cries of Blood

But I think you already know who was holding the gun. Just think about the fear I felt then. In front of that grim house, with the yellowish light illuminating the snow beneath the window. With two corpses in its basement.

There was no one outside. I turned off the flashlight. The exterior of the house looked just as gloomy as when I had left it. I approached slowly, then stopped for a second and counted to ten. My hands and legs trembled, but I pushed the door and went in quietly. If it was Dave holding the gun, I didn't want him to shoot me unintentionally.

Inside was just as I had left it as well – except for one important detail.

Dave wasn't in the living room.

I saw the piece of paper where I had written the police officer's telephone number. The phone was still in the corner, but it hadn't been put back properly on its base. I got closer and placed it to my ear. I could only hear a soft beeping: someone had hung up the call from the other side. I put the phone back down and picked up the piece of paper.

Where was Dave?

It didn't take me long to find out. I heard him crying a few moments later, and followed the sound of his sobs. That shocked me, since I had never seen him cry. Dave was a strong guy, and although now and again he complained, he never cried despite the bad times he'd endured. So, I followed the sound of his mourning from the living room to the kitchen. I could hear him much better there.

His cries were coming from the basement. Someone had turned the light on down there, and the light spilled dimly into the kitchen.

I went down the stairs slowly, trying not to make a noise.

'Don't move.'

For a split second, Sarah's voice froze the blood in my veins. I stopped moving. I thought she was talking to me.

'I told you not to move.'

No, she wasn't talking to me.

I took another step down the stairs, trying not to splash too much. One by one, I went down the steps as quietly as I could.

At the bottom of the stairs I saw Sarah, holding a gun in her hands. It was visibly too heavy for her tiny body, because she was resting it against her chest.

'Please, put the gun down. I beg you, please. I haven't *do* anything to you,' Dave was crying.

'Really, you haven't done anything? Why did you have to come here?! Why did you have to come to my house?!'

'We wanted . . . to find your . . . parents,' he could hardly force out the words to reply to her, making a horrible noise with his blocked nose.

'"*We* wanted"? Where the hell is your dear friend Eva?'

Her voice sounded completely different. She was no longer the sweet and friendly little girl I had first met. I couldn't understand why she had changed so drastically; and much less why she was pronouncing my name with such contempt.

I went down another step, approaching closer and closer behind her back. I couldn't see her face, but I knew that soon Dave would see me, and I was afraid he would betray me with his eyes. But he was too smart for that and kept his expression just the same.

'No . . . She . . . is coming with the police.'

'Excuse me?'

'She is coming with the police. She *go* to the village and . . . she called me and said that the police is coming.'

For a moment I didn't understand what he was saying. The police weren't with me, unfortunately. But a second later I understood what he was doing.

Dave had seen my boots coming slowly down the stairs. And at the same time that he was trying to distract the little girl, he was sending me a sign. It could only mean he had managed to contact Tom Farlane and that the police officer was on his way to the house.

'Liar!' Sarah snapped at him, nonetheless.

'It is . . . true.'

'No, it's a lie and you know it is. Don't try fooling me. I saw that bitch running through the forest. Anyone could have seen her with the flashlight she was holding . . . And you know what? She wasn't with anyone; she was alone.'

Those words struck me deeply. During all the time I had been around Sarah I had never heard her swear. I wasn't even sure she knew what that word meant; she must have heard it during my argument with Stacey. But above all, what struck me most was that she had seen me running through the forest but I hadn't seen her. She must have been hiding among the trees, waiting for me to leave.

Sarah took the gun from her chest and held it in the air, her small arms shaking under its weight.

'Please, don't *shot* me.'

'I'm sorry, Dave, but your girlfriend must be getting her best Christmas present ever, very far away from here. And you . . . ' She began laughing, the same way she had done when I was arguing with Daniel and Stacey. 'You, lovely Dave, are going to die.'

'No . . . please . . . I *do* whatever you want, but please don't kill me . . . ' Dave sobbed, splashing noisily at the water.

The roof of the corridor vanished from my sight as I took a final step, and I saw the room in full. I didn't care anymore about the corpses, their blue flesh surrounded by blood. What mattered to me was seeing my friend's face as he begged for his life.

I will never forget it. I have never seen anyone beg as fervently as he did that day. Kneeling on the floor, the water up to his chest and his hands together, raised in front of his face.

Anyone would pray to God in a situation like that, even Dave, who was an atheist like me. And yet there he was, begging like a little boy. His face was covered with tears and mucus.

'No, it's too late for you. You came and saw what you shouldn't have. Was it too difficult to stay with Eva and the rest of us like a happy family?'

'But we aren't family. This is – was – your family,' the boy cried, pointing behind him.

Dave knelt just between the two bodies, just inches away and surrounded by flies.

'Yes, you are right. But do you see that man?' Sarah asked Dave, who nodded and wiped away the tears that rolled down his cheeks. 'That man was bad. And like him, you are going to pay for being naughty . . . '

I couldn't delay it any longer. If I waited a split second more, Dave was going to die. I didn't even bother with the rest of the steps; I jumped with the knife in my hand and landed on the girl, who turned her face just as our bodies collided.

One shot.

One elbow.

The knife slipping from my hands.

My body submerged underwater.

I let out a scream, drowned under the freezing water. The air bubbled from my mouth as the girl hit me in the face with something. I groped beneath the water for the knife, gasping for breath.

I could not let anything to happen to Dave. Not while I had the power to save him.

But the fetid air in the basement was making me nauseous, not letting me breathe. Depriving me of fresh oxygen. Taking away my sense of time, of north and south and up and down, while our bodies clashed underwater. In seconds I had no choice but to give up on trying to recover the knife.

My head burst to the surface and my eyes fixed on one of the pieces of furniture floating around us. On it lay the gun, which the girl had been holding just seconds before, waiting for one of us to claim it.

I hit the girl's back with the flashlight, making her squeal in pain.

I don't really know what happened next. All I remember is running out the front door towards the forest one more time. I was dragging Dave behind me by one arm, while he in turn was howling in pain and could only follow me like an automaton. I hardly let him take a step at a time.

'Come on, Dave, run,' I urged him, shaking from head to toe. Our clothes were soaked by the water and the icy air of the December night was stabbing every part of our bodies with its sharp teeth, making us shiver and stumble. But we had to get away as fast as possible.

That was our only chance. The chance to live. To get out of that house and tell someone what had happened.

'I can't, I can't, Eva . . . I'm going to die,' Dave babbled, trying to catch his breath.

He was weak, practically fainting. I turned to look at him and didn't like what I saw.

His face was not only white as paper, but splashed with his own blood. I looked down and saw his coat was covered in it, and it was increasing by the second. It was then that I discovered the reason for his howls.

'Oh, my God,' I whispered. He had been shot in the arm.

I grabbed the uninjured arm and pulled him on. He was too heavy for me and yet I ran and ran, desperate. I needed to find a place where I could take a look at his wound.

Another shot behind our backs.

A supernatural fear invaded my heart. It throbbed as it has never done since, forcing the adrenalin around my body and giving me the strength to somehow keep moving.

I turned into the forest, still following our earlier footprints.

'*Light* . . . Turn it off . . . ' Dave said, his voice becoming weaker every moment.

The little girl had said she'd seen me running through the forest. The flashlight would let her follow us again. So, I turned it off and we were at the mercy of the timid moonlight, which dimly lit our way.

When we had been running for maybe two or three minutes, almost stumbling every two steps, I looked back. I couldn't see nor hear a trace of the girl anywhere. I let Dave sit down for a moment, his body shivering and his teeth chattering.

'Come on, Dave, calm down. Everything's going to be alright.'

I was rather saying the words to myself. The boy was half unconscious, his breathing shallow and holding a shaky hand to his wounded shoulder. I took off my belt and removed his coat.

'Ok, ok, I'm not going to hurt you,' I promised, being extra careful as I drew his bad arm out of the sleeve of his coat.

The jumper he was wearing, once grey, was now dark with blood. I asked him to cover his mouth and clench his teeth. We couldn't afford any noise. It was enough that we had stopped: with each second we were sitting there the girl was getting a step closer.

I uncovered his arm as well as I could, trying not to make him cry out in pain. I moved his arm an inch at a time, and he groaned in agony. But the noise wasn't loud enough to reveal our position. Even so, I didn't want to risk another minute taking a thorough look at the wound, so I placed my belt around his arm and tightened it as much as I could.

'There you go, Dave, keep breathing. I'll get you to the doctor soon and . . .'

I couldn't say anything else. I didn't want to lie to him. I couldn't promise something I didn't know I could ever do. At least I could prevent him from bleeding to death with the belt around his arm. Now we had to get to the house and call for help from there.

'Dave, wake up,' I whispered, slapping him on the face. He looked back at me with feverish eyes, his strength fading with each word I was saying. 'Tom Farlane. Did you get to talk with him?'

He seemed not to understand me for a second. As I was about to repeat the question, he raised his face and said, 'Yes . . . The police . . . is coming. But the girl *shoot* me . . . I don't know what he *say*.'

'Come on, get up.'

I covered him with his coat, although I didn't think it would make any difference. He wasn't any drier than me, so I grabbed him again and placed his good arm over my shoulders, pulling him to his feet.

Cries of Blood

This time I wanted to be smarter and not follow the same set of footprints.

Another shot, random I guessed, echoed in the forest. A bird that had been resting on a treetop flew into the air not far away from us. That meant that Sarah couldn't be too far behind. Young as she was, the damned girl had taken advantage of those seconds we had stopped.

I pulled Dave along behind me.

We passed near the clearing surrounded by the circle of rocks and carefully crossed the frozen stream. Still, we slipped and fell on the ice. We didn't stop for long, but it was long enough to realise that Dave was leaving a trail of blood behind him.

I felt him growing weaker, barely able to hold his head up. He groped his way forwards, struggling to overcome his inertia. He followed my steps, which weren't very precise due to the poor visibility. The treetops hid the moon almost entirely. Everything was covered by that bleak darkness, but I couldn't take the risk of turning on the flashlight.

Not this time.

'You are going to die.' We heard the girl's voice not far away.

I couldn't turn my head. In the dark we heard another shot hit the trunk of a tree not far from us.

The house wasn't much further on. Perhaps one minute more and we would be there.

'Come on, Dave, run!' I shouted at him now, desperate.

I couldn't let him die. I couldn't let the girl catch up with us. We had to keep our distance, as it was clear she didn't have a good aim with the gun (although her grandfather, the man we had found shot in the forehead, might have disagreed with that if he'd been in a position to express an opinion). If she got close, it would be easy for her to hit us, but not if we were several feet away.

I didn't know how much long I could keep running. My strength was vanishing and Dave's weight on my side was increasing. He was leaning on the same leg that had my ankle screaming beneath me. I wouldn't be able to ignore it for much longer.

'Few more seconds, few more seconds . . . Come on, we're getting home, Dave,' I tried to encourage him, hearing his breathing slowing and his chest making a strange noise.

But not even a couple of seconds after that, he collapsed in my arms, making us both fall in the snow.

'Wake up, Dave, please!'

It was too late. He was all but unconscious in my arms, his face as white as the snow around us.

'I got you.'

Another shot.

Time seemed to freeze.

I had not even a second to react.

I felt something thump into Dave's back and his body slumped in my arms.

I felt the blood splash all over my face.

The warm drops trickled down my forehead.

I looked at Dave inert in my arms. I buried my head in his shoulder, covering my face with even more blood, the salty taste filling my mouth. Giving me all the warmth the boy was losing by the second.

And a horrible noise invaded the forest.

A noise nobody would ever want to hear.

A noise which scared even me . . .

Cries of blood.

Cries tearing my throat with sharp claws, while my tears poured down my cheeks and mingled with the blood. Blood which came out of my mouth, spat out with each cry.

I couldn't lose him. Not him. Not like that.

And I kept crying, heartbroken, seeing that Dave wasn't showing any sign of life. His face was so white.

I realised that it had begun to snow as a small and perfect snowflake fell onto my arm. It melted instantly, so fast I thought I had imagined it. I lifted up my face and saw other snowflakes falling. But I couldn't see Sarah. She had disappeared.

'I'm right here,' she told me, next to me.

I turned around so suddenly that I dropped Dave's body on the snow and let all my weight fall onto the girl. She didn't expect it and fell, groaning with fear. I found the gun and hit her around the face with it. Simultaneously she elbowed me, blinding me momentarily. I grabbed the gun, my hands slippery with Dave's blood. When my eyesight cleared, I saw the girl a few feet away from me.

But . . .

'We're saved,' I suddenly muttered.

Sarah didn't ask me what I meant; she followed my eyes to see what I was looking at.

We were just a few feet behind the house. My house. And above the roof I could make out the lights from the patrol cars at the other side of the building, bathing the snowflakes that fell from the sky in flashing beams of a bluish colour.

They had come just in time.

We were finally saved. The police had heard my cries and they were coming over, their flashlights lighting up the darkness. Sarah turned to face me.

'One day I will find you and we will end this, just the two of us.'

She then turned and began to run between the trees.

'Noooooo! This ends right now!' I cried with all the air in my lungs, spitting out blood, and I pulled the trigger with all the strength in my hands.

I pulled it once, twice, three, four times.

16. Final questions

Eva closed her eyes for a moment, letting a tear slide down her soft cheek. It glittered in the light of a sunray that slipped between the blinds.

When she opened her eyes, she saw Julia's face next to hers. The woman had got up from her seat and thrown her notes and diary on the floor. She held her gaze for a second and then Julia was welcoming her into her arms, crying too.

'It's alright. Everything's in the past,' Julia whispered.

Eva wiped her tears with the tissue Julia offered her.

The presenter asked Sam to stop filming while the two women held each other. Eva let the tears flow, unable to contain them anymore. She no longer minded having other people see her cry; opening up so completely in front of two strangers didn't bother her.

She had held her emotions in check for too long.

After a few minutes, they both returned to their seats. Eva wiped away the tears which still rolled down her cheeks. Even Julia had mascara all over her face. When Eva felt confident enough to continue, she made a sign to Julia, who asked her husband to turn the camera back on.

'Thank you for staying with us,' the woman thanked her audience, looking into the camera. The way she was looking at the device now seemed different to Eva somehow. 'This programme is coming to an end. We have been following the true, previously untold story of Eva Domínguez, the survivor of a series of horrific events that took place two years ago in the area around the village of Guildon Forest.

'But don't worry, there are still a few last questions to be answered,' Julia continued after a short pause. She looked at the young girl with tenderness and said, 'Tell us, Eva, what happened after you pulled the trigger of the gun?'

'Nothing. Nothing happened,' the girl said, her frustration clear. 'I know it's not something anyone should say, but I wish I'd had just one bullet left in that gun. Sarah had used them all. So when I pulled the trigger, not even a single bullet came out.'

'I don't think anybody would blame you for saying that.'

'Well, it's true. I would have loved to put a bullet through her the way she did with Dave.' Eva closed her eyes, holding back her tears once again.

'So did Sarah escape then?'

Eva knew perfectly well that Julia knew the answer; yet she replied. 'Yes, she did. She got out of there like a bat out of hell.'

Julia frowned and pursed her lips.

'Couldn't the police find her? What about the officer you'd spoken to, Tom Farlane?'

Eva knew her answer wasn't really necessary. 'Tom Farlane wasn't there. Dave had been in contact with him and asked him for help. He asked him to go out there immediately and told him quickly about the corpses. But Tom was off duty right that minute, so he called it into the station.'

Six police officers, Eva continued with a strained voice, had got to her house as fast as they could. Snowploughs had swept the snow from the roads that day and the surface had been gritted, so it hadn't been difficult for them to make good time. But the officers that showed up had almost no details of their situation.

When they got to the house, they found the front door open and went in. They searched all the rooms. They'd expected to find four youngsters and a little girl. But what they found instead were the two corpses of Stacey and Daniel, and the dog's bloodstained body. They even found the lonely teddy bear and the girl's bloodstained clothes under the sofa.

'Two plus two makes four,' Eva summed up, crestfallen. 'I don't blame them for thinking the girl had been mortally wounded, or that we had killed her, or – or I don't know what other scenario they built up in those seconds. What I can't forgive was how they treated me,' she continued. 'When they heard the gunshots and my cries, they went running to the back of the house. And they arrived just in time to see me holding the gun, covered in blood from head to toe. There was no child in sight; only Dave, bleeding to death on the snow at my feet, and the gun in my hands.'

'They mistook you for the attacker then?'

'Yes, they did, but I don't blame them for that,' Eva added quickly. 'I would have thought the same with that image in front of me. They approached me while I was still aiming the gun in the direction the girl had run, and they disarmed me. The next thing I remember is everything going crazy. I was struggling in the arms of an officer who was trying to separate me from Dave, while another policeman was trying to examine his wounds.

'I was knocked to the ground and they handcuffed me. I didn't understand what was going on when they told me I had the right to remain silent and put me in one of the patrol cars. I could only shout Dave's name.'

'And they took you to the police station,' Julia summarised.

Eva nodded. She looked out of the window and noticed a bird that had perched on the balustrade outside.

'They held me in there for half an hour, more or less, in an interrogation room. I didn't understand anything at all. How could I have been arrested and taken away from Dave? Where was he? I just wanted to be with him. And, even though I felt safe far away from the little girl, I knew that with each passing second I stayed locked in there, without anybody listening to me, she was escaping. I didn't want to waste any more time with solicitors, so I just tried to get to the point.'

'Didn't the police listen to you?'

'Well, yeah, after they asked me for the hundredth time where the "damned girl" was. I asked them not to raise their voices and to explain what on earth was going on. I asked them why they'd arrested me. Not that someone normally walks around with a gun and covered in blood, but was that a crime?' Eva asked no one in particular; she wasn't expecting an answer. 'It was then I was told why I had been handcuffed and arrested.'

'Because they thought you had killed your two friends, the dog and the little girl,' Julia guessed, writing more notes.

'That's right.'

Eva gave the presenter time to finish writing. The plasma screen was now off. She was grateful it no longer showed the footage from the security cameras. She didn't have to look at those images of her friends and Daisy piled up in the middle of the garage anymore.

'At first I struggled to digest what they were saying. I defended myself as best as I could, although even the most innocent person would feel guilty in that room. The officers who interrogated me were professionals and they knew how to do their job. It's not like it is in films. No one assaulted me or smoked a cigarette in silence while they analysed me, or anything like that.

'I told them my version of events, from the beginning. They asked me so many questions; even more than you have.'

'Well, they're the police; I'm just a TV presenter – among other things.' Julia gave her a sad smile.

Eva smiled back. Getting to that point in the interview it felt as if a great weight had been lifted from her shoulders. No matter how painful the truth was, she would never have to carry that weight again.

'I told them that if they didn't believe me, they could watch the footage from the security cameras for themselves. They could even read my diary, which I still had in my shoulder bag. Obviously, they didn't give a damn about my diary then, although they ended up needing it later on.'

'But they could count on the most obvious evidence from the security cameras,' Julia said.

'Yes, they could. I told them I wanted to make a call, as was my right. And I called my mum.'

'Who, I guess, didn't understand anything at all,' the presenter interrupted Eva to laugh towards the camera, her manner oddly out of place.

'No, to be honest, she didn't. But she told me where the hard drive from the security cameras was and I left her to speak to the police.'

Julia took a moment to briefly write something in her notes. 'Ok, so once they managed to watch the security videos . . . '

'Well, when they finally got to watch them,' Eva continued, her voice low and full of rage, 'it was at least two or three hours later. Too late for them to send the police officers who had remained in the house after Sarah. They never found her,' the girl finished abruptly, looking straight at the camera for the first time.

'I see,' was all the presenter said for a while. Then, 'So after making it clear that you were innocent, what did you do next?'

'Officer Tom Farlane came to see me. He gave me, very politely, the only answer I needed.'

'About Dave,' Julia muttered with right intuition.

Eva smiled, wiping away a tear she hadn't been able to contain. 'Yes. He took me to the hospital immediately. Someone took a look at my ankle and later on I was allowed to see Dave. Luckily, neither of the bullets touched any arteries or caused irreparable damage,' she said. Her smile was bitter, but it was still a smile.

Julia let a few seconds go by. 'Tell us, Eva, what happened to Dave Campos? There has barely been a word about him in the media, just the occasional vague comment.'

'Dave had lost a lot of blood by the time he arrived at the hospital,' Eva explained, her smile erased. 'The police had got him there just in time. A few more minutes and perhaps he wouldn't have been alive to tell the tale. He was taken into surgery at once and then he slept right through the night. I stayed by his bedside. When he woke up, he wasn't the Dave I knew.'

'What do you mean?'

The girl hesitated for a few seconds, during which she took the opportunity to moisten her throat with a sip of water. 'As I said, he was lucky. And he recovered from the wounds quickly, considering the circumstances. But it wasn't his arm or back, where the last bullet hit him, which were left damaged. It was his mind.

'I'm not sure exactly how to describe it; I'm not a doctor. But the blood didn't reach his brain properly. And that's what made him go into shock. And when he woke up, he didn't know his own name.'

'Amnesia?'

'Yes,' Eva confirmed, serious. 'I stayed with him for as long as the doctors would let me. Two days later, my mum arrived at the hospital along with Dave's. They took care of everything: all the mess in our house, the paparazzi and police officers. And the two of them forced me to go to a hotel near the hospital. Apparently, my continuous presence in Dave's room wasn't good.'

She took another sip of water and then a deep breath, leaving an empty space inside her after all those words she had left unsaid for so long.

'A week later, Dave had made great progress. The doctors were very encouraged by it. At the beginning he could only speak in English and had no memories of his mother tongue. But a few days later he woke up and began to speak in Spanish again, as if nothing had happened. He remembered who he was, and he recognised his own mother, and even my mother and me.'

'So, what is the problem then?' Julia asked, registering Eva's severe tone.

'His amnesia subsided into what doctors call a lacunar amnesia,' Eva continued hesitantly.

It had been two years now, two long years during which Dave had lived with his condition – and she hadn't visited him once. But that wasn't something she was prepared to talk about.

'He remembered everything: his name, his family, his past, how we had met, why we were in Scotland and not in London. Everything, except what happened.'

'I suppose he's improved since then; or is the damage irreversible?'

'No, it's not irreversible; but after two years, he's not making any more progress. His mum couldn't afford the treatment costs for a specialist institution, so I said I'd cover the costs of a good one in London, not far from where I live. At the end of the day, what happened to him is my fault.'

Julia slammed her notebook shut, leaned forwards in her chair and said, 'Don't you ever say that again, do you hear me? Only Sarah is to blame for what happened. No one else.'

'I know that, but he didn't want to go to Scotland in the first place. He wanted to stay home alone but I convinced him to come with us.'

'Well, let's leave Dave's case to one side, shall we?' the presenter proposed, leaning back again in her seat. 'It's clear enough, not only from your version of events but from the irrefutable footage from the security cameras, that you're not to be blamed for anything that happened.'

Changing the subject, Julia now asked Eva about the corpses she and Dave had found in the basement.

'As I said, the woman's body was Yäel's – the real Yäel, that is. The man was her husband, George. As the girl said in one of the videos,' she pointed at the plasma screen, 'her dad had died a few years earlier as a result of drug use. He'd taken an overdose, and her mum had died in a car accident. It was after that happened that custody of Sarah went to Yäel, her grandmother.'

'What about the name in the nightgown? It wasn't the girl who was called Yäel, but her grandma,' Julia remembered.

'I don't know,' Eva admitted. 'I suppose it must have belonged to the woman when she was a child. We found the name and presumed mistakenly that it was the girl's.'

'I don't know if I am the only one wondering about this – indeed, you mentioned earlier that you had your own questions – but how is it possible that Mrs McGregor didn't tell you anything about the family? You lived just a few minutes' walk away from a house where those people had been living for the last three years, isn't that right?'

Eva frowned. This was beginning to feel more like an interrogation than a TV interview.

She took a deep breath and let the air out slowly through her mouth. And she told the woman how Yäel and her husband had been squatting in that house. It had been built about ten years earlier, but whoever had built it had never lived in it. That was why Yäel and her husband had kept a low profile, scarcely going into the village. But Mrs McGregor had carried out a thorough investigation and had spoken to a neighbour, who happened to have met Yäel a few years back. Even Mrs McGregor had seen Yäel with the little girl in her shop once.

It had been a day like any other, far too long ago for her to recall it perfectly. But the details she received from her friend, about Yäel always wearing flowery, long dresses or bad taste prints, matched perfectly with what she remembered. It was enough to bring it all back to her. The girl, Mrs McGregor said, had been playing outside the shop and came in with a dead bird in her hand.

'A dead bird?' Julia asked, puzzled.

'Don't ask me,' Eva shrugged. 'I can't tell you if Sarah was already crazy then. But there was something about her, as Mrs McGregor remembered, that made Yäel not want her granddaughter to be seen in public. Besides, they were squatters in that house; I don't think they could afford to let others see them very often. I don't know. To be frank, no one has been able to tell me anything about Sarah, except that she was almost seven years old when we found her.'

'And what happened with the police investigation?'

'I ask myself that same question,' Eva answered coldly. 'They used the images from the security cameras as the most recent picture of her, along with the ones they found at her grandparents' house. There was supposedly an operation to track her down. But after these last two years, no one has heard anything from them; not my mum, nor any of my friends' parents, nor Mr or Mrs McGregor. Even I haven't heard any news.'

Julia looked surprised. 'Not a single thing?' Eva shook her head. 'But a girl of that age needs a roof to sleep under, food, maybe even medicines and visits to the doctor. How is it possible that no one has ever seen her?'

'If you are waiting for an answer,' Eva warned her, frowning, 'I'm afraid I don't have one. The only thing I can tell you is that I hope she fell into a well, or that a fox attacked her and she died. She doesn't deserve anything else,' she added, seeing Julia's shocked look.

'Speaking of atrocious deaths,' Julia said, softening her voice, 'were the deaths of Sarah's grandparents investigated?'

'Of course they were. The police might not be any good at giving you answers on the phone, but they're great at telling you about investigations into deaths.' Eva's tone was sharp. 'But they didn't say much that I couldn't have guessed from seeing the bodies.

'The man had been accused not only of abusing alcohol, but also of being violent. Apparently, he was very controlling towards Yaël. The autopsy confirmed he'd been violent towards her; there were countless bruises all over her body. And only a man with the strength of her husband could have made the cuts on her neck. According to the angle of the bullet in his brain, the girl must have found him in the act and shot him.'

'That seems plausible enough. But from where did she take the gun? The man had been fired from the police. If he had taken a gun from–'

'Oh, the gun wasn't from the police. It didn't match the calibre of any of the weapons they use. Anyway, as you know, only specialist firearms officers carry guns, and the presence of guns throughout the UK is pretty limited. No one knows where he got it from. He didn't even have a licence.'

Julia reviewed her notes. She flipped through one page after another, reading what she'd written. She drank from her glass of water and looked intently at Eva.

'So, the man used to mistreat his wife and abuse the girl. One day, for whatever reason, he killed his wife, but had an unpleasant surprise when the girl was behind him with the gun in her hands. She killed him with an accurate shot to the forehead and hid the gun in her teddy bear. And after that, you found her.'

'Actually, no,' Eva answered, confusingly. 'It seems that the bodies were in too advanced a state of decomposition for Sarah to have left the house immediately,' she clarified. 'Supposedly, she stayed in the house for a few more days afterwards, although it's not known exactly how many.'

'Was it so difficult for the forensic team to know when the grandparents had been killed?'

'Yes, indeed. The rate of decomposition depends on dozens of factors, and it's difficult to estimate the hours or days that had passed before the girl left the house. She just stayed there, doing who knows what, in what kind of emotional and psychological state we can only imagine. They assumed she was forced to leave the house when she had no more food left. And it was then that we found her – which would explain why she devoured each and every meal we gave her.'

'Why tell this story now?' Julia asked, abruptly changing the subject.

'I've already given you my reasons away from the cameras. But I know that people at home might be wondering the same thing,' Eva affirmed sadly. 'It's been two long years since then, and in all that time journalists from across the continent, even in America, have been sullying my name and that of my family. For two long years I have tried to run away and forget everything. But in the end, it doesn't matter where I go, because every single day I hear new, macabre stories from people who have no idea about the truth.

'No one has stopped to think that they're not only hurting me and my family,' Eva continued after a deep breath, 'but also Dave's. His parents have to live with their son unable to completely recover from his amnesia. And then there are Stacey's and Daniel's families, who for so long have suffered from the dozens of lies told about their deceased children. And I was there; I went through it myself and I know what happened out of sight of those security cameras. There's nobody better than me to tell the world what really happened.'

Julia looked at her notes again, searching for more questions. Eva wondered if she hadn't already asked enough.

She herself had suffered that agonising feeling of emptiness she knew the presenter was now experiencing. The difference between them was that Eva had lost her former boyfriend and her friend, and had as good as lost her best friend; while for Julia this was a massive opportunity, Eva's first and last interview with the media, an opportunity which would catapult her career into the stratosphere without her ever having to feel that terror, coldness, loneliness, suffering, pain, confusion . . .

It had been two long and painful years since those events, and Eva had tortured herself with questions through all that time.

But the case would remain unsolved.

If no one had yet answered all those questions, nobody would ever be able to.

'I know that it may not be what you expected, but I can only tell what I saw with my own eyes and what I was vaguely told later. And, at least now everyone will know the truth and stop spreading lies around.'

After a minute of silence, Julia accepted those words and looked straight at the camera and thanked her audience once more for following Eva's story through the two parts of the interview. She provided the contact telephone numbers for the police in Scotland and said that photographs of the girl would be available on the TV channel's website: anyone who believed they had seen her should call the police immediately.

'How do you feel?' Julia asked Eva. They were stood on the balcony of Julia's office. The interview was finished and Sam had removed the microphones from their dresses.

Eva took a long puff on her cigarette. It had been so long since the last time she smoked, but after that tedious and exhausting interview, she thought she deserved one. She exhaled the smoke slowly, feeling her lungs empty. She felt a little dizzy for a few seconds.

'At peace. It was something I needed to do, even though it's brought back so many things I'd never like to have to say again. I hope I don't get any more nightmares.'

'I'm sorry, sweetheart, but this is something that you're going to carry with you for the rest of your life.'

Eva stared back at Julia, her expression somewhere between amused and hurt. 'Oh, thank you.'

'For what it's worth, I don't think I'll be able to forget those videos either,' Julia assured her. 'I hope you've got some good advice for how to forget about them.'

Eva took another puff of her cigarette. 'Well, if you hadn't fucked up big time in Almería, I would have said my grandma would have welcomed you with open arms. But she called me a few weeks ago and told me that you were a "puta loca",' the girl quoted in Spanish, laughing.

'My Spanish is good enough to know what that means,' Julia said laughing as well, half choking on the smoke of her own cigarette.

They went back inside when they'd finished. Julia apologised once again for the trouble she had caused and invited Eva to her house to talk more over a cup of tea; but Eva had plans and didn't feel like talking, so she declined the offer politely.

When she took a step out onto the street, she felt fresh and new. It was as if somehow she had left her past behind in that office. An inner peace, just as she had described to Julia, filled her heart and mind now.

She allowed herself to enjoy her anonymity for as long as it lasted, unconcerned by the woman walking in the opposite direction who was glancing jealously at Eva's nice clothes. She knew the time would come when she would have to avoid the streets and crowds; once the interview was broadcast people would start talking about her and recognising her all over again, thanks to the dozens of paparazzi who would certainly harass her everywhere she went.

She walked onto Whitehall Street in no hurry and waved to attract the attention of a taxi driver.

'Where are you going?' asked the driver, who didn't seem to recognise her.

Eva smiled. 'It's time,' she muttered to herself. And then she gave the driver the address of the psychiatric institution where Dave had been staying for the last two years.

She was a girl who fulfilled her promises.

It was time to pay him a visit.

Epilogue

The light was fading on the horizon, the dull orange tone giving way to the night. The cars and buses were suffering their ongoing fight against the arrogant pedestrians who crossed the streets without looking, ignoring traffic lights and zebra crossings.

Julia was one of them, crossing the street in a hurry and turning the corner of the hotel, almost running over a couple who were walking at their own slow pace.

One of the two doormen standing beneath the rounded, dark blue and gold canopy of The Ritz Hotel's main entrance attended her politely. He opened the door for her after telling her with whom she had to speak.

She approached the reception desk.

'Good evening, welcome to The Ritz Hotel. My name is . . . ' the smiley receptionist began, but as soon as he recognised her he was speechless. After a pause, he said, 'Julia Stevenson, is that right? I understand that Eva Domínguez is expecting you.'

'That's right,' the woman replied, her tone brusque and her eyes serious.

'Would you like me to escort you to her room?' the receptionist asked in the same polite voice, keeping his smile pinned to his face.

Julia nodded and followed him across the lobby.

He walked in front in an uncomfortable silence. They walked up the pristine and ornate staircase, but Julia didn't pay any attention to its grandeur. She almost forgot to thank the man when they arrived at the door to the young actress's room.

Once he had disappeared back down the stairs, she knocked on the door. She was hoping to be received by the young girl herself; but seeing those brown eyes, which even after so long she recognised immediately, took her by surprise.

'Hi, Julia,' Olivia Domínguez greeted her.

But she had no time to process her astonishment. Behind the mother appeared the daughter, who threw herself into Julia's arms crying and shaking.

'What is it? What's happened?' Julia managed to say over the young girl's sobs.

'Ah, Eva, let her enter and remove her coat,' Olivia said with a thick Spanish accent.

Julia made the girl sit on a sofa in the living room and covered her with a blanket. Behind them came Olivia, who took Julia's coat and handbag and placed them on a chair.

Only the dim light that filtered through the curtains illuminated the room, so Julia took the liberty of lighting a lamp by the sofa. The girl sat there, crying inconsolably.

'Please, Eva, tell me what has happened,' she asked her again, taking her in her arms. 'I couldn't understand a single word of what you said over the phone.'

Eva blew her nose and wiped her tears with the tissue her mother held out for her. Tremors shook her body as her sobs subsided. She took a deep breath and began to speak slowly. 'Yesterday, after we finished the interview at your office, I visited Dave at the psychiatric institution where he's staying. It was special. We hugged each other and felt so happy that we were together after all this time.'

She paused to blow her nose a second time and tried to breathe as best she could.

'He's changed so much since the last time I saw him,' Eva continued. 'I spoke with his doctors and they told me he's still in a state of denial about what happened, a state he doesn't seem to want to come out of. I told you yesterday that he suffered an emotional shock that produced amnesia, which eventually diminished into a lacunar type. And he doesn't remember anything about what happened at the end of our stay up in Guildon Forest.

'Overall, the day with him was good, although it was difficult seeing him like that. He was as fragile as a child. In fact, he behaved as if he was one. And he asked me so innocently why I hadn't gone to see him for so long.'

'Did you answer him?'

'No, I couldn't. The doctors had recommended not talking at all about those days. They said he always turned violent when they tried to do so. And I couldn't stop myself from crying when he asked me about Daniel and Stacey,' she said, also not able to hold back her tears now. 'He thinks they still have some kind of friendship, and he's angry with them for not even sending him a letter.'

Julia was listening carefully to the young girl's faltering words, all the while looking at the mother. She felt uncomfortable that she was the one hugging the girl instead of her own mother.

'But if everything went well, why have you called me sounding so hysterical? What's happened?'

Eva leaned forwards and threw off the blanket, abruptly. She got up and stood next to the window.

'Sara has appeared,' the young girl muttered.

'Beg your pardon?' Julia said, looking at the mother and daughter.

Eva turned and looked at her through eyes that were wet and tired.

'Apparently, today a girl of about eight or nine years old showed up there, saying I was coming in a few minutes and that I had asked her to wait for me in the room with Dave. The receptionist refused to let her in at first; but in the end the girl succeeded with her excuses and convinced the lady to let her go up to Dave's room.

'When Dave saw her stepping in his room he panicked and began to shout hysterically. The doctors had to sedate him. It was after that they called me.'

Julia remained silent, absorbing the story. Neither the mother's eyes nor the daughter's gave any indication that the whole thing was a joke. No, there was no doubt that Eva's words were true. 'How's Dave now?' she asked.

'You can see for yourself,' Eva answered, pointing to a door next to the bathroom, her chest still heaving and her breathing no better than before.

Julia didn't understand what she meant. Was Dave on the other side of that door? It was Olivia who explained that, indeed, the boy was in the next room, sleeping peacefully.

'Has she taken him out of the institution?' Julia asked Olivia, who merely nodded.

'No one dared to stop me. I was the one who got him there of his own free will and with his family's consent. So, when I arrived, after they had told me what happened, I took him out of there. He's still completely knocked out by the sedatives,' Eva concluded. 'And I hope they don't bother calling me or his mother. They have caused him enough suffering with their incompetence,' she said, looking between Julia and her mother.

Julia didn't know what to say, and Olivia looked as if she felt the same way. It seemed that this story would never cease to amaze her.

'I called mum first; but when she came, neither of us knew what to do.'

'But why haven't you called the police? I can't help with this: I'm only a journalist.'

The two of them looked at her with a strange gleam in their eyes.

'There's something else you should know,' said Eva, whispering as she entered the room where Dave slept. She returned a moment later with something in her hand. 'Before she left, Sarah left something on Dave's bed.'

She closed the door and the three of them sat on the sofa. Julia reached over and loosened Eva's clenched fingers. A crumpled piece of paper lay in the palm of the girl's hand. Julia picked it up and asked, 'Do you mind?'

'Not at all: this is what you're here for,' Olivia affirmed.

Eva just nodded, exhausted by the hard day.

Cries of Blood

Julia tried to straighten out the piece of paper. She discovered it was a letter. A letter from Sarah, the little girl who had made the four young actors live through their worst nightmares two years ago. The little girl who had apparently showed up out of nowhere at the institution where Dave had been staying and left that piece of paper on his bed.

The handwriting was bad, but it was well drafted and, Julia believed, very well thought through:

Dear Eva,

It has been a long time since we've seen each other.

Too long, I would say.

I promised you that I would find you and we would end what we began.

It doesn't matter where you hide: I will always be near you and Dave.

Next time we see each other, it will be the last.

Regards,
Your dear Yäel :)

P.S. I miss Johnny.

Acknowledgements

I owe my gratitude to the many people who have helped making this book a reality. I would like to pay tribute to the many wonderful souls who have shared with me their time, talent and support.

First and foremost, my thanks to Claire Cooper for her passion, dedication, knowledge, patience, each and every one of her marvellous corrections, recommendations and her almost FBI like inspection over the first translation draft of the book. This edition would not exist without your hard work. Where there are errors, they are my own.

Thanks to Marina Kiriacou for the greatest book cover any author could wish for, her patience and her unselfish interest in helping me getting this edition just right. I hope everyone goes and checks her work at www.marinakphotography.com.

For sure a million thanks to my dearest friend Pablo Lillo. Not only for being a friend at a time of need, but for encouraging me to be brave enough and share with the world what years ago was just an idea.

My thanks to another first supporter, Sarah Rowe. She became so captivated by the little girl in this book that I ended up having to change her name midway!

My many, many thanks to Angelines Lena for believing in my evil side. No one better to feed my crazy imagination as her with her many stories, such as the one when she was a small child . . . walking barefoot in the mountains.

Thanks to my many good friends at the Spanish TV series "Física o Química", specially to Patricia Domínguez, Roberto Hoyos and Gema Cobo. I'll forever cherish our many impromptu car trips around Spain which, unintentionally, led to this story.

Thanks to my aunt Conchi and my friends Hania and Pilar for being the first readers of the original manuscript. I'm horribly in debt to you due to your majestic ideas, sharp analysis and for helping me get the details where they should be.

Huge thanks to the Scottish Police for very kindly and patiently attending my very suspicious and not so brief call from all the way in London. Unlike Eva, I'm forever grateful for making me feel the safest person alive on each and every one of my trips to Scotland.

A very special thanks to all family members and closer friends for your unconditional support, no matter what. I'm the luckiest man to have you all with me.

And last, but not least, to every one of my old and new readers around the world . . . Thank you for reading and sharing my book with your friends. Without you, all this would certainly not be happening.

About the author

Christian Martin is a Spanish actor and writer originally from Madrid, Spain.

His debut book "Cries of Blood", a suspense/thriller novel based mostly in Scotland, UK, was also published in Spanish under the title "Llantos de Sangre" by Max Estrella Ediciones.

Currently, he's working on book two on the "Cries" series.

On the little screen you might have seen him on: "Sketch Up", NottsTV (UK); "Física o Química", Antena3 (Spain); "Amar en tiempos revueltos", TVE (Spain); and on "De Buena Ley", Telecinco (Spain).

He likes to read a large and diverse range of books. Between his favourite authors you'll find Laura Gallego, John Verdon, Diane Setterfield, J.K. Rowling and Dan Brown.

If you'd like to hear more of Christian, you can do so by following on:
-Goodreads - Christian Martin
-Instagram - @christian23martin

Printed in Great Britain
by Amazon